BG

AMON

FRIENDS

Dearest Gill, this is quite different to the others & set in lovely Bristol – not Cornwall for once! Thanks so much for your friendship + generosity. There are not many like you. Kath xxxx

Katharine E. Smith

Katharine E. Smith

HEDDON PUBLISHING

First edition published in 2016 by Heddon Publishing.

Copyright © Katharine E. Smith, all rights reserved.
No part of this book may be reproduced, adapted, stored in a
retrieval system or transmitted by any means, electronic, photocopying,
or otherwise without prior permission of the author.

ISBN 978-0-9934870-4-0

Cover design by Catherine Clarke

This is a work of fiction. Names, characters, businesses, places, events
and incidents are either the products of the author's imagination or
used in a fictitious manner. Any resemblance to actual persons, living
or dead, or actual events is purely coincidental.
No part of this book may be reproduced or transmitted in any form or
by any means, electronic or mechanical, including photocopying,
recording or by any information storage and retrieval system, without
written permission from the author.

www.heddonpublishing.com
www.facebook.com/heddonpublishing
@PublishHeddon

About the Author

 Katharine E. Smith runs Heddon Publishing - an independent publishing house. She also works as a freelance proofreader, editor and copywriter.

She has a degree in Philosophy and a love for the written word. She works with authors all over the world and considers herself extremely privileged to do so.

A Yorkshire-woman by birth, Katharine now lives in Shropshire with her husband and their two children.

Other books by Katharine E. Smith

Writing the Town Read
Looking Past

For Mum and Dad, for everything

AMONGST FRIENDS

2003

The big bang

The explosion had reverberated around Lawrence Weston, bouncing off Long Cross, into the woods of Blaise Estate and over the industrialised waters of Avonmouth Docks. Days after the event there was talk of it being heard all the way over at Fishponds. Right then, though, right after it happened, the neighbourhood was still for just a moment. People, animals, birds alike.

Then a dog began to bark, then another, and another. The birds began to call once more; slightly nervously at first, it seemed, but soon they were back to exactly as they'd been before Mike's house had blown up. It was as though it had never happened, for them at least.

It didn't take long for Mike's neighbours to begin appearing on their street. They came out into the summer evening, some already in pyjamas and slippers, shuffling nervously into the road, gathering a few metres away from the scene of the explosion. More than one held a phone in shaking hands, calling the Emergency Services, although the sound of sirens coming closer assured them help was already on its way.

What kind of help could truly be provided was another matter. The house gaped open, displaying a cross-section which included the kitchen and lounge downstairs and part of the bathroom, landing and a bedroom upstairs. It reminded some of the older residents of the Blitz, when Bristol had suffered its fair share of German raids.

"Oh my God!"

"Are you OK?"

These exclamations were among the most common at first, until people re-found their voices and, it seemed, their thoughts.

"Was 'e in there, d'you think?"

"I dunno, 'aven't seen him all day but I've been down the Mall this afternoon."

"D'you reckon we should 'ave a look?"

"No, don't be stupid, look at the place! You're lucky it's just his place, you'll need to get someone to check yours over, being next door an' all."

The street was a cul-de-sac lined either side with near-identical largely ex-council houses. Many, including Mike's, had been bought during Margaret Thatcher's Right to Buy scheme in the early 1980s and, while some were now owned by housing associations and saw a steady coming and going of tenants, for the most part the people who lived there had done so for decades. They knew each other, if not intimately then reliably. Knew where each other worked, which of the more elderly neighbours required a hand with shopping from time-to-time, and they facilitated a reliable support network without being in each other's pockets, or houses, too much.

"What if 'e's in there 'urt, though?"

"Ambulance'll be 'ere soon enough, and the Fire Brigade – in fact 'ere you go."

The ever-growing crowd of people; many coming from neighbouring streets now to join the throng, looked in unison to the corner of the road where three fire engines, lights flashing and sirens still blaring, turned one by one into the close. Police cars soon followed, and two ambulances.

A stern-looking policeman with thick salt-and-pepper hair and an impressive moustache took control, ushering the people back while a couple of younger officers put up the requisite cordon.

The residents, still shocked, moved backwards like an unusually obedient flock of sheep.

In the warm glow of the summer evening, the Fire Brigade assessed the situation before a number of officers entered what remained of the house, to the hushed gasps of the onlookers. Overhead, slowly and somewhat incongruously, drifted a group of hot air balloons, making their gradual descent, perhaps looking to land on St Bede's school fields. A common enough sight on a clear Bristol evening but too bright and frivolous above the scene of devastation.

"What do you reckon caused it, then? Unexploded bomb?"

"More likely a gas leak, I reckon, that mate of 'is, you know, runs Westbury Gas, 'e's been round a couple o' times this week. Mike said 'is boiler was playin' up."

"Fuckin' 'ell, can't 'ave done much of a job fixin' it. Remind me not to use Westbury Gas again."

"Shush!" Maddie, the mother of Eammon, who had made this remark, admonished her son and his mate Freddie. Mike's mum, Emma, who owned the house, had been a good friend to her before leaving for sunny Spain. Maddie could feel her heart thudding in her chest as she waited anxiously for the firemen to come back out. It couldn't be long, surely. It wasn't a big house.

An unclear communication on the police sergeant's walkie-talkie had him suddenly summoning the ambulance crew, who entered the building, accompanied by a further two of the Fire Rescue crew.

"Shit." Maddie's face went paler still. Eammon moved closer to her and put his arm round her.

"It'll be alright, Ma."

She smiled weakly while Bella, the renowned gossip of the street, joined the conversation, picking up the thread about Lee Lewis, owner of Westbury Gas. "Well I don't know 'ow good 'e is at 'is job but I don't reckon 'e can be much of a 'usband judging by the amount of time 'is Mrs 'as been round Mike's place."

Maddie smiled politely, "Can't say as I've noticed," she lied, "but I don't suppose now's the time for that kind of talk anyway."

Bella glowered. How dare that little upstart Maddie Connolly talk to her like that? But there was no time for an argument as Bill from 39 nudged her and heads turned as one once more to see a fire officer exit the property, followed by the ambulance crew. Grim-faced, they carried a stretcher on which lay a zipped-up body bag.

The crowd fell silent as the birds around them sang their evening songs, bidding one another goodnight.

The big night out

Lee opened his eyes, grimacing as his head, then the rest of his body, recalled the previous night. He and Mike had definitely been hitting it hard, but that had been the point. A night for old times' sake, like nights long-since past. They'd been through a lot together, there was no denying it. From primary school, through secondary school, and beyond.

He'd wanted one last night to remember. Not many people would have thought it but he was just a big softie at heart.

The night had started tamely enough; a couple of beers at Elbow Room on Park Street. Mike, who hadn't seemed overly enthusiastic at the idea of their boys' night in the first place, had tried to persuade Lee to go somewhere quieter. Cheaper, more like. Lee had brushed Mike's protestations gallantly aside, saying that the night was on him.

Reluctantly - and quite ungratefully, Lee thought - Mike had agreed to go along with him and so they'd met up, had a couple of pints of expensive lager and played a couple of games of expensive pool.

Mike had seemed a bit on edge initially but the beer had mellowed him a little and Lee's suggestion of them trying to chat up the hot girls who were drinking at the bar seemed to put Mike even more at ease, though he had made some wimpy excuse not to do it. It had been a carefully planned move on Lee's part, that suggestion, and quite a clever one. Lee's supposed plans for infidelity would put his so-called friend's mind at rest about his own recent behaviour. He had probably even justified it all to himself, Lee thought scornfully. But he pushed the thought aside, reminding himself it was important that the two of them had a good time. Those girls really were pretty hot, though. Maybe he'd come back next week. Not with Mike, though.

After whipping Mike's ass at pool, Lee suggested they head on down to the harbourside. "Go on mate, a pint at all of 'em. We'll start over the other side at the Shakespeare, then one at the Arnolfini and on to the townie bars after."

Mike, who had been drinking more slowly than Lee, opened his mouth to refuse but again, the spineless bastard had offered short-lived resistance. "Alright, but I can't be too late out."

"Big day tomorrow, mate?"

"Something like that."

You don't know the half of it, mate.

"Boiler still playin' you up?"

"Yeah, it's a bit better since you came round, but I still think I can smell gas from time to time. Probably imagining it."

"You don't want to risk that, though, mate. Tell you what, I'll drop in tomorrow mornin', take a quick look. Leave us a key, above the back door like you used to."

"Oh, erm, don't worry, Lee…"

What was this? Mike having some kind of crisis of conscience?

"No, mate, I insist, you don't wanna fuck about with gas. I think we're goin' to 'ave to take another look at that pipework, you know. I'll sort it for you."

"OK," Mike seemed reluctant but Lee had made sure he couldn't refuse his kind offer. What possible reason could Mike have for neglecting the safety of his home? Especially if Anna was going to be moving in.

At the bottom of Park Street they walked past College Green, scene of many of their teenage nights out. The two of them and Anna would join up with a large group of kids from across the city and in the summer they'd sit out on the grass well after dark; smoking, drinking and singing. In the winter they would congregate under the arches of the building, sitting on the cold stone and discussing festivals that the majority of their parents would never let them attend.

The old place still attracted teenagers with bottles of cider, illicit cigarettes and guitars.

Mike smiled across at a small group sitting under one of the trees. "That could be me, you and Anna, ten years ago."

"Yeah, what were we like, eh? Ripped jeans, stripey shirts, long hair, Nirvana tops. No offence, mate."

Lee hadn't been able to resist that one. Whereas his own style had changed with his life, inheriting the family business at the age of 21, Mike looked like he hadn't changed a bit. Although the ponytail was gone, he often let his hair grow longer and unkempt, and was usually sporting some kind of unplanned stubble. Yes, he still had ripped jeans and had even been known to wear his old t-shirts. He still loved the music. The Wonder Stuff, Nirvana, The Cure, The Levellers, Primal Scream, Sugar. These were the bands of their youth, but Mike had seen no reason to give them up as the years had progressed, whereas Lee had moved on to the clubbier dance scene, possessing an impressive record collection and, whereas he had once dreamed of being a bassist in an indie band, he now fancied himself as a professional DJ.

In contrast to Mike, Lee was usually immaculately dressed and groomed. He favoured the expensive labels that could be found in the shops of Park Street.

"None taken, you twat," Mike grinned and somehow the tension which had been simmering unseen between them eased with the insult.

Lee found himself smiling and an uncomfortable feeling

rose up in him, like a crick in his neck. He refused to acknowledge it for that way lay defeat, retreat, destruction. He had made up his mind, made his plan, and was well on the way to winning this little war. It was no time for friendship.

Despite his determination, by the time they were in the Arnolfini, the conversation between them had returned to the way it had always been. Good-natured winding up leading to full-on, outrageously rude accusations and insults. They had talked about music, work, Mike's mum and her Spanish partner, their friend Suzie and her new baby, school, football, their fellow drinkers. The one subject they did not discuss was Anna.

At the end of the night they'd shared a taxi, first up to Lee's house in Sneyd Park and then on to Mike's in Lawrence Weston.

"Take this, mate," Lee had pushed a twenty-pound note into Mike's hand.

"No, no, it's too much. I can pay the taxi, anyway, you've bought everything else."

"I insist, mate, I insist."

Unusually, the pair hugged before parting ways. It wasn't just the drink making them emotional; both were thinking of how they were betraying the other.

Struggling to pull himself out of bed with his stomach churning, Lee crossed the soft, thick carpet of the bedroom which had been his father's and opened the curtains, letting the morning sunshine sail through the floor-to-ceiling window his dad had insisted on when the house was built. His house was surrounded by tall old trees but just visible between them were the Downs, their usually green grass slightly brown from the summer's heat, and beyond them the Avon Gorge and the world-famous Clifton Suspension Bridge.

Anna had left for work some hours before. Lee had grunted something as she'd gone. Silly bitch. It was her fault, coming between him and Mike. It could have been brilliant when his old mate had returned to Bristol but she'd put paid to all that. No doubt spinning some kind of sob story and turning on the charm.

Ah well, fuck her.

In the en suite, Lee pushed his fingers into his throat and threw up. One brisk shower later in his state-of-the-art bathroom and he was ready to face the world. He made some proper coffee and a fry-up, setting himself up for the day. It was going to be a big one, after all.

Down in Lawrence Weston, he drove slowly past the end of Mike's close, checking that his friend's car wasn't there. Affirmative. He drove up to the parade of shops to buy a pack of Marlboro red then back down to Mike's, where he parked his van in full view of the street. Leaning nonchalantly on the bonnet, Lee proceeded to light up a cigarette, knowing it would only be a matter of time before one of the neighbours came by.

It was a leafy cul-de-sac, the trees in the neat front gardens busy with small garden birds. High above, swallows and swifts shrieked their urgent, high-pitched cries to one another as they whirled about. Lee thought about Emma, Mike's mum, putting out cat food for hedgehogs and one long hot summer when she'd spent many an evening sitting in the dark in the lounge, waiting for a badger which had become a frequent visitor, sneaking down from the woods at Kingsweston for a snack of peanuts or dog food.

He and Mike had usually been up in Mike's room, having a crafty fag and discussing music – or, more often than not, the girls in their year. They had been good times, Lee thought wistfully, but he was snapped out of his reverie by a movement at Mike's neighbour's house.

Bingo. It was that woman Mike's mum had been friends with; Maggie or something.

"Alright?" he smiled as calmly as he could. Despite himself, his heart had increased its rhythm and he hoped she couldn't tell.

"Oh hi, love, are you looking for Mike? I think he's at work."

"Oh yeah, I know, I just come down to check 'is boiler. Been playin' up; thought I sorted it the other day but Mike said 'e thinks there's still a problem. You 'aven't noticed any suspicious smells?"

"Well, yeah – plenty. But not anything like gas, if that's what you're getting at!"

She smiled at him openly and he laughed along with her. She wasn't too bad, actually; would have been pretty fit twenty years ago.

"I know what you're sayin'! Well, no worries, I've got a key so I'll just pop in and make sure it's all lookin' OK."

Mike had left the key as agreed. *Idiot.* Lee was in and out of the house in minutes and, as he'd hoped, there was the neighbour, coming back from the shops with her paper.

"Everything OK, love?"

"Well I think that boiler's on its way out, and a bit of pipework could do with an update by the looks of it, but I can't get 'old of Mike and I can't do anythin' without 'is say-so. I'll 'ave to wait for 'im to call me back. A dodgy boiler's a bit of a worry, though, so if you do notice anything like a strong smell of gas, will you give me a bell? I'd 'ate anythin' to 'appen while Mike's out at work."

"Course I will. Thanks, love." Maddie smiled as Lee handed her a card before hopping into his van and driving away, a grin a mile wide on his face.

This was going to be piss-easy. He swung his van back into his expansive driveway and tapped another cigarette out of his packet. His nerves were tingling, with excitement, and self-righteousness. Tonight, justice would be done.

He slid out of the van and lit up, wandering his garden while he smoked right down to the filter. The deep drags mixing with his nerves and residual hangover had the effect of making him nauseous. He stubbed the cigarette out on a fencepost and unlocked his front door, footsteps echoing on the wooden floorboards in his empty house.

He made another strong coffee and took it upstairs, sneering at himself in the mirror as he took in his transformed image. Gone were the smart Cult Clothing trousers and lightweight jacket; now he was lumberjacked up, with a checked blue-and-red shirt and ripped jeans. He pulled on a cap. Fucking hell, he looked like... well he looked quite a lot like Mike, actually. That wasn't necessarily planned, but it wouldn't hurt.

He had some time to kill till the next stage of his plan so he settled down in his den and stuck *Grand Theft Auto* on his new slimline PlayStation 2, thinking he'd put some of his nervous energy to good use.

The den was a huge room – a third reception room, really – and his father had used it as an office. In a gesture of rebellion to his dad, which he'd only felt able to make posthumously, Lee had gutted the house and made it his own. Well, his and Anna's officially, he supposed, but she'd never have lived there if it wasn't for him, the ungrateful bitch; it wasn't her parents', was it? He'd let her use his old bedroom as a dressing room and study. After all, if she had her own space, all the better for him; she wouldn't be cluttering up his. She'd decorated it herself, after getting his permission of course, and it was a pretty girlie place which he didn't spend much time in.

Other than that, the house had a proper manly feel to it. The first thing you noticed when you walked in was the highly polished black-and-white tiled floor of the hallway. Strong dark-tiled bathrooms and cloakroom, with a shiny white-and-chrome kitchen with dark slate tiled floor. There were black-

and-white photos throughout the house – nothing familial, rather stark scenes from films Lee loved or shots of Bristol, Hong Kong and New York; his holy trinity, he called them.

He settled down on a beanbag and prepared to cause some mayhem.

A few hours later, Lee was waiting on Blackboy Hill for the number 40 bus. He cursed his rumbling stomach; it seemed to be twisting with nerves, and his head had developed a tightness like a band being slowly squeezed around his forehead. He pulled the cap down over his eyes, praying he wouldn't see anybody who would recognise him.

He breathed a sigh of relief as he swung himself round the top of the bus stairs onto an empty top deck then took a seat at the very front, slouching so that if anybody came up he'd be almost obscured from view.

The bus jerked away from the stop and moved slowly up to the Downs, busy with early evening dog walkers, joggers, kids with kites, mothers speed-walking with buggies. It was yet another hot, clear day and the air seemed to shimmer over the Avon Gorge.

Down the bus went, very close to his own house. He could have got on at a closer stop but he wanted to disguise his every movement from now until he returned home later. He also wanted to remove any risk of bumping into his neighbours dressed as he was. He had a reputation to maintain, after all.

By the time the bus had reached Shirehampton he had a few fellow passengers upstairs, but nobody had paid the slightest bit of attention to him. Nevertheless, he could feel his palms becoming sticky, and his breathing quicken. It wasn't too late to back out, he thought, but as quickly as that had popped into his mind, so had his father's voice.

Don't be a puff, they've been taking the piss out of you for months.

Lee swallowed hard. He knew his dad was right. Step

down now and it was game over. He'd have known his wife and his supposed best mate were having it off and let them get away with it. Even if nobody else knew, he would, and that knowledge would gnaw away at him.

He hopped off the bus in Lawrence Weston, his anger freshly returned, and sloped along to Mike's. This time he had to be quick. He did not want to be seen, though hopefully if any of the neighbours got a glimpse of him they'd just assume he was Mike.

The day had been so hot that there were patches of melted tarmac on the road. A group of kids were sitting on a grass verge with a few cans of Blackthorn, talking and swearing loudly. They paid him no heed.

He made a quick assessment of the cul-de-sac and, satisfied it was empty, headed straight for Mike's place. It was just as it had been that morning. Remarkably, suspiciously, tidy.

Keeping the place clean for his girlfriend, Lee thought to himself. Mike was renowned for his untidiness. Clearly now he had a woman on the scene – *my* woman, thought Lee – he had decided to make an effort. Or maybe Anna had been cleaning for Mike. An involuntary growl came from the back of Lee's throat at the thought of this.

Checking the clock, he could see he had a couple of hours till Mike was due back. He'd said he was on the late shift, which ended at nine. It'd take him half an hour to get back from work. There was plenty of time.

Lee wasted no time in locating the boiler. He admired his previous subtle handiwork. A bit of damage here and there, the perfectly fine pipework replaced with some older, rustier stuff Lee had taken from a house on another job, and the leak would look like the result of an aged system.

Lee pulled his mask from his rucksack. He was going to

have to be very careful that this didn't blow up in his face. *Literally,* he chuckled to himself. He switched off the electricity at the mains then walked towards the stove. His heart was beating double-time. Pulling the mask down over his mouth, he carefully turned on each of the gas hobs, one by one. He opened the oven door and turned the gas supply on for that as well. He could hear the hissing of the gas; unchallenged by any ignition, untamed, it crept into the room. Lee imagined it curling into corners, sneaking through the gaps in the cupboard doors. Wrapping itself around the pots and pans. This was its day.

Be quiet, he silently commanded his heart. He had known that this would be difficult. There was a chance he would change his mind. To steady his nerves, and reinforce his resolve, he walked out of the kitchen, closing the door behind him as he went into the hallway. An unexpected, vivid memory of Emma came unbidden to him. Almost an out-of-body experience; she opened the door to twelve-year-old Lee; sullen, unkempt, broken-hearted, and opened her arms out to him. Despite her busy life and her small house, Emma had time and space for everybody. Lee gulped at the memory. Could he really go through with this, knowing what it would do to her? *Push it back, push it away.* Backing out now would mean giving up, giving in; letting Mike win. Letting his girl go off with his once-best friend. That just could not happen.

Lee trudged up the stairs, ever mindful of the time. He had to allow enough for the gas to get everywhere, so that when Mike got back all it would take was the flick of the light switch – right inside the kitchen door – and BOOM. He made a mental note to turn the electricity back on in the kitchen.

There was a radio on in Mike's room. Why was Mike still using his little kid's room? Lee scoffed at the thought. Emma wasn't here to claim the meagre 'master bedroom' (no en suite). Mike needed to grow up. Get his hair cut. Get a proper job. Lee winced slightly at the thought that none of that was going to happen now.

A sharp, stabbing pain in his chest took Lee by surprise. He sat back on Mike's bed, half-noting the way he'd wrinkled the duvet and somewhere in the back of his mind thinking that he'd have to straighten it out before he left the room. He was too busy catching his breath, however, to really take that thought in. What was going on? Was he having a heart attack? A high-pitched sound confused him until he realised it was his own wheezing chest. Tears were suddenly streaming down his face. He pulled the mask to one side. What the fuck had happened to him? What was he doing? Planning to kill his best friend. To *kill* someone. And for what? For looking after their other best friend. Something Lee had promised to do when he married her but he'd failed. He'd let her down; he'd more than let her down, in fact. He felt a familiar self-loathing flood into him and he crumpled forward, his head in his hands, sobbing and nearly retching at the thought of what he was doing.

He sat that way for some minutes, thinking he should just let Mike find him, let him see what had become of him, and then do whatever he wanted – kick the shit out of him, take him to the police. Whatever. He was a total fuck-up, no better than his dad. His bastard, bullying dad.

But then he spotted it. Just out of the corner of his eye, nearly obscured by the duvet which almost reached the floor. A piece of lined A4, crumpled but the familiar handwriting unmistakeable. Lee leaned forward, ignoring the pain in his chest. He picked up the paper, smoothed it out. Read his wife's words – which said nothing much yet said it all and renewed his resolve. He read the words again and again, like a mantra, feeling his breathing slow down and a sense of calm righteousness take over.

Mike, here's the last of my stuff. I still can't believe this is real. Anna xxx

It was starting to get dusky outside, the long summer evenings already shortening. Lee knew he would have to get going. He pulled on his mask again and even then, as he made his way back down the dark staircase, he could smell the gas that was leaking through from the kitchen.

He crept in, wondering why he was tiptoeing. Slowly, he turned off the gas supply to the hobs and the oven before he wiped the handles clean. He checked the electrical appliances to make sure all were turned off before he reconnected the electricity. Slowly, he eased the switch down, holding his breath. The clock on the cooker started flashing but that was all. He was nearly home and dry. One last look then, holding his breath, he removed his mask, slid it into his rucksack and reached into his pocket for his wallet; he'd need some cash for the bus back home. Shit. His wallet. Where was it? He looked around, swearing. It must have come out of his pocket when he was sitting on Mike's bed – which he hadn't straightened up, either, he thought – although, really, who was going to notice that? Checking his watch, Lee saw it was only 8.27. Mike still had half an hour of work to go. There was no need to panic.

Lee slipped quietly and carefully through the kitchen door, closing it gently, as though the slightest movement would cause the house to collapse. He had to stop himself from switching on the light in the hallway and laughed at himself. That was a close call. Gently, quietly – although there was nobody around to hear him – he began retracing his footsteps.

What if his wallet was not in the house and he'd dropped it on the street? Either way, he needed it. It wasn't just the money he needed to get home; although he'd carefully manipulated the situation so that the neighbours had seen him earlier that day, he didn't want any evidence of his presence on the premises. Nothing that could link him to his friend's death.

Leaving

Anna was finding it difficult to work out the last few items she should take with her. She and Mike had planned this carefully in the hope that their preparations would go unnoticed and she didn't want Lee to become suspicious at the last moment.

Over the previous few weeks, whenever she had the chance, Anna would drop a couple of items off at Mike's. There was now a neat pile of clothes on his spare bed, which would go into the travel bags they had chosen and ordered online. In a smaller case were Anna's few really cherished possessions. Among them were a necklace which had been her grandma's, a book of poems which Mike had given to her when they were at secondary school, and her old school shirt - signed by both Mike and Lee, and about forty other children in their year. To Anna it signified the happiest time of her life – *so far*, she tried to persuade herself.

In the top drawer in Lee's office was her passport, along with his. Ever since she and Mike had hatched their plan, Anna had been desperate to take it, to know she had it safely in her possession, but this was the kind of thing she knew Lee would notice and so she had left it, the knowledge of its presence – its vulnerability – gnawing away at her. Every day she had checked it was still there, if Lee was out at work or having a cigarette in the garden. Her heart would beat wildly as she crept into his office, even if she knew he was not at home.

Now, the time had come to take possession of the passport.

Her stomach was churning at the thought of what she was about to do and she could not wait for the next twenty-four hours to be out of the way.

It was hard to believe that this was to be the last night in this house (she had never been able to think of it as home). The last night of her marriage. And unbelievably, Lee had chosen this night to ask Mike to go on a night out.

"What?" she'd exclaimed a couple of days earlier when Mike had told her.

"It's OK," he'd assured her, "in fact possibly even quite good. It means you get the house to yourself and can make sure you've got everything you need. You can drop the rest of your things off at mine and be back home in bed before Lee gets back. I'll make sure we stay out late and if there's any problem, I'll let you know. Kind of perfect, really."

"Except you have to go for a night out with Lee."

"Don't worry about that."

She slipped her favourite hoodie and a pair of jeans into the bag, followed by underwear and a pair of sandals. Her toiletries would have to remain in the bathroom so as not to arouse Lee's suspicion. They were just things, she told herself, and, as Mike liked to say, they did have shops in Spain.

Trotting down the stairs, Anna looked about the house in disdain. This was his place. And before it was Lee's, it had been *his*. She thought of Scott with the utmost dislike. Hate, in fact. Although Scott had long since left this world, his strong, manly body withering away before their eyes, he was still there somehow. In Lee, in the house she shared with Lee. An overbearing presence, as he had been in real life. She was sure that if it wasn't for him, Lee could have turned out differently. In spite of everything, she couldn't help but care about her husband and grieve for the boy he had once been.

She opened the door of Lee's study, feeling his strong

personality in its dark colours and stark walls. Her heart in her mouth, she opened the filing cabinet carefully, imagining the passport gone. She exhaled in relief. It was there, exactly where it had always been. Taking it quickly, she shut the drawer carefully - although there was nobody in the house to hear - then picked up her bag in the hallway and walked outside, locking the door behind her.

Theirs was a dark driveway, even on days of sheer sunlight, as the tall trees - meant to keep the house out of view of the road - seemed to close in on it, separating Lee and Anna from the rest of the world. It was worse in the winter, somehow; even though the fallen leaves meant there was a bit more sky to see, the naked branches reminded her of strong, cruel arms, barring her way.

As the slight breeze rustled the leaves high above her, a pair of blackbirds flew low across her path, chattering wildly to each other. She would miss the birds, she thought. They were one of the few things she did love about the house, and the one redeeming feature of those tyrannical trees, as the fearless birds happily nested in them, the woodpecker even daring to tap away at the thick coating of bark.

Anna's relief was short-lived as she drove out of their drive. From here on in, she knew she would be on edge until that plane was in the air, with her and Mike safely on board.

The only person in Bristol other than Mike who knew Anna was leaving was her friend and now boss, Suzie. As she drove down Parry's Lane, Anna thought back to their goodbye earlier that day. It had been hard but Suzie had been nothing but supportive; in fact, she had actively encouraged Anna to get away.

Equally hard was not saying goodbye to her other friends and colleagues. As nurses at the children's hospital, through necessity and shared experiences, they had all grown close over the years. Anna had worked there since she graduated and knew that her job and the people she worked with were what she would miss most about life in Bristol.

She had wanted to tell people how much she had loved working with them, but she knew she had to be strong and keep this secret as close to her chest as possible. The fewer people who knew, the better. Suzie had accepted her resignation but nothing had been said at work. Anna's position had already been filled, her replacement starting the following day. "I'll handle it, Anna, don't worry. Once you're safely gone, I'll tell them... something. I'll tell them you didn't want to leave them."

It had made Anna cry.

Mike's cul-de-sac was quiet and Anna was thankful for that. She had parked up around the corner, and gone through the allotments behind his house, into his back garden and through the door into the kitchen. There was a faint smell of gas again. Momentarily, she felt annoyed at Lee who had said he'd fixed the problem with the boiler, but then she reminded herself that it really didn't matter. They could speak to Emma about it and get it sorted when they were safely out of the country – they probably wouldn't ask Westbury Gas to do it, though.

How different Mike's house felt to the one she shared with Lee. It was far smaller and much more modest, but it felt like a real home. When she had first come round after Mike's return, she had been struck by how little it had changed since their school days when she, Mike and Lee would hang around after school or at weekends, before they were old enough to go out. Emma had been the most welcoming of the parents, and the most relaxed. She had seemed to remember what it was like to be a child, and a teenager. Anna wondered if Emma had changed much, and whether they would still get on OK. After all, Mike's mum had seemed to have a soft spot for Lee and had always been sympathetic to his situation. Growing up, Anna had often felt a bit left out as Lee was always staying over at Mike's whereas she, being a girl, would have to leave, often just as it seemed things were starting to get fun. Emma would drop Anna off at her house, where her mum would be working away in her study, and her brothers more often than not out living their older, more grown-up lives. Her dad, of course, would be away with work. Anna remembered the sinking feeling of returning to her tall house, echoing with emptiness, wishing she'd been able to stay in the warm, dark confines of Mike's room where he and Lee were no doubt carrying on playing Sonic and listening to tunes.

On the rare occasion that both her parents were at home, and not working, Anna would greet them and they'd look up from their books, smile vaguely at her, but rarely ask what she'd been doing, where she'd been, who she'd been with. They had seemed to Anna like polite acquaintances who happened to share a house.

She swung herself up the small staircase to Mike's spare room, where his giant rucksack now lay next to her holdall. This really was it. She laid her clothes carefully on top of the others and zipped the bag shut, then tucked her passport into the outside pocket.

She used the toilet and, as she was washing her hands, caught sight of her reflection in the bathroom mirror. Her face was flushed and her eyes seemed to have a slightly wild quality. There were dark rings below them, which was nothing new. People usually put it down to her night shifts at the hospital but in truth it was the nights at home - lying awake, unable to sleep until Lee got back, anticipating his return and what mood he might be in. It was only once he was snoring away at her side that she felt safe enough to sleep. Night shifts were like a break to her, the small room where she was sometimes able to have an hour or two's sleep a haven. She knew that people envied her lifestyle; she had a good-looking, successful husband, and wanted for nothing materially. If only they knew the truth.

She splashed water on her face and looked her mirrored self in the eyes. Time to be really strong.

Outside, despite the warmth of the evening, Anna found her teeth started chattering. She pulled her cardigan around herself and hopped back over Mike's garden fence, returning to her car.

It seemed that everywhere held a memory as she drove back to the house. The primary school where she, Mike and Lee had first met. The small park where they and their other friends had first played in the playground together, later graduating to drinking cider and smoking Benson and Hedges. Even now, the smell of a freshly opened packet of cigarettes could transport Anna straight back to those days.

Taking a detour past Blaise Estate, Anna drove through the outskirts of Henbury, on through Westbury-on-Trym, up to the Downs. She bypassed the turn-off for her house and skirted the expanse of grass - now a subdued brown from the heat of the summer – and parked at the viewing spot for the Clifton Suspension Bridge. There was the ever-present ice cream van, and an older couple standing near the fence, talking quietly and intimately. A family were seated on a bench, the children's faces coated in ice cream and the parents laughingly trying to clean them up. Two visions of possible futures which would not be hers. Not in Bristol, anyway.

She still felt cold, she realised, and pulled away, circling back around the Downs until she came back to her turn-off. Although she knew Mike would have told her if there was any problem, she still felt nervous that Lee could actually be at the house when she returned. It was the same fear she experienced on a daily basis but this time accentuated by the situation.

As she drew back in between the trees it felt like they closed in behind her, but she was relieved to see the house in darkness.

"Hello?" she called doubtfully into the empty hallway, to no response.

What to do now? It was only just after nine but she couldn't sit still. There was nothing she wanted to do in this house except leave it.

She put on the kettle and made a cup of tea then scraped out the bread bin, thinking she would feed the crumbs to the birds. A farewell to them. She felt bad for leaving them with Lee, who she knew would never think of putting out food for them, of giving them water in the icy depths of winter. Still, they were survivors and probably had plenty of other gardens they could visit.

In the secluded garden she listened to the distant sounds of the city she had grown up in. The odd motorbike speeding along the Portway, the sound of its roaring motor carrying up through the clear night. The laughter of kids out on the Downs, swearing at each other but affectionately. Anna envied them their age; that golden age, she thought of it, when the world began to open up and adults began to treat you with just the smallest bit of respect. Organising your own social calendars, staying out late. First kisses, first drinks, first everything. It was a time of tumultuous emotions and the utmost assuredness that you knew everything, and everything you knew was right.

There was so much that she would miss about Bristol, Anna thought sadly. But she had to go.

She bid a silent farewell to the birds, many of whom were retreating to their nests for the night, and scattered the remnants of crumbs across the lawn. They could enjoy them for breakfast in the morning.

Treading wearily upstairs, Anna showered and brushed her teeth, put on the shapeless, baggy pyjamas she had taken to wearing, pushed her mobile under the side of the mattress, and got into bed.

Turning the light off, she lay with her eyes wide open, aware of every creak; any possible noise outside which could signal Lee's return home. She checked her phone, which had full signal but no message. A good thing. She and Mike had agreed that unless there was any problem, they wouldn't make contact until they saw each other in the early hours of the morning.

"And then," Mike had said, tucking a loose strand of her hair behind her ear, "I'm going to get you away from this place."

"I can't believe it, I can't."

"It's true, Anna," she had been reminded of his earnest teenage self. "We're going to get away from here and once you're away, you'll be safe. I'll make sure of it."

Sure he was going to kiss her, Anna had closed her eyes, but instead he had pulled her into a strong, brotherly embrace. She had tried to work out if she felt disappointed. She definitely felt a flood of warmth. Mike made her feel safe, although he seemed to be constantly at pains to point out to her that he wasn't rescuing her: "I'm just offering you a route out of here. You'd do the same for me."

"I know," Anna had laughed, "I don't think you're the macho type."

"Thanks very much!"

"Sorry, Mike. What I mean is, you're not the caveman type. You're being a good friend. A great friend. The best."

"That's it, I am. And I want you to know that I don't expect anything from you. I just want to know you're safe. That's what will make me happy."

Anna thought about what Mike was saying. She was glad, really, that he wasn't complicating this with love, romance, sex... any of those things. But despite his protestations that he wasn't rescuing her, that this was her decision and he was just *enabling* her (she could hear Emma's influence in these words, she was sure), all she had wanted to do was lean into his warm, fleece-covered shoulder and fall asleep.

She pushed the phone back and ran through the plan in her mind, double checking everything to make sure that she hadn't left any clues for Lee to find. He would be drunk when he got in, anyway, but even so. It would be silly to have got this far and then let a moment of carelessness give her away.

The tickets were at Mike's, as was her passport, and their bags. No, she reassured herself, nothing here looked out of place. Even if Lee were to pull open her wardrobe doors, nothing would seem amiss. She had taken the bare minimum.

She closed her eyes, trying some deep breathing to relax.

Perhaps she had drifted off. She was woken by a slam of the front door and immediately pulled from her reverie into wide-awakeness. Lee's keys clattered onto the sideboard in the hallway and she heard him go into the kitchen, where he made no effort to behave quietly - clattering glasses and noisily filling one from the tap. A cupboard door opened and there was the rustling of a bread bag. No doubt he was making a sandwich and leaving the tidy room in a mess. As if he would ever tidy away after himself. He knew she would be up before him the next day and would diligently clear up his clutter as she always did. She had tried leaving it a mess once, to see if he'd take the hint, but she had ended up paying for that.

She thought she could hear him muttering to himself, then he was in the hallway, kicking off his shoes and coming up the stairs.

This was the time of night that Anna surpassed herself with her acting skills. She turned over so she wasn't facing the door, and began the carefully practised deep breathing. As he flung the door open and the light fell on her, she moved slightly, as if disturbed in her sleep; inwardly terrified. It was a huge effort not to revert to her previous nervous, shallow breathing, but by the sound of it, he was paying her no attention. She heard him shedding his clothes then felt the bed dip violently as he got in, pulling the majority of the covers over himself.

Within minutes he was snoring and Anna was free to go to sleep but she knew that night that she wouldn't.

In the early hours of the morning she slipped silently from the bed, taking her phone out from under the mattress and tucking it up her sleeve. She padded softly down the hall to her room, where she'd laid out her uniform, and dressed herself as if for a normal day at work.

With no time, or stomach, for breakfast, she took her keys and her handbag and left the house. She had primed herself for this. She had no wish to take a last look around and she couldn't chance a last glance at Lee. She didn't want to; she wouldn't miss him, as such, not the Lee he had grown into, but she knew that she would miss the Lee he had once been for the rest of her life.

Today was the day she was walking out of his life forever. She opened the oversized oak door into the awakening day, the light falling onto the gleaming tiles. She stepped outside and she smiled.

Bristol, June 2003

Discovery

Lee kicked the garage door, hurting his foot and cursing himself as he knelt to examine the dent. His dad would have gone mental about that. The thought actually made him feel slightly better. He gave the door another kick. *That one's for you, Dad. Bastard.*

He wasn't a good husband to Anna; he knew that, really. He hadn't been faithful to her, and he knocked her about. It was wrong, he knew it and sometimes – often – he saw Scott in himself and he hated himself. But he wasn't all bad. He earned a good living, and Anna wanted for nothing. And he loved her. Anyway, it wasn't like he hit her every day. It was just that she made him so angry sometimes.

Sometimes it was her unwillingness to stand up to him that enraged him, and sometimes it was the very opposite. What had been unforgiveable was her thinking it was OK to trick him. She'd tried it once, with those pills, and now she was at it again but even worse.

He didn't know whether to laugh, shout, cry, scream... what?

His wife and his best friend were having an affair and they thought he was so stupid that he wouldn't notice. Them with their university degrees; well, he was earning five times as much as either of them. More, probably, now that Mike was doing crappy call-centre work.

And why did Anna think he wouldn't see her sneaking

things from the house? It was so obvious, that time he'd walked into her room and seen her hurriedly stuffing some books into a drawer. She had bookcases for books, drawers for underwear, tops, that kind of thing.

"What're you doing?" he'd asked nonchalantly while inside him a series of alarms was going off.

"Oh, just tidying up. You know, trying to keep things as... we like them."

It was true that Lee did insist on a tidy house. Well, it was such a place that it shouldn't ever be untidy.

He had smiled at her, but taken note. Yes, Anna was often nervous around him these days. He felt bad about it if he let himself but it was better to shrug it off – after all, it wasn't altogether a bad thing, he mused. Good to keep her on her toes. But she had been different just then. Less nervous, if anything. Acting, he thought.

Later that day, when she was cooking tea, Lee had checked that same drawer and seen the books were no longer there. He had quietly checked the rest of her room and there, under the chest of drawers, was a small bag, with what looked like those same books, a couple of CDs, and one of her favourite tops, too.

He had gone downstairs to have tea with her, switching on the oversized TV so that they wouldn't have to talk to each other, but every now and then he'd sneak a glance at her. Something was up, but he didn't want to give his hand away so he ate quickly, as usual, leaving his dirty plate and glass on the table. He had gone to the fridge, got himself a yoghurt and noisily eaten it, then gone to his study. He'd wait and see what she did next.

"I've got to leave for work a bit early, I promised Suzie I'd drop a book round to hers."

"OK. What time you going to be back?"

"Same as usual. It's night shift so I should be back just before you go to work."

"Right. See you later."

Lee had looked out of the window to see Anna walking to her car, carrying her usual bag, although it looked more full than it normally did. A quick check under the drawers confirmed that the bag he'd found was no longer there. He ran downstairs, grabbed his keys off the hook, and leapt into his car. From the end of his drive he could just see Anna's car going left; the wrong way if she was going to Suzie's.

Lee followed at a distance, drumming his fingers impatiently as he got stuck at some temporary traffic lights at Druid Hill. He knew, though. He knew where she was going and suddenly it felt like he had always known it.

To make sure, he carried on along Shirehampton Road, though he could no longer see her car. In the dusky evening light, he drove that route he knew so well, past Kingsweston House, down to Long Cross, where he turned right. He drove almost automatically, and there, as he'd known it would be, was his wife's car. Parked boldly and brazenly for all to see, in front of his best mate's house.

Lee slammed on his brakes, causing the driver behind him to sound their horn, and the one behind them likewise. The sharp sound made him think quickly. Rushing in and sorting Mike out would be Scott's way of doing things. Immediate, angry revenge, the satisfaction short-lived. It would also, Lee quickly reckoned, cement the relationship between Mike and Anna. Sticking his middle finger up at the driver behind, he drove on.

Bristol, May 2003

Decision time

Under the spreading chestnut tree, Mike took Anna's hand in his.

"We can do this, Anna – *you* can do it, I should say. And more than *can*, you *should*. You must. You can't spend any more of your life like this."

She looked into his earnest eyes, and suppressed an inappropriate urge to laugh. It was just that, in all the time he'd been away in Spain – doing a bit of travelling, learning a new language, meeting different people - it seemed he had not changed a bit. Yet she and Lee had remained in Bristol, the place they had all grown up, in the same jobs for years, and they had changed immeasurably.

She bit her lip. "I just don't know, Mike. I know I have to do something. But this – well, it will break Lee's heart..." Mike snorted at this and she acknowledged his point: "I know, I know. I suppose more than anything I'm thinking what if something goes wrong? What if he finds out – or finds us? He'll kill us."

"He won't find out. I've got a plan, I know exactly what we can do. Even if he guesses we've gone to Mum's, he's got no idea where she is. Spain's a big place."

"I don't know, Mike. I just don't want to drag you into all of this."

She sighed. He let go of her hand and put his fingers under her chin, turning her face to his.

For a moment she thought he would kiss her.

"You haven't dragged me into anything, Anna. I've come to you with this idea. I can't live happily knowing what he's doing to you anyway, so maybe this is me being selfish. Don't laugh," though he smiled himself. "Listen, what's been going on isn't right. You know it and I know it. If it was happening to somebody else, you'd be telling them what I'm telling you. It's just lucky that I'm in a position to help, that's all. Don't think about it any longer, just say you'll come with me."

Beyond them and the lush green field sat the industrial port of Avonmouth. The fat chimneys puffed out smoke, which drifted in lazy, fat clouds. Was there a message there? Anna chided herself. The message she needed was right there, being delivered by the man, the friend, who sat beside her. *Leave this life*. That was the message and she couldn't ignore it.

She nodded. "OK."

Mike hugged her to him and she felt his warmth through the soft, well-washed shirt. He smelled of something unfamiliar and she thought for a moment of how he and Lee had used to cover themselves in Lynx body spray when they were younger – and how she herself had commandeered a can of the Oriental fragrance for herself.

"Right then," he relinquished his grip, "we'd better get planning."

From his rucksack, Mike took his notepad and a sharp pencil. He always had some form of writing apparatus with him, in case inspiration struck or he happened upon the scoop of the century. He looked at the poem he was working on and flipped the page over, starting his and Anna's escape plan on a clean sheet.

"I can't tell you how happy I am that you said yes. I know you still care about Lee. I do too, believe it or not, but Anna, nobody can treat you – or anybody else – like that and get away with it. Maybe you'll change your mind about telling the police when you're away from here?"

She shook her head. Mike said no more on the subject but he knew he wouldn't let it lie. They couldn't leave Lee free to behave this way to some other poor woman. *One step at a time*, he told himself.

"OK, so when we get to Mum's you're to have the apartment I was in. There's plenty of space for me at her place." He could see Anna open her mouth as if to object but there was no time for objections so he ploughed on. "I'll book our flights. You're not to give me any money for anything, or Lee might notice. We can sort out cash later if necessary. What you can do is start to think about what you want to bring with you, sneak out a couple of things at a time. I'll get you a new bag which you can keep at my place. I'll give you a key and you can drop round on your way to or from work, or on your lunchbreaks, so Lee doesn't notice anything. I know it's a bit tight but you should be able to get from work to mine, dump your things then head straight back. If we give ourselves two months, do you think that will be enough time for you to get things in order?"

"I'll have to hand in my resignation. Work my notice."

"I know, but luckily you've got the best boss in the world."

Anna smiled. "Suzie's going to be happy when I tell her. She's never wanted me to be with Lee. She didn't say it outright at first but I could sense it."

"She's not daft, is she?"

"No, she wanted me to come out to Spain with her but I couldn't, and she knew Lee wouldn't let me come without him."

"I know, she said she'd asked you. That was when I really realised things weren't good with you and Lee. She was so worried. I know you'll miss her, and little Barney. They can come and visit, though; Jamie too, of course. I know it's going to be really hard for you, Anna. It's easy for me, I can just walk out of that crappy call-centre any time I like. Some of the people are OK but I don't think we're going to be lifelong friends. You're going to need to keep it between you and Suze, you know. The fewer people who know about this, the better."

For a moment, Anna looked at Mike and thought perhaps she was wrong; maybe he had changed. She had never known him so forthright and sure of himself in the past.

Unaware of her thoughts, Mike continued, "We'll book flights for early morning if possible, make it look like you're just going to do an early shift. You should be able to leave the house in your uniform as if you're going to do a normal shift then come straight to me. You'll have to leave your car somewhere round the back, we can give Suzie the key – or post it to your mum. We'll get a taxi to the airport. I'm going to try and make it look like I'm still around – maybe leave some lights on and the radio or something."

"Wow, Mike, have you thought of everything?"

"I don't know, I really don't know, but I think I've got the basics covered. We just need to be really careful with communicating. I know you delete messages straightaway anyway but we can't mention any of this anywhere on email, text, anything that could get into the wrong hands. Let's decide the date now and work towards that."

He wrote in large letters '27th July 2003' in the centre of the piece of paper. Then he circled it, drew stars around it, and fireworks, and Anna, forgetting her worries for just a moment, felt her heart might explode with happiness.

"9.15 is perfect, mate, I'll come and meet you straight from work." When Lee had called to arrange a night out, Mike had been surprised and worried but he quickly came to realise this was the perfect chance to make sure Anna had time to get herself sorted. The timing couldn't have been better. He beamed down the phone.

He wanted to call Anna immediately, tell her the flights were booked, but he knew she'd be at home, possibly with

Lee. He would have to wait until she was at work.

He checked himself as he'd had to so many times lately. She was his friend. Lee was his friend too, but Lee was behaving like a bastard. Mike couldn't afford to be thoughtful towards him right now. Anna, though... well. Had he always loved her? He wasn't sure. He'd loved Suzie once, he was sure he had, though she always said he hadn't: "Not really," she had said more than once, "not that kind of love."

That statement had seemed mysterious to him, but he thought he knew what she meant. He had loved being with Suzie, fancied her like mad, from the first moment he'd set eyes on her. Since then there had been Silvia in Spain, but that had fizzled out – despite her dark eyes, which seemed to twinkle with mischief, and waist-length black hair, which sent a shiver across him whenever it brushed his bare skin. Anna and Lee – and their relationship - were the reason he'd left Bristol. It wasn't just Lee's change of attitude towards Mike, or what had happened on the stag do. Mike knew that he couldn't cope with them being together; his once-best friends had become something very different.

He and Anna had missed their opportunities, he thought; opting instead for Lee, and for Suzie, at different times, on dark, potent nights years before. Now he had to be careful.

Despite his protestations to the contrary, and the warnings from Emma and Suzie, he couldn't help but feel that he was rescuing Anna. But that sounded so... patronising. She was perfectly capable of rescuing herself but he could tell she was scared. When he'd realised what was going on with her and Lee, he had been practically apoplectic. He had felt a deep, growing, *manly*, anger, which had taken him by surprise.

It wasn't an ownership thing, whatever the Germaine Greers of the world might suggest. It was pure outrage that one human being could treat another in that way, and these feelings were only magnified by the fact that the people in question were his two childhood friends.

He just wanted to get Anna out. No matter what happened - or didn't happen - between the two of them in the future. He knew that he must not mix any of this up with his feelings for her. Those had to be irrelevant. They weren't running away together in the traditional sense.

It was enough that he had her trust. That, from somebody who must find it near impossible to trust anybody, was a huge compliment.

2002

Last Christmas

When she was a child, what Anna had enjoyed most about Christmas was the run-up to it; the plays at school, the carol concerts. She had been swept up in the expectation and hope. The reality of it was so different to the Christmases she read about in books, or saw on TV. It was true that it was one of the only times of the year that all her family were together but in Anna's book this wasn't necessarily a good thing.

Her dad would be back home but bored and irritable. He and her mum would drink too much, argue, and sulk. Meanwhile, her brothers would hole themselves up in one or other of their bedrooms, sharing their love of music, computer games, films, which they never considered Anna might equally enjoy, or at least want to be a part of.

When her grandma was alive, those had been the best Christmases. She always had time for Anna. She would play with Anna's new toys with her, help her build make-believe worlds for her cuddly animals and Sylvanian Families, but once her grandma had died, Anna felt very much alone. Christmas would bring good presents – great ones, and generous, but it was expected that Anna would then take these presents and occupy herself with them while her parents cooked, drank, and argued.

Many a Christmas day was spent sadly but wholeheartedly wrapped up in a duvet, nose in a book, transported into somebody else's world. There was something about *A Little*

Princess which particularly appealed to Anna. She could feel Sara's loneliness, and admired her determinedly correct behaviour in the face of adversity.

Anna had gone from the Harper family Christmases to those of the Lewis family, with nothing in between. When Scott had been alive, he had ruled the roost. He, too, had used Christmas as an excuse to drink, and had been at turns exuberant and bad-tempered. His presence had cowed Lee, who had been sullen and depressed, and Anna had been unsure of how to act. She had busied herself with preparing Christmas dinner, as had seemed to be expected of her anyway.

Now it was just her and Lee and he seemed to have done his best to fill Scott's boots. This year, he had invited Mike to join them and had insisted that he and Mike go to the pub while Anna prepared the dinner – despite the fact that she had been on night shift and only arrived home at breakfast time.

She had enjoyed the feeling of being out and about in the city that morning; it was unnaturally quiet – to the point that it could have been unnerving if she hadn't known what day it was. Of course there were the usual homeless people, still asleep or knocked out by their chosen intoxicant, hunched in doorways and on steps. Other than these poor souls, the city seemed deserted. She had driven home, yawning, thinking of the children she'd looked after; how despite everything – drips, chemo, amputation in one case - they let the magic of Christmas in.

At least Mike would be there today; it had been hard to imagine a whole day spent with Lee otherwise. It would no doubt have ended with tears.

Mike had looked between his two friends, trying to decide what to do. There was no way Emma would have let this happen; it had always been his and her shared responsibility to cook. Since he was old enough to remember, he'd been involved in some way, and he had loved standing in the kitchen on a chair, mixing the stuffing or, when he was older, peeling potatoes and carrots, listening to carols and singing along with his mum.

Anna, however, had just smiled. "Go on, have a drink, this should be ready by the time you get back. I've got a nut roast for us, Mike, and yes, Lee, turkey for you."

She smiled, laughingly, but Mike felt annoyed for her. Why was Lee making her cook the whole thing – and, adding insult to injury, making her cook meat? *She's a vegetarian, for Christ's sake,* he thought, but he knew Lee's mind did not work like that. *She don't have to eat it,* he could imagine Lee saying.

"Thanks, Anna, that sounds lovely." Mike had smiled and taken his coat, feeling guilty.

Mike and Lee had walked across the Downs to the Port of Call. It was a drizzly, unseasonably warm day and Mike was beginning to think it couldn't feel much less like Christmas if it tried. However, he was glad of Lee's choice of pub. The little steep backstreets around this part of Bristol always reminded Mike of Cornwall. He was happy to soak up the festive atmosphere in the bar and thought it might be a relief to Anna to have some time to herself anyway.

"Happy Christmas, mate," Lee plonked two pints on the table.

"Happy Christmas. It's nice to be back."

"Yeah, like old times, eh?"

"Yeah," Mike clinked Lee's glass with his but couldn't help thinking that it couldn't be more different from old times.

After he'd bought a round in return, Mike suggested that they go back and help Anna finish preparing dinner.

"No, let's have another, eh? She'll be OK," Lee said, already pulling his wallet out.

"It just seems a bit... leaving her alone... it's Christmas day, Lee."

"I know, and that's why I want another pint with my best mate."

"OK," Mike had sighed, knowing all too well where this was going. Lee was soon back with a pint each and a whisky chaser. "OK," Mike said again, "But after this we go back to Anna."

"We'll go when I say, mate. It's my 'ouse, she's my wife." Lee's attitude had turned on its head suddenly, his eyes glaring into Mike's.

"Well I'm not going to drink any more, not now. It's not fair..."

"*It's not fair on Anna,*" Lee mimicked.

"No, it's not," Mike felt angry himself now.

"Don't be such a fuckin' Mummy's boy."

"I'm not," Mike flashed back, "I just don't think it's right."

"Fine. We'll go back, then." Lee finished his pint quickly, washing it down with the whisky, and grabbed his leather jacket. "You comin', then?"

Mike downed his whisky, leaving the majority of his pint, and the pair of them made their way in silence back across the Downs, the rain now coming down heavily.

"You're soaked!" Anna exclaimed when they got in. The house was full of the smell of Christmas dinner and the lights on the tree in the hallway twinkled merrily. Still, there was something amiss.

Anna fetched towels for them both then the three of them sat down to eat. Mike and Lee sat opposite each other, Lee glowering and Mike making polite conversation with Anna. She could clearly see something had happened but, not wanting to tip the heavily teetering balance any further, sportingly kept up her side of the conversation.

Lee kept the bottle of wine close to his place and poured himself top-ups liberally. Mike saw Anna glancing up from time to time and thought that her expression was one of increasing concern.

However, Lee surprised them both. "Sorry, I'm being a

prick!" he burst out, then raised his glass, grinning. "'Ere's us three back together again and I'm sulkin'. Anna, this dinner is lush, and Mike it's good to have you back in Bristol, mate. Merry Christmas."

Mike and Anna glanced briefly at each other before raising their glasses too.

The rest of the day was OK. They drank: Anna moderately, Mike to just short of excess, and Lee to way past any recommended weekly level.

Mike was keeping an eye out for anything untoward. It was clear that Anna was not comfortable around Lee, but he had yet to see anything other than bullying. It made him sad that it had come to this; his two best friends making each other unhappy – well one making the other unhappy, at least; and making himself unhappy at the same time, Mike suspected. Lee was such a forceful personality. Like a gale blowing through the house, Emma used to say. He'd lost some of that when his mum had left, but now that Scott was out of the way, it seemed he had recovered some of that strength. Like he'd inherited a part of his dad, along with the house and the business.

Anna, however, was quieter than ever. Maybe some people wouldn't notice; she had always been quiet, but Mike sensed that this was somehow different. Still, it was Christmas Day and it seemed to Mike that it might be a chance for happiness. He felt full of good food, and good wine, and nostalgia. These were his friends who he'd known all his life, and the memories they shared were irreplaceable.

He tried to push away the thoughts of what Suzie had told him and Emma, when she'd come out to visit. Though it was clear Lee's temper had become shorter over the years, it was hard to believe that he would hit Anna. Almost impossible, in fact. It had been a hard few years for his friend, thought Mike – a hard life so far. Maybe more than anything, he needed help.

Perhaps Mike could be the one to help him - and Anna, too. He could put his own feelings aside and help his friends, and when it was done he could disappear back to Spain again. The drink was getting to him, he realised, but still – it wasn't out of the question, was it?

Mike went to bed at about 9pm. He'd found himself unable to keep up with Lee in terms of drinking and while Anna prepared a cheeseboard and biscuits, he realised he was starting to feel sick.

"Sorry," he said, kissing her on the cheek, "I think I need to sleep today off. Merry Christmas."

"Merry Christmas, mate," Lee gave Mike a hearty slap on the back. "Here's to many more, eh?"

Mike wobbled up to his room and sat wearily on his bed, reclining so that the room seemed to spin around him. He tried the trick somebody had told him, of placing one foot on the floor. It didn't help.

"You fuckin' what?"

Mike was jolted from his stupor-like sleep by a loud shout. It took him a moment to work out where he was and who was shouting.

"Shush, Lee, Mike will hear you."

"I don't fuckin' care. What are you doin', tryin' to make an idiot of me? No wonder all the blokes take the piss out of me, say I'm firin' blanks."

"I'm sorry, Lee."

Mike moved to the door of his room to hear more clearly. It sounded like Lee and Anna were in the hallway; Anna's voice, though quiet and a bit shaky, was still clear. "I knew it would upset you. That's why I didn't say anything."

"What else are you hidin' from me?"

Mike heard the sound of keys, coins, and God knew what else bouncing on the tiled floor.

"What else is in 'ere, you stupid bitch?"

Mike inhaled sharply. What should he do? He opened his door further, crept onto the landing. His heart was beating in a panic. He wanted to see what was going on before intervening.

"Lee, please, just give me back my bag." Anna's voice was consciously calm, placating.

"Why the fuck should I? I bought it for you and you use it to hide your pills. No wonder I can't get you up the duff. What is it? You sleepin' with someone else?"

"No!" Anna shrieked. "Of course I'm not! It's just you, you'll regret this in the morning. Let's talk about it then, eh?"

"What, give you a chance to make up some bullshit? No thanks."

Mike heard a sharp intake of breath and he crept to the banister, to see Lee with Anna's hair in one hand, twisting her arm with his other.

"You'll take those pills and flush them down the bog, right? NOW!" he yelled.

"OK, OK," Anna said.

"Good." Lee let go of her and pushed her towards the downstairs toilet. "GO ON, THEN."

Mike stood stock-still. What was he doing? Why wasn't he down there, defending Anna? He needed to think. Shortly, there was the sound of the toilet being flushed, and footsteps crossing the tiles towards the stairs. Anna's. He moved back towards his room, still thinking, breathing hard. Then he heard Lee go back into the kitchen, slamming the door.

Anna came up the stairs, her head down. Mike stood in his doorway and she looked at him. She wasn't crying but nevertheless he thought he had never seen anybody look so miserable.

"Don't say anything," she whispered, and went through to her bedroom.

Mike, head pounding along with his heart, retreated into

his room. He couldn't sleep, despite the hangover which was already setting in. Instead he kept vigil, lying awake and listening for Lee's hard step on the staircase. If anything else happened, he would intervene. But Lee never came upstairs and eventually Mike fell into a hard, hollow sleep.

In the morning it was as though nothing had happened.

Anna gave Mike a look as he came into the kitchen, but it was so fleeting he couldn't be sure that he wasn't imagining it. She kept her head down, then, making breakfast for the three of them and seeming genuinely concerned for Lee's self-induced headache.

What Mike needed was time to think, time to make a plan. He couldn't let this go on but he couldn't yet see how he could stop it.

Three's a crowd

"Mike, mate! Good to see you, good to see you," Lee enthused, slapping his old mate on the back and pushing a pint his way. "Still drink the warm stuff, mate? Bet you don't get much of that in Spain."

Bloody hell, Lee thought; the bloke hadn't changed a bit! It was obvious that he'd made a bit of an effort to smarten up for their night out but the stubble, the faded jeans, the trainers… Lee pulled at his own shirt, feeling the reassuringly expensive fabric soft between his fingertips. The two of them had once dressed exactly the same but whereas he had moved on, with the times and his success as a businessman, following his old man's footsteps, for Mike it seemed that time, and fashion, had stood quite still.

Mike smiled. "You're right, it's lager all the way there. And wine, of course. Nice to get a pint of proper ale, though, thanks Lee. Hi Anna," he smiled at the third member of the old school trio, and she smiled back almost shyly.

"Aren't you gonna say nothin', then?" Lee gave his wife a playful push and she winced slightly. He hadn't wanted her to come, to be honest. They didn't often go out together these days; not in years, really. When Mike had phoned to say he was back, Lee had suggested a couple of nights when Anna was on late shift but Mike had stood his ground, kept saying he'd wanted all three of them to get together, so in the end Lee had caved in. It should be easy enough to get rid of her, though.

"It's great to see you, Mike, really." Anna smiled more openly this time.

Lee watched closely. Although he'd been the one to win her, he'd always suspected she had come close to choosing their good friend over him. He'd had to make sure that, once he had her, she never looked back. When he and Mike had fallen out, and Mike had followed his mum to Spain, Lee had been quite relieved. Not that he'd admit that to anyone, of course.

"So how long you back for then, mate?" He took hold of the conversation and made it his. Mike was his friend first and foremost; after all, they were both blokes, weren't they? Nothing good could come of a male-female friendship. Sex would have to come into it somewhere, but blokes; well, they could drink together, go and watch City together, get pissed up and visit Birds of Paradise. Anna wouldn't be into any of that. Mind you, if Mike was still into the same 90s New Man shit, he wouldn't be, either. Lee thought back to the shambles of his stag do. Was that the last time they'd seen each other? Ah well, the rest of the night had been pretty good, from what he could remember.

"I'm not sure, really. I've got Mum's house for as long as I want, so I'll see what happens with work and that. It's good to be back, though."

Mike raised his glass and Lee clinked his against it. Anna, after a quick glance at her husband, did the same.

Soon it was – almost – like old times. They'd met in the Shakespeare, at Mike's suggestion. Lee would have preferred one of the waterfront bars but he had to admit, it was quite good to be back in one of their old haunts. The pub was full of after-work drinkers but in the corner sat a couple of the old regulars, drinking their cider from tin mugs.

"It's so good to be in a proper pub," said Mike. "Spain's full of bars trying to emulate this…" he tapped the wooden partition behind him and gestured to the bar area, "… but nothing comes close."

The conversation was flowing all around and there were regular bursts of laughter from a group of suited blokes at a nearby table. Sometimes Lee wished he got to wear a suit more often; they looked pretty sharp, but he was so glad he didn't have to sit in a fucking office all day, it'd drive him out of his mind.

Lee was aware that Mike wasn't in as strong a financial position as he was, and he liked to flash the cash, so he insisted that the night was on him. "Welcome an old mate back, right?"

He couldn't tell if Mike was happy with this or not, but what the fuck. A hundred quid, two hundred... it wasn't going to make much of a dent. He wanted Mike to see the success he'd made of himself, anyway, while Mike had been trying to make his way in the world of journalism.

"So, bet there's loads of fit Spanish birds, eh?"

Mike glanced at Anna – this didn't escape Lee's notice – before answering. "Well, yeah, no more than here, though."

"They don't like to shave their pits, do they? Dirty bitches."

Lee laughed and Mike smiled, giving nothing away.

"How's your work, Anna?" he turned the conversation towards the third member of their party, who had been sitting quietly.

"Oh, it's really good, thanks, Mike," Anna's eyes looked more alive, somehow, thought Mike, at the mention of her job. "I'm still on the same ward, I still love it."

"Yeah, and I love the uniform," Lee scoffed, leaning over to kiss Anna on the cheek.

Anna accepted the kiss and smiled weakly at the comment.

"Anna doesn't think I take her job seriously, do you, love?"

"I never said that..."

"She looks a bit of alright in that nurse's kit, like I say, but it pays fuck all. Sorry mate, Mike, I know you're not exactly loaded, either."

"It's not all about the money," Mike smiled at Anna and she smiled back, despite Lee glaring at her.

"Yeah, but she don't seem to mind 'avin' a nice place to live and a shiny new car to drive, do you?

Anna looked at the table.

"Mate, I was thinkin'," Lee continued, "why don't you come and work for me for a bit? You were always pretty 'andy. I could do with someone to 'elp on the bathroom fittings, what do you think? Save you gettin' stuck in one o' them call-centres."

"Thanks, mate," Mike seemed to be looking at Anna but quickly moved his glance to Lee. "That's decent of you, I'm going to plug away at the writing, though. I probably will end up in a call-centre but it should just tide me over, I can do some freelance stuff in the evenings then."

"Suit yourself," Lee shrugged then turned to Anna. "She's all pissed off with me for belittlin' 'er job, aren't you?" He leaned over to kiss her on the cheek again. In doing so he also took the opportunity to whisper, "Finish your drink and fuck off, alright?"

She didn't answer but he knew she'd got the message. Lee had some serious catching up, some serious drinking, to do with his mate and he could do without the ball and chain hanging about.

"I'm just off for a piss," Mike said, "Then how about visiting some of the old places? Mr Pope's? The Hatchet?"

"Sure mate, let's make a night of it. Anna's got to go, though, 'aven't you love?"

"Oh no, really?"

Lee was sure that was a look of disappointment on Mike's face.

"Yeah," Anna said, not looking at Mike or Lee, "I've got an early shift tomorrow, I'd better get some sleep. It's great to see you though, Mike. And if you're back for a while I'm sure we'll get plenty of time to catch up."

Mike smiled to hide his disappointment and headed off to the toilet.

Lee grabbed Anna's wrist. "You won't be doin' any catchin' up without my say so, right? And not without me there, neither. You can't just go about with single blokes now, you're married."

"But it's Mike," she began to protest but Lee's grip tightened.

"I don't give a shit if it's the fuckin' Pope."

"OK," she said, eyes down, and he kissed her.

"There's a good girl. Now 'ead off straight 'ome, alright? 'Ere's some cash for the taxi."

Lee pulled a twenty out of his pocket and handed it to Anna, who picked up her bag and left quietly. He watched her go then went to the bar and ordered a couple of grim-looking shots to see them on their way. Maybe he could persuade Mike about Birds of Paradise.

After Anna had gone, Lee went to the bar and Mike watched him closely. There he was, the same old Lee, but he seemed bigger somehow; he wasn't any taller, he couldn't be, but in the years since Mike had last seen him, his frame had filled out. He'd become more of a man, Mike supposed. He remembered the boy's body – the skinny legs, poking out of boxer shorts at Emma's kitchen table, the white, skinny arms escaping black t-shirt sleeves. Lee had once been inseparable from his Nirvana t-shirt, to the point that Anna and Mike had bought him a second identical one half-jokingly, just so he could wash the first one. Now, Lee was smart. His jeans were well cut and no doubt expensive, and his feet - which at one time were never out of DMs – were clad in smart brown... loafers? Was that what they were called?

It was hard for Mike to imagine Lee hurting Anna, but if Suzie's suspicions were correct, he was going to have to do something. It was beyond wrong, and the mismatch between

Lee's bulk and Anna's slender frame meant that real physical damage could be done. Worse than that, thought Mike, would be the psychological damage to Anna. She had not seemed herself tonight, but then it had been a long time since he'd seen her. A lot of water had passed under the bridge and he had, after all, missed her wedding. He hadn't been there for her. Had she wanted him to be?

He watched his friend joke with the barman then come back to the table, grinning, somehow managing to carry four glasses and two pots of expensive bar snacks.

"There you go, mate. Drink up." Lee picked up his own pint glass and took a healthy swig.

"Cheers, Lee," said Mike, realising that he had been watching him perhaps too intently. "Listen, mate, I just wanted to talk about what happened. At your stag do..."

"Ah, don't, buddy," Lee said, "It's in the past. Let's keep it there. I was behavin' like a twat, I'm sorry."

"OK, well I just wanted to say something. Get it out in the open."

"Ha! You sound like your mum!" Lee slapped Mike on the back. "That's just what she'd say but come on, let bygones be bygones and all that. We're older now. Men, yeah?"

"Yeah," Mike said slowly.

"Cheers, mate," Lee pushed his glass to Mike's, sloshing out some of the beer. "To the future."

"To the future," agreed Mike, smiling despite himself. It did feel good to be back. There was something immensely comforting about being with his old friend, like putting on a pair of worn-in shoes. He hoped against hope that what Suzie was thinking was wrong.

When Lee got home, Anna was fast asleep in their bed. He sometimes thought she pretended to be sleeping just to avoid him. He leaned in close to her face, whispering, his alcohol-fumed breath surely enough to make her give the game away if she was taking the piss. "You awake?"

Her even breathing suggested she was genuinely asleep. He considered waking her up, but he'd drunk too much for anything more than falling heavily onto the bed, fully clothed.

The next generation

Anna walked into the maternity ward to see Jacob sitting on a chair by Suzie's bed, his eyes fixed on the small blanketed bundle in the cot. Suzie looked like she was dozing; her bed reclined halfway and her hands resting on her stomach. She had a small smile on her face. Anna thought she had never seen her friend look so beautiful.

"Hi, Jacob," she whispered, and kissed him as he rose to greet her.

"Thanks for coming, Anna, Suze's going to be so happy to see you!"

"I don't want to wake her, though. I can always come back later, after my shift..."

"No need for that," Suzie opened one eye. "I wasn't really asleep, you know. Just resting."

"You deserve to," Jacob said and Anna looked at him, noting the admiration that was written all over his face, "after what you've been through."

"Was it OK?" asked Anna.

"It was... Shit, I was going to say it was fine but it wasn't. It was painful, so unbelievably painful!" Suzie laughed. "But all along, I just kept thinking what it was all about. It kept me going. It was worth it, I can tell you that much."

Anna turned her attention to the cot. "So this is him, eh? Your son." She found her eyes welling up.

"He is beautiful, isn't he?" Suzie asked. "Well I say that; I guess I'm pretty biased."

"Oh, he is, though. So lovely."

As if he knew he was being talked about, the baby sighed and snuffled, the tips of his tiny fingers just visible, gripping the top of the swaddling blanket.

"How's he got his hand out of there, eh? Shaping up to be the next Houdini, I reckon," Jacob said, the pride evident in his voice. He fetched a chair for Anna, from another smiling new mum across the ward. "Your turn next, eh?"

Anna smiled at him, "Not just yet. He is gorgeous, though."

"Can't deny it. Just like his mum."

Jacob gazed at his girlfriend with adoration once more.

"Go and get us a drink, you soppy git! Make yourself useful!" Suzie playfully admonished him.

"Alright, alright. Coffee? You should have decaf, you know, if you're…"

"Just get me a real coffee, this once, eh? Then it's decaf all the way, I promise."

Jacob was about to protest but one look at Suzie's face told him it wasn't worth it. "Anna?"

"I'll have what she's having. Thanks, Jacob."

"OK. I'm going to get a jug of water, too, right?"

"Whatever!" Suzie laughed, "Just get on with it."

As Jacob disappeared out of the room, Suzie said, "He was great, you know, last night. So great. I had a big panic, which I wasn't expecting, but they had to monitor the heartbeat, then I thought it had stopped, and…" her eyes filled with tears and Anna found hers following suit, "but Jacob calmed me down, the midwife thought he was brilliant too, you could tell. And it was fine. As you can see."

"It must be a scary thing to go through," Anna said.

"Yep, scarier than I'd ever imagined. And how people do it without pain relief, I've got no idea. I had the lot – apart from the pethidine. You know how weird people go on that."

"Wow. You're a mum!" Anna said in wonder. "I mean, I knew you were going to be, but while he was still safely tucked away in there, it didn't feel real. Not quite."

"Have you told Lee?" Suzie asked.

"I've left him a message, there was no answer. He's on some big job up in Wiltshire so he's away for a few days."

Was that why Anna looked more relaxed than usual? "Could you let Mike know, too?"

"Sure." Anna couldn't think when she had last spoken to her friend.

"You don't have to, not if it's weird..."

"No, it'll be... it'll be fine."

"Anna?" Mike sounded surprised but happy to hear her voice. "How are you?"

"Oh, fine, thank you, same as ever! But listen, Suzie asked me to let you know she's had her baby."

"She has? Isn't that a bit early? Is she OK?"

"She's fine," Anna smiled at the concern in Mike's voice. Why did he always know the right thing to say – the right thing to ask? Why didn't Lee?

"And the baby?"

"Is fine... and a little boy."

"Ah, I bet he's beautiful."

"He is – and tired out too. He didn't wake up all the time I was there, though I suppose it wasn't for too long. I wanted to let Jacob and Suze have some time together before he got kicked out."

"What's he like – Jacob, I mean?" Mike's tone was serious and Anna felt a sharp stab of... what? Was it jealousy?

"He's lovely," she said airily. "A really nice guy, a bit older than us, and it sounds like he was a star when Suzie was giving birth."

"That's good to know." That sounded like genuine relief in Mike's voice. "I'd hate to think of her with some idiot.

Especially now she's going to be... well, already is, I suppose... a mum."

"No worries on that score, I promise."

"Great. And how are you, Anna?"

"You already asked me that," Anna kicked herself for her defensive tone but she was scared that she might actually want to tell him the truth. How was she? Scared. Miserable. Depressed. Lonely. Trapped. "I'm fine. Same as ever. How are you? How's the writing going?"

"It's going OK, actually, which I've been surprised by. I've had some regular commissions. I'm doing some corporate copywriting, which pays OK, and I've been working on a local magazine. It's not much really, Mum's friends run it, but it's a start."

"It's great, Mike. You always said you needed to build up your portfolio. Isn't that what you're doing?"

Mike, nearly one-and-a-half-thousand miles away, couldn't help but smile at this. Typical of Anna that she'd remembered what he used to say, and that she was trying to buoy him up. "That's exactly right, that's just what I'm doing. But listen, Anna..."

"Yes?"

"I'm thinking I might... I might come back to Bristol. Mum's tenants are moving out at the end of this month and I just think, well, I do love it in Spain but... I don't know... it's Mum's place, really. Hers and Miguel's. Not mine. And I wouldn't mind having a crack at the British press instead. Not the ex-pat one. I think I can do that better if I'm in the UK."

"You're coming back?"

Mike couldn't tell what Anna thought about this from her voice. Was she pleased? He hoped so. "Yes, I think so. I've missed you, Anna."

"Sorry?" For the third time that day, Anna's eyes were full of tears. The emotion had taken her by surprise and she didn't know what to say. Mike back in Bristol? But that could never be. If anybody could see what was going on with Lee, it would be him.

"I said, I've missed you. And Lee." Had he? Mike wondered. Had he missed Lee? He missed the old Lee, it was true; he always had, but did that count?

"Well, it'll be... it'll be great to see you again."

"Great."

Mike asked Anna to pass on his love to Suzie and they said their goodbyes. He had no idea what Anna thought of him coming back but she certainly hadn't sounded delighted. He put his phone in his pocket and turned back to his laptop, suddenly despondent.

On a rainy Park Street, Anna was also feeling glum. As she walked past Christopher Wray, aglow as usual with a vast array of lights and lamps, she thought of Suzie, who had just become a mum. Of Jacob, who was ready to become a dad, concerned for his girlfriend and concerned for his baby – to the point of challenging Suzie's choice of drink! That could probably be a bit annoying, Anna conceded, but still – he was there, and he cared. He had looked overwhelmed, she thought, and she wondered what it might be like to witness the birth of your child – from almost an outsider's point of view.

How helpless a dad must feel as his partner went through agony and all the attention was (quite rightly) focused on her. What could he do? Stand back; step in, having his hand squeezed till the bones crunched, or being snapped at to get out of the way. Some of the parents whose children Anna had looked after had funny stories to tell. It seemed that being back in hospital brought all those memories flooding back – and, Anna supposed, for some parents, seeing their son or daughter so poorly and close to death in some cases, it was only natural that their thoughts returned to the day their precious child arrived in the world.

Anna tried to imagine Lee in that situation; what if she was pregnant? Would he be involved? Come to scans, midwife appointments? Would he watch what she ate, make sure she rested? She nearly laughed out loud at the thought of it. More likely he would just let her get on with it, not change any of his behaviour, and allow her to deal with everything on her own. Which, if she was honest, she would actually prefer to the alternative of him becoming too involved, taking control even more than normal.

Then would come the birth – what on earth would Lee be like at the birth? Would he even be there? She couldn't see it somehow; he was squeamish at the best of times. Would he allow himself to be told what to do by a midwife? Would he step in and rub Anna's back as she breathed through the pain, or whatever women in labour did? Would he look at her with the awe and admiration she had seen written on Jacob's face that afternoon? Try as she might, Anna just couldn't see it.

But Lee wanted children; she knew he did, and he'd be happy to have them soon. "When are you going to give me my son and heir, eh?" (This is how he would say it in front of his workmates, while Anna wanted the ground to swallow her up.)

"Let's 'ave a fuck, see if we can get you up the duff." (This is how he'd sometimes voice it at home after a drink or two and Anna would feel her mouth dry, and her whole body tense up; there was little she would like less.)

"Come on Anna, we should have kids, they'd be beautiful, they'd be the making of us. I'd be a better person if I was a dad." (In a wheedling, pathetic tone that he'd use sometimes when he was feeling sentimental, or guilty, and it seemed possible to Anna that it was worse than his crassness. That he thought having a child would make any difference, to them or to him – especially when he had been that child not so long ago. But somewhere in there was that grain of pity for him, still. The belief that really he wanted to do the right thing.)

Still, Anna had no idea what Lee thought having children

meant. She couldn't see him being one of those nappy-changing dads, getting up in the night to feed the baby so his wife could snatch a few hours' sleep.

No. Most likely, Lee would let Anna do all the hard work – the pregnancy, the birth, the day-to-day care, and he'd sweep in at a moment's notice; scoop up the child and show it off to his mates, claiming the glory.

That was the best case scenario. The worst was history repeating itself all over again. That could never happen to a child of hers.

Almost without thinking, though it was in fact something she had thought about many, many times before, Anna found herself at the side door with the discreet 'BPAS' letters inscribed on it. She pushed the door open to be greeted by a friendly woman, who looked up over the top of her glasses.

"Hello, have you got an appointment?"

"No," said Anna, "I haven't. But I'd like to speak to somebody about birth control."

A problem shared

"It's so good to see you, Suzie," Emma rushed over as Suzie got out of the car, the heat of the midday sun hitting her after the comfortable air conditioning.

"You too!" Suzie laughed as Emma went for a kiss on each cheek. "Wow, you're really Spanish now, Emma!"

"Well, I have to – it's not like in London, all that *lovie, dahling* air-kissing stuff they do in the UK. It's just the way things are over here. Men kiss each other the same way."

"I'm only winding you up; I like it. And you've got a beautiful place."

Emma had got up from her seat on a wide terrace, flanked by the wildly purple flowers of the jacaranda trees, which were shading her from the sun. Just off the terrace was a clear, inviting swimming pool. Suzie longed to strip off and ease herself into the sparkling water but thought she should wait at least a couple of minutes, for the sake of politeness. The sky was a vivid blue, and in a nearby tree she could hear parakeets shouting at one another.

"This place is amazing," she called to Mike, who was lugging her case from the car.

"Not too hot for you, in your condition?" He looked meaningfully at Suzie's swelling stomach.

"Not at all. Well, time will tell, I suppose."

"Oh, you'll be fine," said Emma. "Just make sure you keep those feet up to stop them from swelling. I'm so glad you could come out and visit before your newbie takes over your life. It's going to happen, you know. It's just a shame that Jacob couldn't come too. I'd love to meet him."

"I know, he would have loved to come out but, well, actually it's quite nice to just come as me. You know, it's tricky sometimes when you're with somebody who doesn't share your history; you feel like you need to keep filling them in about things, and like you can't really reminisce, without leaving them out."

"I know what you mean," Emma put her arm around Suzie's shoulders, "Come on, let's get those feet up right now, and I'll get you a drink. I'm sure we've got an awful lot to catch up on."

"What have you got in here, Suze? You're only meant to be staying three days!" Mike called across to them, heaving the case onto his shoulder.

"I've come prepared."

"You're not kidding." As Mike passed into the cool darkness of the house, he grinned to himself, delighted to see his friend – he preferred to think of her as that than his ex, which sounded so dismissive - again.

***

Suzie sat back on her sun lounger, listening to Mike and Emma talking easily in the kitchen. It was amazing how quickly she could feel at home. It was the people that made her feel that way, not the house – although the building was beautiful. Its outside walls were white and its wide roof sloped gently, so as to appear almost flat. Inside, the stone floors were cool and soothing on bare feet, in stark contrast with the blazing summer outside. The bedroom windows were shuttered against the heat of the day. The L-shaped structure formed a bracket around the swimming pool, on the other side of which was the 'granny annexe', otherwise known as Mike's flat.

It was the kind of place people dreamed of when summer was over and the relentless grey of a UK winter was approaching. Nevertheless, Suzie knew she could have been anywhere with Mike and Emma and she would have felt as though she belonged.

Mike sat down next to her, squeezing her hand. "I can't believe you're going to be a mum!"

"I know, neither can I half the time."

"Jacob's going to look after you, isn't he?"

"I don't need looking after!" Suzie laughed. "But yes, he's a good one, if that's what you mean. It was a bit of a shock to both of us; we weren't planning to have a child quite so soon, but it's OK. It's exciting, in fact."

"Good, I'm going to have to come and meet him – and that baby when it's born."

"That's something I wanted to talk to you about."

"I'm not going to be an au pair, you'll have to ask someone else."

"No, you idiot! Coming over. Back to Bristol."

Mike opened his mouth in surprise just as Emma appeared from the shadowy doorway, carrying a tray with three tall glasses and a jug of freshly-made lemonade, fat wedges of lemon and chunks of ice bobbing about at the top. "Here we go."

"Wow, that looks lovely! I think I'm going to like it here," Suzie beamed.

"We do, don't we, Mike?"

"I can see that. You both look so well, with your disgusting healthy tans!"

"Thanks, I think!" Emma smiled. "So how's Bristol? How are Lee and Anna?"

"Bristol is fine! Great, in fact. Well, same as ever really, but it's home, isn't it?"

"It is – and it still is to me; always will be, even though it's bloody gorgeous out here."

"Lee and Anna are a different matter. This is what I wanted to talk to you about, Mike."

"Oh?" Mike's gaze seemed to sharpen, his eyes narrow.

"I'm sorry, I didn't mean to get into this so soon. But it's been weighing me down for so long and seeing you two... I..."

"Don't worry," Emma laid a reassuring hand on Suzie's shoulder, "just let it spill out! What's up with Lee and Anna?"

"I think they're having some problems."

"What kind of problems?" Emma was instantly alert.

"They're... he's... I don't know, not for definite, but I don't think he's treating her well."

"What kind of not well?" Mike sat forward, his face serious.

"Oh God," Suzie took a long sip of her drink, "well, I don't know how to say this really but I think he's bullying her. Maybe even... hitting her?"

"No way!" said Mike.

"I don't know, I don't know, it's a suspicion. Anna's never told me as much. But I know what he's like in terms of trying to control her. He hardly lets her do anything except go to work. Sometimes I'm allowed to go out to the cinema with her but he's always phoning, checking where she is, when she'll get back. It's awful."

"But hitting her – why do you think he's doing that? I know Lee; I know what a twat he turned into, but he's not Scott."

Mike looked at Emma, who glared at him. Suzie didn't notice. "I never really knew Scott," she said, "but I remember what you used to say about him, Mike. I just – why do I think Lee's hitting her? It's kind of lots of little things all adding up to that conclusion. There was one day, when she had a mark on her cheek. That was a while back. I asked her what had happened and she said she'd slipped over in the kitchen, banged her cheek on the side of the work surface. I haven't seen any marks or anything since that, but she keeps herself covered up – in work and out of work. And I've noticed things – seen her flinching when a kid's reached out to her, or pulled her arm, that kind of thing. As though it's hurt her more than it should. But even if I'm wrong about that – and I hope I am – she just isn't happy. I know she's not. He doesn't let her have a life of her own."

"Poor Anna," breathed Emma. "And she just puts up with this?"

"Mm-hmm," said Suzie. "I don't think she knows what else to do. I feel like she's lost some of herself. She's thinner, and sadder, though she's great at work, but if I try to ask her about Lee – even hint at criticising him in any way – she gets really defensive. I don't want to risk arguing with her about it. If we fall out, she won't have anyone. I'm the only friend he lets her see. She's told me before he thinks I'm OK because I've got a long-term boyfriend, I'm not some single girl going out clubbing and on the pull."

"What about her family?" Emma asked.

"Oh God, didn't you know? She's not talking to them – Lee's doing, I reckon. You know they never liked him."

"Well, that's ridiculous! They're her family!"

"I know."

"Oh my God, poor Anna," said Emma.

Mike had sat quietly throughout this exchange. Suzie looked at him, seeing his muscles tensed up, hands squeezed into fists.

"Are you OK, Mike?"

"Hmm? Yeah. No. I just... can't believe this. Except I can, I could see it happening. As soon as those two got together, everything started to change. It was like Lee felt like he owned Anna. All our friendship - I mean the three of us – was like ancient history. And I don't mean to exclude you there, Suzie, you know we all love you too, but the three of us have known each other since we were four years old! Then suddenly I felt like I wasn't allowed to be friends with Anna any more. It was when Scott got ill that Lee really lost it, even though he tried not to show it."

Emma nodded, "I've had the odd letter and card from Anna, but they never really say much. She does say how much she loves her job though, Suzie, and working with you."

"She's just clammed up. You know how intensely loyal she is, and how protective she feels towards Lee. I think she thinks it's her duty, but I also think she's scared. Scared what he'll do if she leaves him; I don't know if it's a matter of being worried for herself or for him."

"He's such a liability," said Emma, looking sad, "I can't believe that little boy has turned out like this - although knowing his dad, I can believe it only too well. That man was a tyrant. Don't look at me like that, Mike. God knows what Scott's own childhood was like but his mum, Lee's gran, was a good sort, wasn't she? Maybe her husband wasn't as nice. Or maybe it was just Scott. Not that any of this excuses how Lee's treating Anna."

"There isn't any excuse," Suzie said angrily, "he's a grown man and he can make his own decisions, whatever his dad was like. I'm just sorry to have to tell you all of this, I know it's difficult to hear this about your friends. You've known each other forever."

"Yeah, but it's not like Lee and I are in touch any more, is it?" said Mike. "I felt like he was just looking for an excuse to get rid of me. I'm amazed he lets Anna see you, Suze; you're a link to life before they got together, and before Scott died. It felt to me like he was trying to forget all the old stuff, people included."

"Impossible when they still live in that bloody house," said Suzie, shivering in spite of the heat. "I hate it there. There is something so cold about it, though it's a beautiful house. I don't really believe in ghosts but it feels like there is something of Scott there, always. I suggested to them both once that they look for somewhere new, to start their own life together properly, but Lee was really annoyed. Anna doesn't get a say in the matter, of course."

"Right. Well this can't go on, can it?" Emma said matter-of-factly. "But what to do? I don't want to just trample in and interfere in their relationship. It's their business, really, but if Anna is scared, like you say, then she's going to need some help. If her own family can't or won't help her then we're the next best thing. What do you think, Mike?"

"I don't know. They're married. It's their relationship, isn't it?"

"But Mike, if he's beating her up?"

"I can't... even though I know what a twat Lee's turned into, I can't believe he'd do that."

"Mike, I would never have mentioned it if I wasn't nearly 100% sure of it," Suzie exclaimed. "You know I wouldn't. I've thought and thought about what to tell you – whether to tell you anything – but I know he's bullying her and I really do think he's beating her up. I do."

"OK. Well, what do we do? Is there no way you can persuade her to leave?"

"She won't listen to me, I've told you. And even if she left, where would she go? She won't go back to her parents', I know she won't."

"If she did, he'd easily find her there," Emma agreed. "That's what they do, isn't it, these men? Get their women back, either by force or by playing the sympathy card. Knowing Lee, and knowing how kind Anna is, I bet he'd go for the sympathy card."

"Bloody hell," Mike put his head in his hands then looked up at Suzie. "I can't believe it. No, I'm not doubting you, I know you're telling the truth. It's just... I know Lee doesn't have much respect for women but this is something else."

"So will you help?" Suzie asked, putting her hand to her tummy as she felt the baby kick.

Emma noticed this and couldn't help smiling. "Yes. We'll

help. You mustn't take this on yourself, Suzie, you need to look after yourself and that little'un. We'll have a think and work out what we can do."

***

By the time Suzie was reluctantly saying goodbye to her friends and the cool, clear pool where she had spent much of the last three days, they had hatched a plan. Mike was still the most reluctant of the three, which Emma put down to his having his nose put out of joint from his two lifelong friends losing touch with him. But he loved Anna; and he still loved Lee to some extent, despite the way they'd fallen out, and he wanted to help them both. Really, he wanted to know that it wasn't true, what Suzie had been saying.

"You're the only one that's going to be able to find out what's really going on," Emma told him, "but it's not your responsibility so think long and hard about whether you want to do this."

"I don't know if I 'want' to, as such. For one thing, I love it out here. The magazine's just starting to do well. The weather's bloody lovely, and I really like living with you and Miguel, of course. But... I don't know... I don't think I can not go back. I won't be able to relax, wondering what's going on, if Anna's OK..."

Mike's flat had been the previous owners' grandmother's. It was perfect – set slightly away from the house, it still shared the garden, terrace and pool, and Mike had come to love the easy-going lifestyle with the siestas and long dinners. Miguel had ensured that both Mike and Emma integrated into the local community with ease, and they now had a mix of Spanish and British friends. The magazine Mike wrote for was a hybrid of Spanish and English; set up by a Spanish-English couple as an attempt to try and bring the two communities together, and help them understand each other a bit better.

As well as writing for the magazine, Mike had helped build up some advertising support from local businesses and he was also making a very modest living from some copywriting. It wasn't much but it was enough to keep him going.

He'd had a couple of relationships; nothing serious, and had started to make friends locally. When he went into Marchena, the nearest town, he would often recognise somebody, and be recognised; at least enough to nod a greeting. Enough to make him feel like he was starting to belong.

Now here was Bristol, his old life, calling him back. The situation had an inevitability to it; he'd always felt deep down that no matter where he went, he'd never break the ties with his home town. And he had no real desire to. However, when he thought of the house he'd grown up in, of Lawrence Weston, they seemed grey and dull in contrast with the rich terracottas, hazy blue skies and bold, vivid sunshine of Spain. Mike loved Bristol – always had, always would – but it had become associated with some bitterness and he wasn't at all sure he wanted to return.

Still, this was Anna. When Mike thought that Lee might be hurting her, and even if he wasn't, physically – he had little doubt that Lee could be treating her like shit - Mike found a deep, burning anger grow in him.

"Right," said Emma, "then I'll let the tenants know we need the house back when their contract runs out at the end of October. Mike, that should give you plenty of time to find a job. Suzie, please keep an eye on Anna in the meantime and let us know what's going on. I can be on a plane in hours so if there's anything urgent, just say. You need to look after yourself so definitely do not go getting yourself into any situations. OK?"

"OK," Suzie had started to feel a relief seeping into her as soon as she'd begun to tell Mike and Emma what was going on. Now she knew she was no longer alone with her fears for her friend.

"Both of you need to try and get Anna to let you in on what's going on," said Emma, "get her to tell you herself. If Lee really is hitting her, then she's going to be scared and, like you said, Suzie, she's so bloody loyal, she won't want to admit to what's going on. And on top of all that, I think it's really important that she doesn't feel like she is being *rescued*. She needs to make the decisions, to know that they are her actions, that she is strong enough to do this. This is about Anna, about making her strong again."

Mike looked at his mum, feeling a flood of love for her rush through him. He hugged her.

"Thank you, Mum."

Emma laughed, surprised and pleased. "What for?"

"Just for being bloody brilliant. As usual."

***

Suzie sat back in her seat on the plane, resting her hands on her bump. There were still three months until Mike would be in Bristol, but he was coming. If she could just keep Anna going until then, she felt sure that Mike could help.

She couldn't help but feel sorry for him, being dragged back into all this. He'd looked happy, healthy and tanned in Spain. Relaxed. His life there clearly suited him. By the time he was back to the UK, it would be the tail end of autumn, no doubt windy and rainy, and he had some work to do – not just in finding a job but in re-establishing his friendship with Lee and Anna, potentially just to break it all apart again.

But Emma was right. Suzie had her baby to think of and by the time October came around, he or she would be with her. What chance would she have then to help Anna? She wouldn't be at work to see her, and she had a feeling that the baby was going to turn her life upside down, take over. It was very welcome to, but Suzie didn't want her friend to then disappear into the abyss of her marriage with nobody to support her.

She gazed through the window at the landscape far below, which seemed smaller yet more vast as the plane soared higher.

1999

The new millennium

New Year's Eve. And not just any New Year's Eve but the all-important Millennium. The night that people had been banging on about since, well, since about last New Year, or so it seemed to Anna. She failed to see what the fuss was about, and she was glad she was working. Although... there was a small part of her which couldn't help wondering – was it possible that something big really was going to happen? That the Millennium Bug – an oversight on the part of computer programmers – might take down the world's computer systems? Businesses going haywire as they lost all the information they had carefully compiled. Banks going bust as all record of the wealth they and their customers had accumulated was wiped clean (and along with it all records of overdrafts and debts). It was unlikely, Anna knew; ridiculous, in fact, but she couldn't deny a slight thrill ran through her at the thought of the world being shaken up, having to rethink the way it worked. Maybe it would even out the vast gap between rich and poor. Now she really was being ridiculous.

Points West had run a piece about people taking their savings out of bank accounts, for fear of the worst happening. A Bristol pensioner had been interviewed, who'd admitted to withdrawing all the money he had ("Not much to speak of," he had laughed wheezily), and hiding it.

"In a sock under your bed?" the interviewer had asked brightly.

"You don't think I'd tell you if I'd done that, do you, son?"

"Ha ha. A shoebox?"

"No, no, only me and my Vera, rest her soul, know."

"And you've done this because of the Millennium Bug..?"

"That's right, don't know if I can trust the computers to keep my money safe, do I? Nice to get on TV, too."

The old guy had grinned openly at the camera and it had made Anna laugh. Not much did that these days.

The worry for Anna was the effect that the Millennium Bug could have on the hospital systems. She thought, too, of what would happen to planes high in the air, if traffic control systems went down. She had a recurring image of planes just dropping from the sky. Thoughts of flying would inevitably turn to thoughts of Mike and she wondered what he and Emma would be doing to celebrate. She hadn't seen him before he'd left for Spain. He had tried to ring her, and Lee too – but Lee wouldn't answer, and had strictly forbidden her from doing so. It had been down to Suzie to pass on the news, and pass on Anna's best wishes to Mike.

Best wishes. It was like she hardly knew him. Sometimes she missed him so much that it made her feel sick. There was a sense of what might have been, could have been, possibly should have been... but that was a useless way to think.

Of course, the Millennium Bug would come to nothing, she thought. So much money had been put into fixing the problem, and it was a manmade problem so surely a manmade solution had been found. But just a small part of her still thought it could happen.

Lee, of course, had a 'huge' night out planned. To be honest, Anna wasn't all that interested. A night out was hardly unusual for Lee, and at least she wasn't expected to join him. Not that he would want her cramping his style.

"You sure you want to work, love?" he'd asked, twirling a

wisp of her hair round his finger; his tone she recognised as the one he used when he wanted something, but didn't want her to know he wanted something.

"Oh yeah, it's fine. Just another day, isn't it?"

"It's the Millennium, Anna! New century. New... well, millennium."

"Ah, but that's just a manmade concept, isn't it? Based on religion – another manmade concept."

"Suit yourself."

She could tell Lee was pleased, really. There was no way he wanted to have his wife tagging along on one of the biggest nights out of his life (as he'd called it).

Bristol, like everywhere else in the UK, and many places around the world, had put a lot of extra effort into planning that year's celebrations. There was to be a flotilla in the city harbour, and a burning boat, Viking-style. Entertainers on the streets and two huge fireworks displays – one earlier, for the children, and of course one at midnight. Anna thought that if she was going to be out, she'd like to be on Brandon Hill, watching the fireworks across the city – not just the big displays but the more modest ones, at people's houses. She could picture happy family gatherings, adults with glasses in hand, children pressing their noses against windows, watching as the bright colours broke into the night and into the first day of the new millennium.

She'd get a view of the fireworks from the roof of the hospital, if she could time her break right, but if she couldn't, she wasn't bothered. Better to work through the night, go home, go to bed, and wake up just like every other day. She wondered what the night would bring and thought of some of the children, and their families, who she was looking after, who probably wouldn't be giving the fact it was New Year's Eve a second thought. As the city streets filled with party-goers, anxious parents would be sitting, fear-filled eyes taking in the details of their child's innocent face. Hoping, praying, that the worst was over, that they could bring their son or daughter home soon. It was heart-breaking, sometimes, working where she did, but everybody there tried to make it the brightest, most positive place it could be. Sometimes it worked.

Hopefully Lee would up so late, and have drunk so much – and taken god-knows-what – that he would stay in bed all day. Anna could take to the sofa downstairs, watch some New Year's Day TV, then be getting ready for work just as he was surfacing. That would be the best start to the millennium for her.

Christmas had been dismal. The two of them in their big, empty house. He had drunk, and skulked off upstairs in the afternoon, putting on his music – his tastes had moved to hard house these days, it seemed – and, judging by the smell of it, smoking a load of weed. At least they hadn't argued.

She had gone round to see her mum and dad for an hour or two and she wasn't sure if Lee had even noticed. It made a change to see her parents together, but as always Anna had felt on the outside and even more so when they began to try and have a Talk with her.

"What's going to change for you in the new millennium, Anna?" her mum had asked.

"I don't suppose anything much will."

Her dad had looked sad. "You're enjoying life, aren't you, Anna?"

"Yeah, sure, I love work," she had started to gabble, trying to cover up the large, obvious fact of her unhappiness, "it's so great working with those kids and their families. Even though it's really sad sometimes. But I love working with Suzie too, and…"

"What about Lee?" Anna's mum asked. "Is he happy? How's he coping with the loss of his dad?"

The questions were putting Anna on edge. It was too little, too late. How could she start confiding in her parents now? Why hadn't they shown an interest before?

"Yeah, he's… I think so. I mean, it must take a long time to get over something like that. And his gran, of course. He's really all alone now, apart from having me, of course."

"You must mean a lot to him," Anna's dad glanced at her mum as he said this, and she got the distinct impression that this was a planned conversation. "But he can't depend entirely on you. And you can't give everything you've got to him. You've got to look after yourself."

Anna was surprised by the tears that blossomed on the surfaces of her eyes. She willed them away and hoped her parents wouldn't notice. She scanned the room, its ornaments, artwork, her mum's piano; all so familiar from when she was growing up but where she should have felt a sense of familiarity – belonging - she just felt that she was, as ever, on the outside.

"Oh, Anna," said her mum, putting her hand out.

Anna sniffed resolutely, wiped her eyes. "I'm fine. Just a bit emotional. Probably pre-menstrual." She hoped to make her dad feel uncomfortable. It didn't work.

"We do worry about you, Anna," he said. "We know Lee's your friend…"

"He's not my friend, he's my husband!"

"Yes, yes, sorry, I didn't mean it like that…"

But it was too late. Anna's back had been firmly put up. "He's my husband, and I know you don't like him. You don't think he's good enough for me. And you don't think my job's good enough for me, either. Well, I'm sorry if I've let you down. But Lee's… well, he's had a tough time, but I know him. I've known him forever. You don't know the first thing about our relationship."

"Anna, don't be like that," said her mum. "We just need to know you're OK."

"Well, it's a bit late now to be bothered about that, isn't it?"

"I'm sorry you feel that way."

"Well, I do. Yes, I do. You weren't bothered when I was growing up, were you? When I left an empty house in the morning to go to school and came back to an empty house in the afternoon. Because you were at work. And you," she turned to her dad, "were away all week. I'll tell you who was around for me then. Lee and Mi…"

She stumbled over Mike's name. Anna tried not to think of him too much. She looked angrily at her mum.

"Darling," her mum tried again to take her hand but Anna wasn't going to give in. "I didn't know you felt like that."

"No, well you wouldn't, would you? Because you never asked. You were never here *to* ask. Andy and Steve were always together and they were out most of the time." She looked to the photos of her brothers and their families – both with beautiful, glamorous wives they'd met on the music scene, both living in London. Successful businessmen now, having left their music careers behind but managing somehow – possibly with a bit of her dad's sway, she suspected – to land themselves well-paid jobs, lovely wives, homes and families. They were still together; still miles from Anna, even now they were on a more even, adult footing. "So it was either come home, do my homework, watch TV, go to bed, or go round to Mike's, have tea with him and his mum and Lee."

She stopped short of saying that Emma had been more of a mother to her. It was wrong to say that, she knew, and she wasn't out to hurt her parents – not really. It just made her so angry that they felt they had the right to criticise her husband. It also touched on too raw a nerve, of course, but she wasn't going to let them know that.

Anna wished she could hibernate through winter, wake up in the longer, lighter days of spring, the big celebrations – with their equally big expectations – out of the way. At least in spring there would be sunshine, and warmth.

Alone in Wales

It was a good job he wasn't the type to feel lonely, Mike thought. He was self-sufficient, always had been. He had Emma to thank for that. He gulped as he thought of his mum, denying the threat of tears as he ran through Bute Park on a grey, misty morning.

Only a month ago he'd been over in Spain with her and Miguel. Whenever he thought of Emma's new home he couldn't help seeing it in bright technicolour. Vast shafts of yellow sunshine, terracotta walls, fat oranges and exaggerated lemons. Green lizards, and of course the endless blue sky. Just the occasional, whimsical wisp of cloud floating lazily, teasingly past.

It wasn't that he didn't like Cardiff. It was a thriving, busy city. He still had a lot of friends from uni here, and there were loads of gigs to go to. But when he went out to work, temping at a city-centre solicitors' printroom, and when he returned home to his small, verging-on-damp flat, he just felt, well, flat.

He hadn't wanted to share a house any more. That had been fun for a time but by the end of his third year he'd known he wanted space. He wanted to know that if his place was a mess, it was his mess – and that if he cleared it up, his work would not immediately be undone by one of his housemates. It was funny, the kind of petty things which came to seem important in a shared house. Somebody nicking the last of his milk, shampoo, toothpaste... whatever. Small things, which Mike would never have thought would bother him, but which somehow in his final year had begun to grate. It didn't help, of course, that he had fallen out with Lee and he never saw Anna any more.

Of his friends from Bristol it seemed ironic that it was his ex-girlfriend, Suzie – from whom he'd parted on not altogether amicable terms - who made the effort to phone and visit him. She would come to Cardiff about once a month, see some of her old friends from her course there, and then get to Mike's in time for tea. Usually they'd get a takeaway pizza; occasionally, if they were feeling flush, go to a student-friendly pub, even when they were students no longer.

"I wonder when you earn the right to be called a local?" Suzie had mused.

"I'm not sure. I don't know if you ever do, with an English accent."

"And dressing like a hippy."

Mike looked at his Levellers t-shirt and Suzie's hair, which was dyed pink that month, and laughed. "Yep, I think we're going to have to be eternal students. What do the hospital have to say about your hair, by the way?"

"Oh, they don't like it. But the kids do. And I keep it well tied back, take all my piercings out, too, when I'm at work. I don't wear any of this stuff," she swept a hand vaguely in front of her face, indicating her heavy black eye-liner and thick mascara. "You wouldn't recognise me."

"I bet the kids love you," Mike said. "And Anna."

"Yeah," Suzie said, "they do love Anna. She's great with them. You can imagine."

"I have to," Mike sighed.

"I'm sorry, mate," Suzie had squeezed Mike's hand.

In a perverse way, Mike was enjoying the way the drizzle was coating his skin, cooling the heat of his exertion. This was his second go around his regular circuit. He had a lot to think about. He found the running helped.

He loved Bute Park – there were so many places to go and hide out, or to lazily wander through. The arboretum was his favourite part, although now it was verging on winter and some of the trees were starting to look sorry for themselves, others proudly shaking themselves free of their leaves, determined to stand strong through the harsh, cold months ahead.

It wasn't enough, though. If he was to stay in the UK, he wanted to be back in Bristol. It was home. There was no other way of putting it. Cardiff had little to offer him, and he'd failed to find any work that he wanted to do there. If he had to do crappy temping jobs, he wanted to be doing them in Bristol. But if he was in Bristol, he wanted to see his friends and he knew that was out of the question.

He recalled the conversation he'd had with Maria and Tony, the friends of his mum's and Miguel's – another Spanish-English couple.

"You should definitely come out, Mike. What's there to stop you?" Tony had asked, laying a friendly hand on Mike's arm.

What had Emma told them? Mike wondered. He looked at her but she just smiled openly, innocently, back.

"We could do with somebody like you working on the magazine, too. We're just amateurs. You're a journalism graduate! You'll be able to get it to where we want it to be."

"Maybe," Mike had laughed modestly. "I've got a degree but the only experience I've had is working on the uni magazine."

"That's more than us!" Maria had smiled. "I am happy with selling advertising, but I struggle with the writing. Tony's no better."

"Hey!" Tony had grinned.

"Well, it's true, isn't it? We are not writers. Michael is.

Tell him, Emma."

"It's up to Mike," Emma said, "He knows there's a place for him here if he wants to come out. But, you know. Sun, a swimming pool, beautiful Spanish girls... what is there to tempt him, really?"

"OK, I take your point," Mike had smiled, but wondered if taking this job with his mum's friends, and taking her offer of a place to live, just made him a loser. He hadn't earned either of those things. Still, when he'd got back to his flat, which had taken an age to heat up because he'd switched everything off during his absence in a bid to save money as well as the environment, he hadn't been able to help comparing life in Cardiff to life in Spain, and finding it wanting.

1998

The wedding day

On the morning of the wedding, Suzie woke up next to Anna. Ribbons of sunshine were twirling through the gap in the curtains of those enormous windows. She turned and looked across at her friend.

Anna was staring at the ceiling. She had been awake for some time; in fact, she had hardly slept.

"Ready?" asked Suzie.

***

Lee woke up at Alex's, his head throbbing and a vague memory of the night before. A woman; a short blonde. She'd been well up for it; all over him, but he'd stopped at a quick fumble in the bogs of the pub. After all, he'd told himself, he was getting married the next day. He'd been proud of his will-power but not beyond having a laugh with Alex about it. It didn't hurt to remind his mates and his employees that he was the man. An alpha male.

Now he was full of contrition. What kind of a man was he turning into? Had he already turned into him? There were echoes of Scott everywhere, it seemed to him – like his dad's shadow had somehow stuck to him, entwined itself with his. Some of his mannerisms, his sayings; they were Scott through-and-through. Every now and then he'd catch a glimpse of himself in the mirror and it was like he'd seen Scott standing there. It was the very worst thing to Lee, and the last thing he had wanted to happen, but sometimes he couldn't control any of it. He just hoped that Anna would save him. He was marrying her, his angel, today, and as he stepped out of bed he determined that he would be different from now on. Better. The man he had always wanted to be; who his mother had wanted him to be.

***

Mike went for a long run around his neighbourhood; feet pounding the streets, Faith No More thumping through his headphones. He had taken up running just after Lee and Anna had got engaged. It was good for him – a way of working out his frustrations. He thought of that scene in *Pride and Prejudice*; the one Anna loved, when Mr Darcy plunged into the lake, trying to drown his frustrations and quench his desire. He laughed out loud, startling the old lady who was dawdling along with her pull-along bag. He was hardly Colin Firth.

He had a long, cool shower when he got back to his flat, letting the cold water prickle his back and massage his shoulder blades. He had the day off work but he had been commissioned to write a couple of articles for a local magazine. The clock on his bedside table read 10.47am. The wedding would be taking place in just over an hour.

Despite the beautiful sunshine outside, Mike could think of no better time to lock himself away in his flat and get writing.

***

Anna looked beautiful. Her simple cream dress was designed to swathe about her figure, just touching the floor so that it rustled slightly as she walked. Lee's eyes filled with tears at the sight of her, walking with Suzie up the aisle.

Anna's dad sat in the front row, with her mum and brothers.

She had told them outright that she didn't want her dad giving her away: it was an outdated, patriarchal tradition, she'd said - which she did believe - but really, she hadn't wanted him to have that pride of place at her wedding, when he had barely been there for her day-to-day life.

Suzie felt nervous; sick to her stomach, really, but she had promised her friend that she would be there for her – *whatever, whenever* – and despite her numerous misgivings, Anna had chosen to go ahead with the wedding.

When they reached Lee and Alex, Suzie took Anna's flowers and smiled at her friend, determined to be positive for her. Anna smiled back, then turned to her soon-to-be husband.

***

No expense was spared for the wedding party. Lee had inherited not only Scott's house and business, but a substantial wedge of stocks and shares, and he was out to impress. Anna's family looked down on him, he knew, and he was determined to let them know that he could take care of their girl in the lifestyle they had accustomed her to. Better, even.

The hotel's function room had been decorated by a wedding planner and her team, despite Anna's quiet protestations that she didn't want a huge fuss. The chairs were wrapped in gauzy cream fabric, adorned with bows. There were huge vases of flowers on the tables, and generous gifts for each of the guests. Lee had given Wendy the Wedding Planner (Anna thought she sounded like a kids' TV character) a budgetary figure and free rein to spend it, which she very happily had.

Anna quietly went around the room, talking to guests, smiling for photos and dutifully answering Lee's call when he bade her come to him.

To all intents and purposes, it was a lovely wedding. Surely nobody – except perhaps Suzie – would have suspected that simmering just below the surface was a wealth of misgivings, suspicions and sadness.

As the day wore on, Lee became increasingly drunk. His speech was expansive, full of compliments to Anna and references to their childhood spent together – neatly cutting out any mention of their third friend.

"I can't believe I'm standing here, next to my best friend, and that she's agreed to be my wife. I'm the luckiest man alive," he sobbed, to a general round of *Aaahhhh*s.

Anna stood up and put her hand on his arm, then they embraced. "Thank you, Anna," he whispered, "Thank you."

She smiled half-convincingly.

The two of them had the bridal suite at the hotel where the reception was being held and by half eleven many of the guests had left.

Anna was sitting with Suzie. "I think I'm going to go to bed," she said.

"Really? Well, I suppose I don't blame you," said Suzie, "you must be shattered. Go on, go and tell your husband."

Anna walked over to Lee, who put his arm around her and made some joke Suzie couldn't hear. He laughed loudly with his mates and Suzie thought how small her friend looked next to them all.

She hadn't mentioned to Anna the new man in her own life – it didn't seem appropriate, somehow, like she'd be trying to take some of the attention from Anna's big day. However, she was happy to think that Jacob would be waiting at her flat for her. It had been a long, emotional day and she wasn't sure she could smile for much longer.

She went to the reception desk to see if they could book a taxi for her, but not before she'd watched Anna walk over and step into the lift in the hotel lobby, the doors closing firmly behind her.

Guilt

"Hurry up, Anna, we need to get going," Lee called into the bathroom. He was taking his bride-to-be away for a weekend at a spa hotel; ostensibly a chance for them both to step back from all the wedding planning, but glaringly obviously a result of guilt.

The shower was no longer going, but all was quiet behind the door. He tried the handle but it was locked.

Since the night when he'd slapped her – he couldn't bring himself to say he had actually hit her; that was the kind of thing his dad did, not him – he'd been a bit more cautious with her. Choosing his words more carefully, and speaking gently.

The morning after it had happened, he had been full of remorse. He had evidently passed out in his clothes on their bed, waking to find Anna's slight frame curled under what little of the duvet she could access, lying precariously at the side of the bed.

"Anna," he'd whispered, sure she was awake. There had been no reply. He was sure she'd twitched, though. "Anna," he'd said more loudly. "I'm sorry, I'm so sorry."

She had turned to him then, her big eyes looking at him carefully. He had looked at her face, glad there was no mark there to remind them of what had happened. "My head hurts."

"Shit, did I... was it that hard?"

"From the drink, I mean."

"Oh. Can I get you some painkillers? Water? Coffee?"

"Paracetamols, please. And some water."

He'd gone off down the stairs; practically bounded, keen to do whatever he could to make it up to her. When he returned to their bedroom, she was still under the duvet, though she had managed to reclaim a bit more of it, and moved further onto the mattress. He sat down next to her and he couldn't be sure but he thought she recoiled slightly.

"Anna, I am so, so sorry. I can't believe I did that. I'm a prick. I'm an idiot." Lee hit his forehead hard then his head fell into both his hands, and he slumped forward. "I can't believe I did that to you. Fuck. I... I don't blame you if you don't want to marry me." He turned his head slightly to look at her.

"I. Well, I didn't say that, did I?"

"I'm as bad as him, aren't I, Anna? I said I'd never be like him but I'm turning into him. I'm turning into a bastard." Lee looked in the mirror and Anna followed his gaze. She could see what he meant. His build was his father's, and the dark, heavy brow.

But those blue eyes, they were Elaine's - his mum's. They leant a lightness to Lee which Scott, with his dark, piercing eyes, had never possessed. Anna, looking at them now, thought she could not let Lee become his dad. She could not let that part of him which came from his mum drift away. He was Lee. Her friend: the boy who had stopped the bullies in their tracks when they were making her school life miserable; the little four-year-old she had sat beside on her first day of primary school. Her lifetime friend. If she left him now he would turn into Scott and that would be the end of Lee. She could not let that happen.

"You're not Scott, Lee," she said gently. "You don't have to be."

She sat up and accepted the water and pills, swallowing both.

"Can I..?" he asked, putting his arms out, towards her.

She nodded and he pulled her to him.

"I don't deserve you," he'd said.

Now, a few days later, Lee felt better about the whole thing. Anna had forgiven him and it wouldn't happen again. It probably wasn't that bad anyway; after all, he hadn't left a mark on her. And it had been a heat-of-the-moment thing. His dad, he had come to realise when he'd been a boy, watching from gaps in doorways or hidden behind the upstairs banister, had taken careful aim at his mum, so that bruises could be hidden under clothing – long sleeves, trousers, polo necks. Scott had been cold and calculating whereas Lee had just been in the moment. Drunk, pissed off – after all, she had taken that card without telling him. It was a crime of passion. That was the term they used, wasn't it? Not that it was a crime, really.

He heard her phone buzzing on her bedside table.

Mike.

What did that prick want? Lee looked at the screen, watched as the answering service picked it up, and waited to see if Mike left a message.

Sure enough, the little cassette symbol appeared. Lee felt tense. Should he..? Of course he should; of course he could. They were getting married, it was fine.

"Hi Anna, it's Mike... sorry, you know that, you can see on the phone, can't you..." slightly nervous chuckle. *What a dick*, thought Lee. "Anyway, I know you and Lee are getting married soon and I just wanted to catch up with you, see how things are going, wish you well and...well, give me a call back if you get a chance."

Delete.

That was that sorted.

Bristol, August 1998

Worrying

Suzie knew something was wrong. She wasn't stupid. When she tried to speak to Anna about it, however, she got nothing in return.

"Everything's fine," her friend told her breezily over the phone, "Just got loads to do now, the wedding's only a few weeks away!"

"I know, but let me help. Please. Tell me some of the items on your list and I'll do them for you. And don't forget to take a bit of time off. You're meant to be enjoying this, you know."

"I know," Anna sounded uncomfortable.

"Look, I'm coming up, come on, let's get this in order, shall we? I'm your best bridesmaid, it's my job."

Anna laughed and Suzie felt relieved but her pleading was to no avail. "No, it's fine, Suzie. Look, thank you and everything. Just let me get everything organised here, and I'll give you a ring in a week or so."

"OK, you're the boss. One week. But then we have an afternoon off. Let's have afternoon tea somewhere, after the dress fitting, OK?"

"OK. That would be nice."

Having had no luck with Anna, Suzie decided to try Lee.

"Hi, Suzie." Why did he sound suspicious?

"Hi, Lee. How are you?"

"Fine."

"Oh, OK, I... hope Anna was alright when she got back on Saturday night?"

"She was fine, why wouldn't she be?"

"Oh, she'd just had... one too many, shall we say? And you and I both know that she can't hold her drink."

"Oh, right, I don't know, I didn't see her when she got in. Seemed OK yesterday."

"Great, well I just rang Anna to see if I can help with anything for the wedding so I thought I'd do the same for you. Do you need a hand with anything?"

"Nope. Think it's all sorted, thanks."

"OK. I'll see you soon, then?"

"Yeah, see you soon."

Something wasn't right. The only other person Suzie could think of to speak to was Mike.

"Hi, Suzie!" At least he sounded pleased to hear from her.

"How are you, Mike? How did those exams go?"

"Oh, OK, thanks. I'm glad they're over, though. Thanks for the card, by the way."

"It was nothing. I just wanted you to know I was thinking of you. Listen, have you heard from Lee or Anna?"

Mike paused. "No, Lee hasn't spoken to me since his stag do. Anna called me a few times and we had a chat but she wanted me to still be involved in the wedding and I told her I couldn't. I haven't heard from her for weeks now. I guess I've pissed her off, too."

"Oh God, Mike, poor you. I knew there was some problem with you and Lee and I know Anna's upset about it but I've got no idea what happened. Can you tell me?"

"I shouldn't say, really, but – oh, fuck it, we fell out 'cos he wanted to go to a strip club."

"Twat. Doesn't surprise me, though. What, and you didn't want to?"

"Not my thing, really – but more than that, it just seemed

really disrespectful to Anna. Maybe I'm just old-fashioned, I don't know."

"Maybe," Suzie smiled, "but that's not always a bad thing."

"It's Mum's influence, I guess. She always says that it's like prostitution, really. Blokes paying women to turn them on. And if men don't think it's cheating, would they think it would be OK to be in a room with a woman taking her clothes off if they *weren't* paying her? She says it's all wrong, blokes think that the fact they're paying for it legitimises it. The money makes it worse, Mum says."

Suzie smiled again, "Yep, I can imagine your mum saying that! I can't believe you're not going to the wedding, though."

"Well, I haven't been invited, have I?"

"Would you go if you had?"

"I don't know, I really don't know."

"Have you tried to speak to Anna about it?"

"I don't think I can. I know it's stupid, she's been my friend as long as she's been Lee's, but she's not just his friend any more, is she? She's going to be his wife."

"She's not happy, Mike."

"What?" Mike's response was sharp. "What do you mean? Is she OK?"

"Oh, she won't say anything to me, but I can just tell. I think Lee's too much for her. You know how full-on he can be, and between you and me he pretty much arranged her hen do."

"Let me guess – a nice quiet dinner?" Mike laughed drily. "Whereas he could go off boozing and messing about with other women on his stag do."

"Got it in one," said Suzie.

"Shit. Well, what can we do, Suzie? Nothing. They're getting married."

"Would you phone her? See if she'll talk to you?"

"I'll try," Mike said.

The hen do

When Anna found out that Mike was no longer going to be best man, she tried to persuade him to change his mind, to speak to Lee; to the point where she felt like she was nearly begging, but he wouldn't have it.

Lee, meanwhile, was stubbornly refusing to have anything to do with their friend. "Prick nearly ruined my stag do," he muttered, "he can apologise to me. I'm not having him back as best man, though."

"So you're having Alex instead, are you?" Anna tutted. "Who you've known for... ooh, about eight months... and who I've met all of twice."

"I keep saying we should go out with him and his missus. Get to know 'em."

"Maybe," said Anna, "but I'm sure he'll understand if you ask Mike again. I don't see how he can't. He must have a best mate of his own? Doesn't Alex think it's a bit weird that you've asked him, when you haven't even known each other a year?"

The blood rushed to Lee's face. "Don't fucking call me weird," he slammed his fist onto the glass top of the table.

Anna looked at him calmly. "Don't shout at me. I was just saying it's not... oh, I can't be bothered." She got up as though to leave, but Lee grabbed her wrist. "Ow, Lee, that hurts."

He let go, his temper diffusing as suddenly as it had built up. "God, sorry, babe. Let's have a look."

"No, it's OK," Anna held her reddened wrist to her. It reminded her of the Chinese burns her brothers used to give her when they were kids.

"Shit, sorry, I've hurt you, haven't I?"

"I'm fine," she said, "don't worry."

This time when she got up, he let her go.

"So what are you doing for your hen do?" Lee asked the next morning. He'd insisted that Anna stay in bed. He'd gone downstairs and she'd opened the door onto the balcony, letting the curtains drift gently in and out of the room on the warm summer breeze. She could hear seagulls shrieking not too far away and she dozed off, imagining she was somewhere by the sea. She hadn't slept well the previous night, thinking of Lee grabbing her wrist. It wasn't like it had hurt her particularly, but it had worried her. It was like she could still feel his grip. Now here he was, bearing a tray with toast, orange juice and coffee, and a single rose in a small glass vase. *Guilt*. She tried to banish the thought from her mind.

"Oh, that's lovely. Thank you, Lee. I don't know – not a lot. Suzie's got something planned, I think we might go to that place in Clifton – the relaxation centre or whatever it's called – then have a meal somewhere with a few of the others in the evening."

Lee already knew Suzie had booked a table on the Glass Boat restaurant; he'd suggested it. It had been easy enough, making Suzie think he was being thoughtful, offering to pay for a meal for eight of them.

"Oh that's kind of you, Lee, thank you," Suzie had said when he'd phoned her.

"But make sure it's a surprise for Anna, eh? I know she's always wanted to go there."

"Of course I will."

Suzie knew exactly what Lee was up to. Yes, it was

generous of him to want to pay for their meal, but she was pretty sure he saw the restaurant as a safe bet – somewhere Anna wouldn't bump into any single men, or get involved in the usual hen do shenanigans that went on in clubs – stupid dares like getting a man to remove a garter from her leg with his teeth. Ridiculous, really, thought Suzie; that wasn't Anna's kind of thing at all.

"I'll pay for you lot to get dropped back at home in one of them limos, too," said Lee.

That confirmed it to Suzie. The groom had now had his pick of venue, and was making sure he knew how and when his bride would get back home. She sighed, but she knew Anna wouldn't mind. It wasn't as though she was into wild nights out. Suzie would just do her best to make sure her friend had a wonderful night.

***

What neither Lee nor Suzie had banked on was Anna getting rip-roaring drunk. Although the afternoon had started off very sedately, once the two of them were in the taxi, heading back up to Anna's to get changed, she had turned to Suzie with a grin. "Fancy some cocktails before we go out?"

"Yeah, sure," Suzie smiled, "I think that's only fitting for a hen do. In fact, if you go home sober, I'll make you have another one."

"I don't think there's any chance of that," Anna smiled.

The house was empty, Lee out with some of his mates down at the Lamplighters. "Town's yours tonight," he had smiled magnanimously. "Don't go too wild, though."

"As if," Anna had returned the smile.

What Lee didn't know, however, was that Anna had planned a little surprise herself. She'd bought a new dress for the occasion – dark blue and short, it clung flatteringly to her figure – and reserved a table at Bohenia at the top of

Whiteladies Road, priming the manager that there would be eight young ladies in need of a serious number of cocktails.

Planning the wedding in such a short space of time, especially following Scott's death and subsequent funeral, had proved to be a strain on both Anna and Lee, and his outburst was not the first time he'd let his temper get the better of him, though it was the first time he'd laid a finger on her in such a way.

Anna knew Lee was feeling the strain of running Scott's business. He was determined to make it a success, to get one up on his old man, even though – as Anna pointed out to him – it wasn't as though Scott was around to see the results.

Sometimes it seemed to Anna that everything was wrong. Getting married was supposed to be a time full of joy. Lee, however, seemed to her full of sadness, worry, and a barely concealed anger, but whenever she tried to talk to him about it, his hackles would rise. He'd almost snarl at her that he was OK. That she didn't understand the pressures of running a business. It was true, but Anna had her own pressures, what with finishing her course and searching for work. She had been lucky in that respect, as Suzie was able to point her in the direction of a couple of vacancies and Anna had been delighted to be offered a job on the same ward as her friend, pending a successful pass.

Only once had Lee let his veneer slide, and he had sunk against her one Sunday evening. For once he had not gone to the pub and she had decided they both needed a break. She'd put her studies to one side, opened a bottle of champagne one of Scott's mates had given to her and Lee when they'd got engaged, and asked Lee to light the barbecue. Together they'd cooked the food, sipping from icy glasses and talking quietly. It must have been back in May, one of the first really warm days of the year, and the evening had given her hope. As they sat side-by-side on a bench in the garden, plates and glasses discarded on the lawn nearby, Lee had kissed Anna on the cheek and leaned against her.

"What was that for?" she'd asked.

"Because I love you. Because you're great, and because I don't deserve you."

"Don't say that, Lee, I don't like those words."

"It's true, though, Anna. What the fuck have I done that I get to be with you? You're a lovely, beautiful, kind person, and I'm just a..."

"You're a beautiful person too, Lee."

He'd smiled wryly. "See, you're kind. Like I said. I'm not a beautiful person. Not anymore. Maybe I was once, before Mum left. Before Dad..." here a sob choked his words, and Anna put an arm round him.

"Lee," she said, "Don't forget that I know you. I know you. I've known you forever. You're having a hard time. Your dad... the business... the wedding. None of it is easy."

"Oh God," Lee had managed to squeeze the words out before his face collapsed and he was openly weeping. "You don't need this, Anna. You really don't. You could do a lot better than me."

Anna had just pulled him to her. It was a pointless refrain which she'd heard before.

Now, as Mike was no longer around and it didn't look like he would ever be again; at least that was how it felt to Anna, she was extra grateful to have Suzie, who was not only able to provide a bit of light relief but was one of the only friends Lee had no problem with Anna spending time with. He found her friends from her course too childish, he said, although in truth Anna thought he actually found them too wild. Not one of them had a steady boyfriend and they regularly blew off steam from their demanding course with drunken nights out. If Lee ever heard them recounting some of their escapades to Anna, he would never fail to comment afterwards, on one occasion calling Libby a slag, because she'd had a one-night-stand.

Don't be such a hypocrite, Anna had thought, knowing Lee's own history only too well, but she'd also known better than to voice that thought.

Anna's family were not happy about her marrying Lee, although they had not said so in as many words.

"Aren't you a bit... young?" her mum had asked.

"Don't you think you should live together a bit longer first?" her brother Andy had asked. "What's the rush?"

Anna had shrugged their questions aside, not really wanting to think about them. It seemed a bit late now for her mum to be showing an interest in what she did with her life and as for Andy, he was a serial monogamist, jumping from one relationship to the next with ease, never staying with one woman more than a year or two. Not the kind of person she wanted relationship advice from.

Those words did keep coming back to her, though.

What exactly was the rush?

Her brother wasn't the first to ask that and Lee had told her that Mike had said those very same words to him. She did wonder the same thing herself sometimes, but Lee had asked her and she'd said yes. She wasn't going to let him down. He needed her.

***

This was her day, though; her night, and she was going to bloody well enjoy it. It was a joint celebration for her – not only of her upcoming wedding, but also the end of her exams. Unless something went badly wrong, she would soon be a qualified nurse.

Suzie and Anna got to Bohenia first, favouring the bar stools over the huge beanbags. "I don't fancy trying to sit on one of them in this dress!" Anna had laughed, pulling at the hem.

"Leave it," said Suzie, "don't keep on tugging at it. You look lovely."

"You don't think it's too short?"

"No! I've told you that about thirty times now. It is not too short. It is beautiful. You look beautiful." Suzie pulled her friend into a hug and kissed her forehead.

Soon the others had joined them, perching on the free stools along the side of the bar. The men at the other end of the room, watching the start of the new football season, cast occasional glances their way, but the girls weren't interested. They only had eyes for the cocktail menus.

"We all choose one," said Anna, "and we get two jugs of each type, then we all have a glass of each."

Bloody hell, thought Suzie, *we're going to be slaughtered before we even get to the restaurant.* She realised she liked the idea. It would be good to see Anna letting go of that careful control of herself, just this once.

"Who's paying for this?" she asked Anna.

"I am," her friend hiccupped merrily, "I've got this!" She pulled out a credit card, which Suzie saw bore both Anna's and Lee's names.

"Does Lee know?"

"No, but he spends enough on drinking," Anna answered resolutely. "Today it's my turn."

Fair enough. Suzie knew Lee wouldn't be too happy but that was Anna's concern and it was good to see her friend with a bit of spark, to know she wouldn't just bow to Lee's will at all times.

"To Anna!" Suzie exclaimed, holding her glass aloft, and clinking it against the others.

Anna smiled delightedly.

So it was that a very merry group of young women made their way to the bus stop on the other side of the road and clambered, giggling, with some difficulty, to the top deck of the number 41.

"I love it here, I love this city," Anna said emotionally, as the bus trundled past Dingles and onwards to the top of Park Street, granting a view across the city centre which was bathed in the gold of the late summer's afternoon. "It's bloody beautiful."

"You're glad you're staying, then?" Suzie smiled at her.

"Yes, I'm... I'm happy."

"You sure?" Suzie looked into her friend's eyes but Anna looked away.

"Course! I've got a beautiful house, I'm marrying one of my best friends, got a job with my other best friend."

"Aren't you missing one?"

"Huh?"

"A best friend, I mean. Aren't you missing a best friend?"

"Oh, you mean Mike?"

"Of course."

"I do... I do miss him," Anna's face was downcast, "but what can I do? I'm going to be Lee's wife. I have to be loyal to him."

"Well, yes, but you didn't fall out with Mike. Lee did."

"Let's not talk about this now," said Anna, and turned to the rest of her friends. "Who's ready for another drink?"

They cheered and Anna pressed the bell. "One at the Mauritania, for old time's sake!"

"Go on, then," said Suzie. "It's got to be cider and black, though."

The lights of the harbourside were shining on the swaying waters as they walked to the restaurant. Anna was trying not to look at them as the motion was making her feel slightly odd. She was having enough difficulty concentrating on walking.

"Bloody hell, the Glass Boat! Thanks, Suze!"

"Well, it's Lee you've got to thank, really. He suggested it. And he's paying for it!"

"As well as all those cocktails? Oops!" Anna giggled.

They settled themselves at the table and Suzie ordered an

espresso for Anna, "Just to perk you up a bit."

Anna did as she was told and downed the scalding liquid. "Argh! Fucking hell! Give me some water!"

A couple of glasses later, she felt slightly better, although the very slight, gentle movement of the boat on the water wasn't helping matters. Still, she did a respectable job of eating her dinner and holding what approximated to a conversation with her friends.

"There's one more surprise!" Suzie said when the plates had been cleared away, and signalled to a waiter. A huge chocolate cake was duly delivered, decked out with whipped cream and sparklers.

"Wow! Suzie, did you make that?" Anna gasped.

"Yes, for you, dear friend," Suzie wasn't feeling altogether sober herself. She leaned over and hugged Anna tightly. "I love you. I'm always here for you... whatever, whenever."

"I love you too," Anna found herself sobbing, and pressing her face into Suzie's shoulder.

"Hey, what's all this, you daft cow? This is meant to be a happy occasion!"

"I know, sorry," Anna sniffled.

The evening wound down quickly from that point onwards. All had drunk far more than they were accustomed to, despite what Lee thought of the student nurses, and they quickly dispersed.

"Peaked too soon!" Samantha said, kissing Anna on the cheek. "Great night, though, thanks for the cocktails!"

"Pleasure," Anna smiled unsteadily, "thank you for coming."

She stood uncomfortably next to Suzie at the dockside and, when the last of the others had gone, grabbed at her friend's sleeve. "Quick, Suze, I'm going to be sick!"

Suzie ushered Anna to the side of the dock, into the shadows of the trees and away from the orange glow of the streetlights, so the sight of her friend throwing up wouldn't put the other diners on the boat off their dinners.

Once Anna had heaved as much as she was able, Suzie stood her up and pulled some tissues from her bag. "Come on," she said, "We've got a limo to catch."

"A limo?"

"Yeah, something else Lee organised."

"Did he? Ahh, he's a good bloke, isn't he? Isn't he?" Anna asked again.

"Yes, of course he is," said Suzie and she looked at her friend's face in the darkness, glimpsing a sadness there, before the slight breeze blew the branches of the trees and Anna's expression was obscured by their shadows.

All was quiet in the limo, much to the driver's relief. He was used to raucous, rowdy women poking their heads out of the sun roof and wolf-whistling at innocent males.

To be fair, it was usually on the way out, not back home, that he had hen dos, and judging by the look of the subdued pair in the back, they'd already done their partying.

"I'll get him to drop you off first, then me," Suzie said, pushing Anna's hair behind her ears and rubbing away the smudged mascara from her friend's cheeks.

"OK. Thank you, Suzie. I do love you."

"You too, Anna. And don't forget – whatever, whenever."

The lights were on at home and Anna found herself wishing they weren't. It meant Lee was back already and she'd rather not see him at that moment. Suzie hugged her. "Tell Lee thank you for the meal – and the limo."

"And the cocktails?" Anna found her smile again.

"Maybe don't mention the cocktails, at least not right now."

As the limo pulled away, Anna stood in the light of the front doorway, finding herself reluctant to go in.

Don't be daft, she told herself, and after fumbling with her key for a few moments, let herself into the hallway. There were Lee's new trainers, lined up neatly on the shoe rack. She pulled her shoes off, trying to produce an air of composure.

"Hello?" she called tentatively.

No answer.

"Hello?"

She walked into the kitchen, thinking it might be a good idea to get a glass of water before going upstairs. Maybe even another coffee. Better to be tired tomorrow than hungover. Her stomach rumbled emptily and she could still taste the faint tang of sick in her mouth, mingled with that of the Extra Strong Mint Suzie had produced from her bag.

"You're back, then?" Lee's cold voice struck her. He was sitting round the corner, on the leather settee.

"Oh, hi! You made me jump!" Anna adopted a bright tone of voice.

"Good night?"

"Y-yes, thank you. How about you?"

"Enjoy your cocktails?" Lee ignored her question.

"Y-how did you know about the cocktails?"

"Nick saw you. Said you lot were making a show of yourselves."

"Well," Anna felt annoyed, "we were just having a laugh. Nothing more, nothing less." She took a glass out of the cupboard. "Where was Nick, then?"

"I dunno, do I? In the bar, watching the footie. He said you were paying for the drinks."

"Er, yeah, that's right."

Anna walked towards the sink. Lee was by her side.

"How did you do that, then?"

"I. I paid for it with our credit card."

Lee's hand swept quickly, smashing the glass out of hers as she was turning the tap on. Glittering shards exploded against the tiles.

"What..."

"You taking the piss, Anna? That's meant to be a joint account. That means me and you, not you and your slaggy friends."

"They're not..."

Anna's words stuck in her throat as Lee pushed her against the worktop.

"I paid for your meal, I ordered you a limo, tried to make sure you had a good time, and that's all the thanks I get."

"Lee, I didn't... I didn't know you were doing those things, and it was really nice of you..." Anna's heart was beating double-time.

"You ungrateful bitch."

She didn't see the slap coming.

"Lee!" Anna's hand flew to her cheek and she felt suddenly, coldly, sober.

He backed off, the fight seeming to have ebbed quickly away, but he was still angry. Still self-righteous. He had been wronged and it was important that she knew it.

"Don't ever do anything like that again. And take that dress off," he added, "you look like a whore."

The stag do

Lee was all revved up. He and Anna had argued that morning - he put it down to the stress of the wedding - and he knew that a good night out was just what the doctor ordered.

Mike had made arrangements, hired a boat to take them on a pub crawl around the harbour. It was a nice idea, Lee thought, and a good way to start the night, but he already knew that it wasn't going to be enough.

He wondered how his mates would get along with each other – there would be Mike, of course, then some of the old lot from school days, as well as a few of the College Green crowd – most of whom had gone on to university and were in the process of graduating or in their first year of work. Then there were some of the blokes from work. The younger ones, not his dad's mates – there had been some animosity between him and Scott's old muckers after Scott's death. In fact, they had pretty much split off and gone their separate ways, only doing a bit of contract work for Lee while he took on a new, younger workforce – some slightly older than him, and a few even younger. The younger ones wouldn't make it past the booze cruise stage.

It was a humid evening. Clouds of midges hung in the air over the water, or followed juicy-looking drinkers as they made their way between the dockside bars. Walking past the Pitcher and Piano, Lee took in the animated chatter of people sitting at outdoor tables; cold glass jugs of sangria, beaded with perspiration, and bowls of tapas creating the feel of the Med. There were women with low-cut, strappy tops, showing off freckled shoulders and sun-kissed arms. Lee stopped briefly, pushing his way through the crowded, sweating room to the bar. A pretty barmaid with a pierced nose and black polo shirt displaying the pub's logo noticed him and smiled.

"Double vodka, please, darlin'." Lee had found that, even though he was still only 22, if he used terms like 'darling' with enough confidence, it lent him an air of gravitas. He could hear echoes of his dad ringing through his voice, but he chose to ignore them. He had decided to take what he could from his dad – borrow his mannerisms, his confidence, and swagger, but shrug off the parts he didn't like. Lee was determined to be better than Scott.

"Neat?" she raised her eyebrows.

"Yeah, it's my stag do. Need a bit of Dutch courage."

"Oh, right," the eyebrows raised again and she smiled at him as she put the glass on the bar, cushioned by a neat black serviette. "Good luck."

"Cheers, love," Lee raised his glass to her but she was already off, serving another of the endless swarm of drinkers whose hot, clammy bodies crowded around the bar.

There was champagne on the boat, beers and chasers in the pubs. Lee had to concede it was a better laugh than he'd thought it would be. Everyone seemed to get along well, and at each stop they got progressively rowdier. There was uproar when Sam, one of the younger apprentices, lost his footing on the ladder down to the boat. Mike managed to grab him just in time.

As they cruised round the harbour, they shouted to the other boats which were following a similar route to theirs, and called out to groups of girls who were tottering along the dockside in high heels and short skirts. Lee loved the summer.

The last stop was the Ostrich and here Lee got his wallet

out, buying a round for everybody before sending some of the younger lads off. "This next bit's not for you lot, I'll see you at work on Monday!"

Mike looked at his friend, having a very good idea of what was on Lee's mind.

"OK, now those pussies have gone," Lee was at his most drunken and obnoxious by now, "let's go and see some tits!"

Some of the others cheered their approval while Mike and a couple of their older friends – Dave and Matt - looked at each other.

The other two shrugged. "May as well," said Dave.

"It is a stag do," Matt agreed.

Mike felt his stomach drop. What should he do? He was Lee's best man; he couldn't bail on the night out now but... a strip club? He knew only too well what Emma thought of them, and he had to agree with her.

Lee came over, as if reading his mind. "Scared what Mummy's gonna say?" he half-teased, although Mike could see a less-than-pleasant glint in his friend's eye.

"No, I'm not scared. But you know it's not my kind of thing. Or Anna's," he added meaningfully.

"Yeah, well, it's not Anna's stag do, is it? Or your mum's."

"Mum's always been good to you," Mike felt his temper rising from somewhere not too far within, "and so has Anna."

"Come on, Mike, don't be a prick. It's just a bit of fun. Some of those birds are lush, you'll see."

"Not your first time, then?"

"No, course not, I'm only human. Come on, let's get some cabs booked, down to Old Market."

"No, you're alright. You lot go on; I don't want to be part of this. Anna's back at yours; think how pissed off she'd be if she thought you were celebrating your wedding like this."

"Oh fuck off, Mike, I ain't 'celebratin' the weddin', I'm celebratin' my freedom. Blokes do a lot worse, you know."

"That doesn't make it right," Mike spat, surprising himself

with his own vehemence.

Smash.

Lee's fist was in Mike's face before either of them knew what was happening.

"You self-righteous twat," Lee shouted while Matt pulled him back. "What's the matter, want Anna for yourself? I know she's the reason you split up with Suzie. I'm not fuckin' stupid. She's chose me, though, 'asn't she?"

Mike felt his face, already red on one side from the punch, flush deeply. "Fuck you, Lee." He stalked off darkly, his hands pushed deep into his pockets.

Lee laughed and called Alex, one of his new workmates, over. "You sort the cabs, OK? And you're best man now."

Mike heard it and laughed at his pathetic friend. The only thing that wasn't funny was that Anna was about to make the biggest mistake of her life.

Cardiff, May 1998

Out of sight

Try as he might, Mike couldn't feel happy about the impending wedding. Putting aside the fact that he might still have feelings for Anna – feelings which he had never had the chance to fully explore as Lee had got in there first – there was something about it which just felt wrong.

What was the rush? He had asked Lee but received a half-answer. They were only twenty-one, for God's sake. Anna still a student. It had crossed Mike's mind that she might be pregnant but realised as the months had passed that this did not seem to be the case.

Mike had started to spend less and less time in Bristol, and he was under no illusion that he was hiding from the whole uncomfortable situation.

Lee's possessiveness over Anna was unspoken but just so evident, to the point that Mike had realised he didn't feel he could actually phone Anna any more. He had started to phone Lee first then ask to speak to Anna. It was ridiculous. She was just as much his friend as Lee's, engagement or no engagement, but their relationship, their forthcoming marriage, had changed everything.

Lee seemed less interested in Mike now, too; he'd become obsessed with his work and 'lifestyle' as he irritatingly called it. He hadn't been to Cardiff in months.

Mike sat sadly in his flat, watching the rain pour from the blocked guttering above his window, and sighed.

Spreading the News

"Best man?" Mike asked, astonished.

"Yeah, mate," Lee's cheery voice sounded down the phone line.

"You're marrying... Anna?"

"Yeah, mate!" Lee repeated his words, laughing. "Who else?"

Mike was quiet for a moment. "Well... congratulations," he said eventually, as manners required.

"Cheers," Lee laughed again. "So will you?"

"What?"

"Be best man, you doughnut."

"Oh, yeah, well, yeah, of course I will."

"Brilliant. Better get started organisin' the stag do, then, we're goin' to tie the knot after the summer. Once Anna's graduated."

"Wow... so soon... what's the rush?"

"Yeah, well, there's no point waitin'. We've known each other all our lives. Got a nice big pad to move into now as well, 'aven't we?"

"Have you?"

"Oh yeah, that was the other thing. Dad's dead. Want to come to the funeral too?"

Mike's mind was still reeling when the phone went again. As his housemates were out, he decided to answer it, hoping it would be for one of them. He wasn't in the mood to talk.

"Hi love," it was Emma.

He knew his mum would know something was up. He'd told her as little as possible about when he and Suzie had split up, and how he felt about Lee and Anna getting together, but she knew. She always did.

"Hi Mum," he put on his cheerful voice.

"Are you OK?" she asked cautiously.

"Yeah, fine," he shot back defensively.

"OK," she sounded like she had something on her mind. That was good, it would take the attention away from him.

"Are *you* OK?" Mike decided to try and turn the tables.

"I am, I'm fine thank you, Mike. I'm... well, I'm great, really. Mostly."

"Oh?" This sounded interesting.

"Well, you know I was out in Spain for New Year..?"

"Yes," Mike had gone back to Cardiff early; spent Christmas in Bristol with Emma, then returned to the quiet, cold student house with its bare walls and threadbare carpets, foregoing New Year's Eve partying in favour of working on his dissertation.

"Erm, I don't know... oh, I'm just going to say it. Miguel's asked me to go and live over there with him."

"Shit," Mike laughed.

"Why are you laughing, Mike? That wasn't the reaction I was expecting."

"Oh... nothing, it just seems that it's a day for big announcements. I assume you're saying yes?"

"Well I haven't, not yet, I wanted to talk to you about it first. But I would like to. If you don't hate the idea."

"Mum," said Mike, "I do not hate the idea. I think it's brilliant. You've spent the last twenty years looking after me – and my mates – it's about time you did something for you."

"But... well, thank you, love, but what about you? What about you and me, I mean? I wanted you to be able to come home after you graduated; at least to know you had the option. I don't suppose you want to be coming home to Spain."

"It's actually quite tempting right now," Mike laughed again, "but don't worry, Mum. I'll be fine. Maybe I'll even stay on in Cardiff."

"Well, I wanted to let you know that I'm going to keep the house, maybe rent it out – if you don't want to come back to it, I mean. I want to make sure things work out in Spain before burning my bridges over here. Not because I think things will go wrong but because, well, it's been just you and me forever, hasn't it? Maybe I won't like living with somebody else. Maybe I'll find I miss Lawrence Weston so badly that I have to leave the sunshine, fresh oranges, swimming pool in the garden…"

"Hmm, yes, that sounds likely."

"Oh, Mike, you need to know that wherever I am there's a home for you, always. If you did want to move to Spain, of course you could. Miguel knows it's me and you above anything else."

"Thank you, Mum," Mike felt tears spring to his eyes.

"Now, what's this other news you've had, then?"

The proposal

Scott took a long time to die. Even when he was ill, in fact all the moreso because of his illness, he managed to have everybody bending to his will.

Lee in particular took it badly, which was not surprising, but had Anna worrying so much that by the end of the first summer of Scott's illness, her resolve about leaving Bristol crumbled and she decided she would transfer her course place, move in with Lee, and help him take care of Scott.

Scott wanted to be at home so Lee and Anna spent much of their time there at the house by the Downs. It felt more cold and sterile in that house than ever, Anna thought, with the endless supplies of medication and efficient, though friendly, nurses coming and going. Anna split her time between lectures, placements, looking after Lee at his flat - which she had moved into - and looking after Lee and Scott at the house by the Downs. At the end of a long day she would occasionally sink into a hot, bubbly bath and lock the bathroom door – the only chance she had of any time to herself.

She barely had time to think, and she was glad of it as she knew that if she did stop to consider her current predicament, she would only find questions. How had she ended up in this position? She'd been well on her way. Out of Bristol, on her nursing course, sharing a lovely flat with a friend - she had been becoming independent!

It was just easier not to think sometimes.

Lee, on the other hand, felt he had never been happier. It sometimes seemed wrong to him, with his dad being so ill, but as the cancer had slowly taken Scott in its sharp, icy grip, he had become less scary. The once big, all-powerful man seemed emasculated by having to spend much of his time in bed and do as he was told by the regular stream of women who could let themselves in and out of his house. He was too weak to stop them and they just cheerfully ignored his protests. Lee watched all this with a sense of satisfaction.

In addition to his dad's weakened state, Lee had a woman in his life. Someone he knew he could rely on. Well, he'd thought that before about someone, but he did his best to push that thought out of his head. Anna was not his mum, he told himself, just as he was not his dad. Anyway, since he'd bought Anna a mobile phone, he could phone her any time; check where she was, who she was with... He just wanted to make sure she was still there.

"Hi babe," he'd croon.

"Oh hi, Lee, is everything OK? Is your dad OK?"

"Huh? Oh yeah, he's fine... well, you know..."

"Oh, OK, great, listen, I'm just about to go into a lecture. I'll see you later, OK?"

"Yeah, I'll be up at Dad's after work, see you there?"

"Oh, I don't know today. I was hoping to go to the library. I'll probably have to work a bit late tonight. You know I've got loads to do for my course. I'll see you back at home, OK?"

Alarm bells rang in Lee's head. Working late. That was what they always said, wasn't it? No, no, this was Anna, he told himself. Anna. He would take a deep breath, hold it, picture her face. She wouldn't fuck him about.

"OK."

"I won't be really late. Look, just call if you need anything, OK?"

He would.

Aside from the odd moment of doubt, however, Lee was

enjoying himself. He did feel sorry for his dad, at times. It wasn't much fun to watch the old man fading away, but worse things happened to better people.

Like Anna, Lee was also working hard, picking up the reins from his dad, trying to make sure the business stayed afloat. He'd heard some of the other blokes taking the piss out of him – a kid trying to take over the running of the business, but that attitude had done him a favour, really - driven him harder to succeed, and so he was doing. And once he'd got the hang of things, they might just find that they regretted taking the piss. In the meantime, he'd moved himself from a hands-on role to sales. He'd read up on business management and structures and thought he could see how it was done. They had regular customers, which kept things ticking over, but Lee found that he was getting drawn into the business. He wanted to develop it. Make it better, bigger, and, crucially, do so before his dad died. So that Scott could see that his son was a better man than him, in every way. A final, long-awaited *fuck you*.

So it was that Lee started to go after bigger contracts. He made contact with the council and the social housing department, and started to undercut his competitors. His height, looks and easy charm convinced many to take a chance on him, although perhaps if they'd known his age they may have thought twice. Still, Lee had well and truly got the bit between his teeth and, one thing he did have to be grateful to Scott for, he had a healthy, longstanding business to back him up.

"Dad, wake up," he said one day when he got back to find Scott lying, sleeping and dribbling, on the settee. Lee took in the saliva, drooling from the corner of Scott's sad-looking mouth and pooling on the pillow, with distaste. He knew it was a bit cruel waking his dad up, returning him to his pain, but there was a lot of time to make up for and not much time to do it in. "I've got us a contract for the new council houses."

"Wh... what?"

Scott was confused by sleep and a cocktail of medication.

"I said I've got us a contract working on the new council houses – and some of the existing ones. You know, like you said you were going to do?" Lee was playing the dutiful son – *look at me, Dad, I'm doing this for you* – but he knew, he just knew, it would add to Scott's feeling of failure. "Starting in the New Year. Brilliant, eh?"

He walked over to the window and opened the curtains, the bright autumn sunshine making Scott's sore, tired eyes blink. So this was how it felt to be in control, Lee thought. He loved it.

These were the better moments for Lee, when he felt like the strong one, like he didn't need his dad any more, but there were plenty of dark nights – especially those when Anna was working shifts for a placement – when he would be staying at his dad's house, in his old room, and would lie soaking his pillow in tears at the thought of losing his old man. The bastard. The wife-beater. The bully. The only dad he would ever have.

Emma was a great source of support during Scott's illness, not only to Lee but to Anna and also to Scott himself. She would visit him, when most of his former friends and acquaintances seemed to have already given up on him, as though he was already dead. Lee was surprised by this. He hadn't thought that Emma really knew his dad, but he also thought he shouldn't be surprised. Emma was one of life's genuine people, like Anna; someone who thought about other people, often before herself.

He, of course, had no idea that she knew Scott far better than he could ever have imagined.

Lizzie, Lee's gran, was taking her son's illness particularly hard and it seemed that she had aged years in the course of a few months. "Nobody should have to see their child die before them," she had said quietly to Emma when they had crossed paths on those sparkling black-and-white tiles in Scott's hallway.

Emma had put her hand on the older lady's arm, feeling the frailty beneath the jacket, noting the bony knuckles and liver-spotted skin, the tired eyes. "No," she said, "they shouldn't."

In the end, it didn't come to that. Lizzie died in late autumn of 1997, and Scott died in February 1998, three days after his son turned twenty-one. Scott Lewis succeeded his mother by just three months.

For a while during his illness, he had seemed to rally around, to perk up – almost – although his frame was thin and looked breakable, Anna thought. She had arranged a few days out for him – nowhere too far – but she wanted him to get something out of what life he had left.

One day they went to Brean Down, where Lee insisted that he and Anna went walking on the headland, leaving Scott on his own at the café below, sitting in his wheelchair with a blanket over him. Every bit the old man, only he wasn't old. He was 47. Despite everything, Anna felt desperately sorry for him.

"We can't leave him, Lee. Sorry – Scott, I didn't mean to talk like you're not here. We're not leaving you alone, though. It's freezing cold, and how are we going to know if you need anything?"

"Ah, 'e'll be alright, won't you, Dad? Come on, no point comin' all this way just to sit round with this miserable old fucker." Lee's face broke into a grin, as though he was just joking with his dad, but there was something cold in it.

Anna opened her mouth to protest but Scott put a hand on her arm. She was embarrassed to find she had to stop herself from flinching.

"Go on, kids," Scott had grinned ruefully, his voice throaty and his accent thick. "Go on, son, stick it to your old man, Lee. God knows I deserve it."

So they had gone, but Anna found she could hardly talk to Lee. He had revealed a cruelty which she had never known before. Yes, he could be hot-headed, aggressive, confrontational - but not cruel. She put it down to the stress of the situation, but she couldn't forgive it, not quite.

When Lizzie died, Lee seemed broken. He took it out on his dad and it had been Emma who had taken Scott to his own mother's funeral, as Anna had needed to support Lee and he had absolutely refused to have anything to do with Scott.

"It's his fault, Anna, don't you get it? He chased Mum away, and now he's made Gran ill. Killed her. I hate the fucker, I really hate him." He had choked on his tears and Anna had just held him.

She often thought of Lee's mum and wondered what had happened to her. She didn't doubt that Scott had been a terrible husband and, if Lee's stories were true, which she also didn't doubt, then the woman really had no choice but to go. She knew Scott had sometimes half-suggested to Lee that Elaine had run off with somebody else but Anna couldn't see it. As she remembered her, Lee's mum was quiet, timid, and kind. Anna was certain it was Scott who had driven her away. However, Anna could never imagine being able to leave your own child, and especially with a man who was more than capable of violence.

Somewhere inside, she had a half-acknowledged idea that when Scott was out of the way, they might be able to trace Elaine, but when she'd mentioned this idea to Suzie, on one of their now too infrequent nights out, Suzie had been against the idea.

"She'll find him, if she wants to. If she can."

"What do you mean, if she can?"

"Well… whatever. I mean, we're assuming she's still alive."

"She was only young, and it was only a few years back, so I'm guessing she will be. Unless, you don't mean..?"

"What, that Scott did away with her?" Suzie laughed but then looked serious. "No, that's not what I meant at all but… fucking hell, no, that's ridiculous."

Both went quiet and concentrated on sucking their cocktails through their straws.

Then Scott died. After a very long, gradual and painful deterioration, which seemed to speed up towards the end, like a video on fast-forward, thought Anna, he just stopped breathing one night, when nobody was with him. Anna was on shift and Lee was starting a job early, so it was one of the nurses who found him, who dealt with the necessary arrangements and then phoned Lee to let him know.

Anna came off shift to find a message on her voicemail: "Bastard's gone. I'm at the house. Love you."

She felt a cold shiver run through her, and pulled her coat tightly around her as she walked into the winter morning. The city was only just waking up and streaks of pink and orange pushed through the otherwise grey sky. A few seagulls were squawking and the traffic was already humming with people keen to get to their desks early.

Anna decided she would walk to Scott's. She tried to ring Lee but there was no answer. It wouldn't take too long, though, and she felt that she needed it. A last bit of time to herself before life would be all about Lee. Not that she minded, and she completely understood, but she wanted to prepare herself, make sure she was ready.

As she passed over the Downs, her boots crunched across the frosty grass. Over there, on the far side, behind those trees, was Scott's house. And in that house was Scott, dead. She had seen death first-hand, more than once, thanks to her course, but it had never been anybody that she knew. She shivered again.

At the house, she pushed open the front door and saw muddy footprints across the tiles. Next to the kitchen door, Lee's work boots were cast aside. She called to him but heard nothing. There was nobody in the kitchen so she went upstairs.

In the quiet of the house, her footsteps sounded large, her breathing amplified. Her heart was beating fast and she could feel its pulse pounding in her head.

She found him – them – in Scott's room. Scott, or the body of the person Scott had been, settled peacefully on the bed. Sunken cheeks, bluish eyelids closed. The lack of rasping breath struck her. The peace. In the chair by the bed sat Lee, his head in his hands. He looked up at her when she came in and she could see his eyes were rimmed with red but when he saw her, he smiled.

"Marry me."

1996

Bristol, 1996

Moving on

Life had changed for Mike. He no longer saw Suzie, or only very occasionally. She was wrapped up in her course and, unbeknown to him, still getting over their break-up. Although she had acted sensibly and strongly, she'd loved Mike. She still did. But he didn't need to know that.

Anna, too, was now absent from his life for much of the time. He had been shocked when, towards the end of January, she and Lee – well, Lee really – had announced that they were a couple. A proper couple.

Although Mike had seen them kissing, he hadn't really thought that it would go anywhere. Lee was renowned for lasting no more than a month or two with any girl – if that - as poor Flic was evidence of, but this time Mike saw something different in his friend. The way Lee held Anna's hand, went to the bar for her, watched her if she walked across the pub to go to the toilet. There was something almost proprietorial about it all, thought Mike, but he knew that his thoughts were born of jealousy and he wasn't sure he could trust them fully.

So it was that Mike threw himself into university life. He went out more with friends from his course, joined a band, took a role on the university magazine. All of this he did resolutely. It was time to move on.

Meanwhile, Anna was spending more and more time back in Bristol, at weekends at least. Lee had found a maisonette just off Cheltenham Road which Lizzie had helped him finance the purchase of. The flat had large rooms which needed decorating, having been a student rental for the previous ten years. It had been left in a state of disrepair but with his and Scott's contacts, Lee was in a good position to get it sorted.

"Stepping out on your own two feet, eh son?" Scott had got the saying slightly wrong but Anna, who was sitting at the end of the table when Lee had told him, had thought he looked sad. She caught herself almost feeling sorry for him. The feeling was only fleeting.

"I think it's the right thing to do, Dad. I really appreciate your help, and the job, and everything, but if I get this flat now I'm getting a foot on the property ladder." Lee knew he could appeal to Scott's financial astuteness. "I could have bought it outright by the time I'm thirty."

"My son with his own place. Fuckin' 'ell, I s'pose I'm proud of you," Scott had stood up and pulled Lee into an awkward hug. Neither looked comfortable with the situation.

"Thanks, Dad."

That had been the end of February, just after Lee had turned nineteen, and by the end of March the place had been gutted and worked through by a range of tradesmen who owed Scott favours - and also with some financial assistance from Scott. Lee hadn't told Scott that he'd also received some help from Lizzie, although he wasn't sure why not.

Anna was enjoying adding the finishing touches – Lee had been happy for her to choose colour schemes as he wasn't the slightest bit interested. She had opted for plain colours throughout – paint, not wallpaper – which she thought would provide a calming, comforting feeling. Grey-blue in the bathroom, cream in the bedroom, a very subtle green in the lounge.

The kitchen was small, but the sink was situated below the window, which looked across the road to another, similar house. Anna would sometimes stand at the sink, washing up, and watch their neighbours, a family of five, eating dinner together. Two boys and a girl, like her family, only the kids were closer in age and these people looked like they enjoyed being together. They always seemed to be laughing, Anna thought. Whenever she saw her mum and dad, who lived just down the road from Lee's place, there seemed to be more and more of a struggle to find things to talk about.

It was a relief to come back to Lee, and his flat, and the comfortable existence they shared there.

The windows of the flat looked out towards the city centre and Anna loved nothing more than to sit on the window seat on the top floor, where the roof pitched and the ceiling sloped down on either side of her. She could watch the sky change colour, as the sun set somewhere behind her, and gradually turn dark as Bristol revealed itself, illuminated, before her. Although she fancied herself as a country girl; someone who loved wildlife and fresh air, there was something about the sight of the city at night which at once comforted and excited her. So much life, she thought; so many lives. All those lights out there signified homes, offices, shops, restaurants, bars, clubs. Places with people. It was immensely reassuring to know that she was so far from alone. At the same time, she acknowledged that with all of that came bad things – out there, amongst those lights, awful things could be being acted out. Violent relationships, fights, robberies. Broken homes, neglected children, loneliness, sadness, death. But it was real and it was out there and it was by no means all bad. Mingling with, and hopefully vastly outweighing, the bad, there was happiness, love, friendship, creativity. People snuggled up on settees, watching TV together. Children tucked into warm beds, their rooms lit by soft nightlights. A first date, the couple with no idea that one day they would celebrate their ruby wedding anniversary. Friends creating memories that would still make them smile when they were old and infirm. All of this was vivid to Anna and she wondered whether, if she were to leave Bristol as she planned to, she could ever feel the same about anywhere else.

Lee would often be playing on his Nintendo 64 while Anna was in her spot by the window. There would be music in the background; more often than not, Massive Attack's *Blue Lines* album. Lee was happy to keep the noise of his games to a minimum and there they would sit, together but not together. Often, they would eat a takeaway, maybe have a drink or two, but Lee wasn't interested in heavy drinking anymore. The flat, the independence, and maybe even Anna – if she wasn't flattering herself too much – had done him good. He would see Scott at work, and have a drink with him occasionally at the Lamplighters, but that was it. Anna knew that this was the over-riding factor which had changed Lee's life.

She tried not to think too much about their feelings for each other. Whether hers were right or wrong. She pushed thoughts of Mike aside, although she'd been shocked when she'd realised that he and Suzie had split up. The timing couldn't have been worse, it happening the very night that she and Lee got together. Had she known, would she have acted differently? Anna wasn't sure, but it was futile to think that way. She had chosen Lee, and he her, and they had settled quickly into this sedate lifestyle. It was comfortable, and comforting. She was enjoying it.

In February, on Lee's birthday, they had slept together properly for the first time and Anna was surprised to find that she had been intensely moved by it, to the point of tears. Her experience of sex to that point had been fairly limited and unexciting but Lee surprised her, not least that he – who until very recently she had only ever considered a friend - could make her feel that way. However, the sex didn't seem to be a big thing for them, despite their age. They had found something else that they had been looking for in each other and that was what bound them more tightly than anything.

Lee sometimes cried himself, when they did have sex, and Anna would just hold him. "I love you, Anna." He would look at her with those blue eyes; almost worried, it seemed to her.

"I love you, too."

He would fall asleep with his head on her shoulder and she would lie awake for a while, watching the shadow of the trees move gently on their ceiling, cast by the orange glow of the streetlight.

One day in May, shortly before her exams, Lee said, "Move in with me."

"For the summer?"

"No, properly. For good."

Anna chose her words carefully, "I'd love to, and I will spend most of my time here in the summer, but you know I've got to go back to Cardiff in September."

"You don't."

"I do. I love my course, you know that."

"You can transfer to Bristol."

Anna felt herself prickle a little. She didn't want to transfer to Bristol. She had gone to Cardiff precisely because it was a first small step in leaving Bristol.

"I don't know if…"

"You can, I've looked into it."

"Oh, right, that's really lovely, Lee, but…"

"Don't you want to?"

Anna pushed down a rising feeling of annoyance. "It's not a case of that. Well, I suppose it is…"

"Thanks a lot," Lee interrupted her again, pushing back his chair angrily.

"Don't be like that, Lee."

"I'm not being like anything." He pulled out a packet of cigarettes from his pocket and lit one, not looking at her.

"You are, it's not… I don't know. Well, we've only been together for a few months, for a start."

"But we know each other. We've always known each other. We want to be with each other. I do, anyway," he said sulkily.

"I do too, Lee," Anna put a hand on his arm, which he shrugged away. "But you know I don't want to live in Bristol."

"I thought you'd got over that shit!" Lee half shouted. "Now we're together. Or don't that mean nothin' to you?"

"It... oh, don't be stupid, Lee."

"I'm not stupid!" He slammed his fist on the table and got up.

Anna was shocked. She'd seen Lee lose his temper before, of course, but only when he had been drinking. She swallowed hard and looked at him, doing her best to stay calm.

"I didn't mean it like that. I meant, of course it means something to me. It means a lot. I just, I want to get away from Bristol. From my parents, anyway. See somewhere new, be myself."

"But if you move in here you will be getting away from your parents."

"Not really, Lee. Not like I need to. For one thing, they're only about three minutes down the road."

"Oh, do what you like," he huffed, and went into his bedroom, slamming the door.

Anna silently cleared away their plates, wrapping up the pizza and putting it in the fridge. She got herself a glass of water and took her seat by the window, thinking hard. There it was, the city. Her city. She pushed the catch and hoisted the window so that the sounds and the smells of the place assaulted her. Somewhere, church bells were ringing. Down on Gloucester Road there was endless traffic, and out of sight, somebody shouting - whether for fun or in fear, she couldn't tell. This was familiar, what she'd lived with all her life, everything she'd known, until she'd left for uni. She loved it, but she couldn't come back. She couldn't. Could she?

In the end, the decision was made easier – or harder, depending which way you looked at it - by Scott.

Anna had returned to Cardiff the day after her argument with Lee; him still sulking as he dropped her off at the station. She had gone to kiss him but he'd turned his head so she just got his cheek. She sighed and discovered thoughts of Mike sneaking into her head. She wondered what he was doing that evening, but it was no use. She couldn't talk to him about this; he was her friend and Lee's, and Anna had already made a pact with herself not to get him involved in anything to do with their relationship.

Suzie, however, was a different matter. It had been a while since they had spent any real time together and Anna found herself hoping that her friend would be at home and in the mood for a night off. As Anna hopped off the bus she'd caught from the station, she felt a lightness in her step. It was a lovely thought, spending an uncomplicated, relaxing evening with her friend. She stopped at the little shop on the next street from theirs and picked up a bottle of wine and a tube of Pringles. The shopkeeper smiled, recognising her. This place was beginning to feel a bit like home, too, she thought. Maybe anywhere could if she just put in the effort.

As she rounded the corner, Anna saw Suzie's little battered red car parked on their street and smiled. "Suze!" she called as she opened the door to the flat, "Are you in? I've got wine."

Suzie appeared in the hallway before Anna had even taken her coat off. She looked worried. "Anna," she said, and her tone of voice grabbed Anna's full attention, "Lee rang. It's his dad. He's in hospital and it sounds like it's serious."

New Year's Day

There were many times in the following years when Anna wished that 1996 had been very different. She supposed it fitted the phrase 'starting off on the wrong foot', as it certainly had. What had she been thinking of, letting Lee kiss her? What had she been thinking of, kissing him back?

The answer to both those questions was that she hadn't been thinking. She had drunk more than she was accustomed to and she was a bit stoned; something else she'd not had much experience of. And she cared for Lee deeply. He was her lifelong friend, and he needed her. He'd said so and she'd known it. Had she been a little older and more worldly-wise, she'd have known that he didn't really need her in that way. In fact, when she took on that role in his life, she was less use to him than she could have been as a friend. Because it changed everything.

***

Beautiful Flic, who was in the same halls of residence as Mike, had remained sleeping innocently, beautifully, while Lee - her boyfriend - and Anna had kissed and exchanged words of love and, slightly uncomfortably, passion in the room across the landing. She had not stirred when the front door had slammed and Mike had followed in Suzie's footsteps. He had walked all the way home to Lawrence Weston, passing drunken revellers, ignoring their shouts, inwardly fuming at his two best friends, but also at Suzie, and more than anything at himself.

When Lee and Anna heard the door slam, they jumped, and pulled back from one another, guiltily. It was like a fog clearing and Anna had looked at her friend's face, feeling... what? Desire? She didn't think so. She thought, when she looked back, that it was maybe something more akin to pity, but whatever it was went hand-in-hand with a strong bond, a loyalty, and a need to do the right thing. How she kicked herself in the years that were to come.

They did not sleep together that night, not in the sexual sense, but they lay together, holding hands, on Scott's bed. They felt shy with each other but both were gaining in strength from the other's presence. Lee felt safe and loved in a way he hadn't in years... maybe ever, he thought. Anna felt strong, and noticed, and needed. Important.

When dawn broke, Lee snuck back into his room and Anna went the way of Suzie and Mike, stepping through the solid oak doorframe, headlong into the first day of the cold new year.

They had agreed not to tell anybody what had happened. Lee still had Flic to deal with, and Anna had voiced her concerns for Mike's feelings.

"Why would he care?" Lee's words were slightly spiky, she thought.

"Well, I don't know, really, but I suppose it might be weird for him."

"Why? He's with Suzie."

"Yes, I don't mean in that way." Somewhere deep down, Anna wondered if that was exactly the way she meant, but she buried the thought deeply. "I just mean, well, it's always been the three of us, hasn't it?"

"Yeah, it still will be. He can be our best man!"

Anna had laughed, but that moment was when she recognised a fairly small but hard and undeniable seed of doubt. *Bury it,* she told herself, willing herself to ignore it, refusing to fully acknowledge it. Forgetting that seeds still germinate beneath the soil. "We'll see."

As she walked carefully down the icy pavements of Zetland Road that morning, taking small steps and holding on to the garden walls she passed, she recounted the words in her head. She thought of the kiss. *Kisses,* she corrected herself. Tried to recall how she'd felt when they had happened. There was something warm, friendly, familiar, although she had never kissed Lee before in that way. It contrasted with a sense of otherness, of a friend – somebody she had thought of as a brother - becoming something different. Lee had cried. She had felt a warm tear run from his cheek onto hers and she had pulled back, letting his head fall onto her shoulder, and he had cried. She concentrated on how good it had made her feel to be wanted, and needed. How could she possibly turn to him now and say she had changed her mind?

For Lee, there was no doubt. Anna was his angel. She always had been. Why had he not seen it before? She was the one who had been there for him when his mum left. She had been the only person he could tell about his dad. She had even taken the blame for him that time when Scott had nearly caught him smoking weed. When Mike had gone off with Suzie, it had been Lee and Anna all the way. The other girls were meaningless; it had just taken him a while to realise it. Now he had Anna, there was no way he was going to let her go.

Flic returned to her parents', ashen-faced, on New Year's Day. Lee had wasted no time in breaking up with her, doing so as he made her breakfast and she sat at the kitchen table, crying and head throbbing.

"It's because I made a fool of myself in front of your friends, isn't it?" she'd sobbed.

"No, it's not, it's not. It's just... New year and all that. I had some time to think last night."

"I know it is, I made an idiot of myself, I'm sorry."

"Listen, Flic, it's not that, I promise. It's just... it's been really good..."

Flic, rubbing her tears away, had sidled up to him, slipping her arms around his waist and looking at him with those big brown eyes. Despite a couple of half-hearted protestations, Lee hadn't been able to resist. She looked good – her long, bare legs escaping that shirt of his dad's - which he'd better make sure he washed before Scott got back. Well, what was the harm of one more time – for old time's sake? Lee made up his mind that this would be it, his final fling before he committed himself to Anna fully.

Thinking it meant that it wasn't over, Flic gladly went back upstairs with Lee but afterwards, he got up and pulled his trousers on. "Come on, that toast's goin' to be cold."

Flic had followed him back downstairs, dejected, and retrieved her own clothes from the tumble dryer, thinking sadly how she had chosen them especially, spent her Christmas money on them, to impress Lee. She put them back on, and nibbled some toast, then sat quietly watching TV until it was time to go. The worst thing was, Lee seemed so happy.

Lee had the house to himself after that, Scott not being due back until the following day. He felt more relaxed, more sure of himself, than he had in a long while. He phoned Lizzie.

"Happy new year, Gran!"

"Oh, hello love, happy new year to you, too! Did you have a good time last night? Didn't drink too much, did you?"

"No... well maybe a little bit."

"Oh you!"

"Gran…"

"Yes, love?"

"I've been thinking about what you said… about getting my own place… did you mean it?"

"Yes, I did. Of course, love. I know your dad's house is lovely but I know my son, and it can't be easy for you, living with him. Your friends have got their own flats at university, haven't they? Why shouldn't you have your own place, too?"

"You're a legend! Thanks, Gran. I'm going to get a paper and start looking."

"No time like the present, eh?" she chuckled, relieved to think of Lee escaping Scott's grasp at home at least. She loved her son but he was overbearing and she'd seen Lee lose his way since Elaine had left them. Lizzie had always felt she could only ever watch from the sidelines, but now she had a way to help her only grandchild. "You find one you like, and let me know. I'll come and have a look with you if you like then we'll see about a loan for the deposit. Might as well get you on the housing ladder now, eh? You'll have it all paid off by the time you're thirty, the way you're going!"

Lee smiled, warmed by his grandmother's words. Gran and Anna. Two women he could trust, who loved him no matter what. No doubt about it, 1996 was going to be his year.

1995

Bristol, December 1995

New Year's Eve

The turning of a year means different things to different people. For some, it is an excuse for a night out; for others it's a reason to stay in, huddled under a duvet and trying to ignore the midnight fireworks; for others still, it's a chance to take stock of the previous year, to plan ahead and to wake up on the first day of a fresh new year with a clear head and a great resolve to do things better. For the four friends from Bristol, the end of 1995 was an excuse for a night out; at least this was how it seemed on the surface.

Mike had borrowed Emma's car to pick Flic and Lee up in town. Although Lee had his own car, he'd wanted to meet Flic and take her for lunch. Mike knew Lee would want a beer and, as he and Suzie were heading to Lee's house that afternoon anyway, he'd agreed to give Flic and Lee a lift up there.

Emma was more than happy for Mike to borrow her car; in fact, she was more than happy, full stop. Miguel had come over on the day after Boxing Day and she had been busy showing him around Bristol. Ashton Court, Blaise Estate, Cabot Tower, the Observatory, the docks, the Industrial Museum. Mike wondered if Miguel might have had enough of the tourist information, but he seemed happy to go along with whatever Emma had planned and she was in her element, showing off the city she loved.

Miguel was slightly older than Emma, with smooth, olive skin and black hair tinselled with silver. Mike and Miguel had met a few times now, in Spain, and they liked each other. Miguel had an infectious laugh, and a relaxed, confident air. He had a family too; two daughters who were married, and his first grandchild on the way. His ex-wife was still a friend of his, and he lived in a small town with his extended family all around him.

"Miguel, Spanish for Michael, eh? A great name!" Miguel had smiled and grasped Mike's hand warmly the first time they'd met.

"The best," Mike had agreed.

Even Sandra, Emma's mum, liked Miguel. Her initial reaction to her daughter 'taking up' with a divorced Spaniard was that it was a holiday romance destined to go nowhere but now she too had been to Spain to meet him and she was charmed, and convinced, by him. "He's a good man," she'd told her friend Ella, "He's divorced, yes, but his family love him; he's certainly not neglected them. Oh, and did I mention he's very good looking?" Ella had giggled.

Now, on New Year's Eve, in contrast with the preceding days, Emma and Miguel were planning to stay in. They were not taking stock, nor hiding from fireworks; they were celebrating each other and being together. They could have been anywhere.

"Are you sure you won't come and join us at the Vic Rooms? Miguel might like it!" Mike had said.

"Have you ever been to a Spanish New Year's Eve party?" Emma had said, "The Vic Rooms is unbelievably tame by comparison! No crazy idiots holding lit fireworks in their hands, or mouths. Honestly, Mike, I've had my fill of being in town for New Year, I think it's better left to you young folk."

Mike had smiled and tutted at the term, then hugged Emma and shaken Miguel's hand. "See you next year."

"Yes, happy new year. Wish Suzie, Anna and Lee a good one as well, please."

"Will do."

It was a bright, blue-skied day and Mike took his time driving as he headed to Suzie's house. He was thinking about her, and how she'd been since Christmas. Something didn't seem quite right, he thought, but he wasn't sure what. Maybe it was being back with her family, which he knew she found stressful. He was so grateful for his own mum, and their uncomplicated relationship. Suzie, Lee and Anna had all been brought up in homes with two parents, yet none of them had as happy a home life as his.

Then his thoughts drifted to Anna. She had endured Christmas, she'd said with a wry smile when they'd met up on Boxing Day. Her mum had bought in a lavish meal, no expense - but every effort - spared. Anna now had her own word-processor; a gift from her parents, and Mike had suffered a twinge of envy but it vanished quickly as he looked at her expression and thought of the personal gifts his mum had chosen for him. Evelyn Waugh's *Scoop*, *(What's the Story) Morning Glory?* – the Oasis album which could be heard blaring out from pretty much every bedroom in the halls of residence, but which Mike had been unable to afford a copy of - as well as *Definitely Maybe*. Even though Emma looked at the Gallagher brothers with disdain - and Mike did too, if he was honest. She'd also got him a pack of Reporters Notepads, as the packet said, and a very expensive-looking pen.

"A pen," Emma had said ruefully. "I know it's not what every eighteen-year-old dreams of..."

"Mum, I love it! I love it. I will take it, and one of these notepads, everywhere. Thank you, Mum."

He had money from Sandra, which he'd already spent on Park Street, on a new hooded top. It was maroon, made of thick, fleecy material. He'd worn it every day since and had visions of himself wearing it while sitting up late in his room back at uni, working on assignments and lyrics. He hadn't written much apart from essays since he'd gone to Cardiff but

1996 would be the year he really got into his writing. That was Mike's resolution.

Suzie was waiting at the bay window of her parents' living room.

"Mike's here!" she called up the stairs.

"OK, love," her dad called back. He and her mum were lying in bed, watching TV. She'd taken them a cup of tea each earlier and pulled back their curtains.

"Hey!" her dad had exclaimed, "We're having a lie-in!"

"Yeah, but it's a beautiful day out there. You can lie in bed and look at what you're missing!"

He'd laughed, though she hadn't known if he would. "OK, love. Have a good time tonight, eh? Look, there's a tenner on the drawers over there, why don't you take it? Get some drinks for you and your friends."

"Happy new year!" she shouted now, and heard her dad's reply but nothing from her mum whom, she assumed, had fallen back to sleep.

Suzie grabbed her coat and slammed the door in her rush to leave her stifling home. She climbed into the car, leaning over and giving Mike a peck on the cheek.

"Where to, Drive?"

"Whiteladies first – pick up Lee and Flic, then back to Lee's. I've got a few beers in the boot, and Lee reckons he's got something special for us all."

"Champagne?"

"I'd like to think so but I'm always suspicious when Lee says something's 'special'."

"Hmm. I hope he keeps a lid on it tonight, maybe Flic will be a good influence."

"Let's hope so."

"What about Anna?" asked Suzie, who had actually already spoken to Anna that day.

"She's going to meet us at Lee's, she's meant to be having

lunch with her mum and dad at Brown's or something. Says her mum wants her to wear a nice frock." Mike laughed.

Suzie smiled thinly. "Sounds like a nightmare!"

"Oh, Anna's used to it, she's good at being the diligent daughter."

"I suppose."

"What are your mum and dad up to tonight?"

"Hmm, let's see... Dad's probably cooking chicken and chips and Mum will be drinking a bottle or two of cider. Just for a change."

Mike looked over at Suzie. "Are they OK?"

"They're fine. They're just... Mum and Dad. Look, Dad gave me a tenner, though!"

"Brilliant. Anna's got some cash too, she said. Maybe we could get some champagne, after all."

"She's probably drinking champagne right now, at Brown's."

Mike cast a sideways glance at Suzie, wondering if he'd detected a hint of... what? Sarcasm? Jealousy? "She might be, but she won't be enjoying it. Says she's out with her parents' friends and their boring, stuck-up son."

"Oh yeah? Best she fancies him really."

"No, I don't think so," Mike answered quickly.

"I was only joking," said Suzie, the atmosphere in the car quickly chilling.

Mike kept his eyes on the road and turned the radio on.

Lee and Flic were waiting on a side street near Clifton Down shopping centre.

Mike rolled his window down, "Hop in!"

Suzie had to get out so that she could push the passenger seat forward. She climbed into the back, followed by Flic.

"Hi Mike, hi Suzie," Flic chirped. "Have you had a good Christmas?"

"Not bad, thanks," said Mike.

"Good, thanks, how was yours?" Suzie seemed to have perked up again. She was definitely having some funny mood swings at the moment. It would be good to get back to Cardiff again, get things back on an even keel.

"How are you, mate?" he asked Lee, who was putting the passenger seat back in place and clambering in. Mike could smell spirits on his friend's breath. "What have you been drinking?" he asked, deliberately light-hearted.

"Oh, we had a bottle of wine with lunch, didn't we, babe?" Flic agreed, "And I just had a cheeky scotch with a coffee."

"Ooh, wine, coffee, very posh!" Suzie said. "Was it a good lunch?"

"It was beautiful," Flic gushed, "I've been completely spoiled!"

"Well, you deserve it."

Mike smiled slightly at his friend's slick manner. He could see Flic settling contentedly on the back seat. He caught Suzie's eye in the rear-view mirror and she grinned at him. Just that look made him feel more relaxed.

"Home, James!" Lee said and Flic giggled.

"Whatever you say, sir." Mike pulled the car out, casting another sneaky look in Suzie's direction via the mirror as he did so. She was looking out of the window.

Lee's house was its usual immaculate self. The hallway tiles gleamed and the lights on the Christmas tree twinkled.

"Wow!" Flic gasped.

"I'd forgotten you hadn't been here before," Mike said. "It's a bit grander than my house... and yours, eh Suze?"

Suzie looked at him. "Yes. Anna's is nice though, isn't it?"

"Oh yeah, Anna's house is lovely." He turned to Flic, "It's an old town house, three floors, you know. There are amazing views from the attic rooms. The only problem is, her parents live there!"

"Oh, doesn't Anna like her parents?"

"It's not that she doesn't like them," Mike began.

"She hardly sees 'em. They're well into their work and a right pair o' snobs," Lee cut in.

"Her mum's not so bad," Mike said.

"She's a silly bitch. Always 'avin' a go at Anna for what she's wearin', thinks nursin' ain't a good career choice."

"It's a great career choice," Mike moved to put his arm around Suzie but she moved away.

"OK, shall we talk about something else?" she said, "Anna will be here in person soon enough."

There was a beat of silence then Lee magnanimously spoke up, "Let's go through to the kitchen, get drinking!"

"Can't you show me your room first, Lee?" Flic pulled at his arm and looked meaningfully at him.

"Er, yeah, course. You two go on through," Lee grinned at Mike and Suzie. "Make yourselves at home. There's beer in the fridge and vodka on the side. Help yourselves."

Through the kitchen window it was evident that those earlier blue skies were being slowly muffled and smothered by a blanket of grey cloud. The back garden looked sparse, stray brown leaves blown into corners and a lone robin hopping across the mud, looking for worms.

"What's up?" Mike asked Suzie.

"Nothing, I'm fine." She stiffened.

"Well, I can tell you're not." Mike wandered to the fridge and opened it up, extracting a beer for himself and some orange juice for Suzie's vodka.

"I am, everything's fine," Suzie snapped.

Mike sighed and handed her a glass. They sat and sipped their drinks in silence, trying to ignore the giggling and banging sounds from the room above.

Not long after Lee and Flic had returned downstairs, slightly flushed and smiling, the doorbell went.

"That'll be Anna," said Mike, getting up.

"I'll get it," Suzie said firmly. She walked through the hallway to find Anna, rosy-cheeked and bearing boxes of takeaway pizza.

"I thought you'd just been for lunch?" Suzie asked.

"Well, if you can call it that. The plates are massive but there's hardly any food on them. My dad enjoys being ripped off!" Anna smiled, kissing Suzie on the cheek. "Happy new year... nearly."

Seeing Anna's warm smile had the effect of diluting Suzie's bad mood. She returned her friend's kiss. "Happy new year to you, too!"

"I thought I'd bring these to soak up the booze," Anna whispered to her, "I take it Lee's started already?"

"Good move," Suzie whispered back, "Yes he has, although there's been a break in proceedings as he and Flic have been upstairs for a while, getting reacquainted, shall we say?"

Anna smiled. "Why does that not surprise me?" She hung up her coat on the banister. "Scott's definitely not around, is he?"

"No, Lee said he's visiting his new girlfriend in Brighton."

"Thank God for that!" Anna walked through to the kitchen. "Who wants pizza?"

**

"Shall we play some drinking games?" Lee asked, a string of melted mozzarella drizzling onto his chin.

Anna looked at Mike, as did Suzie.

"Great idea!" said Flic.

Before any of the others had a chance to protest, five shot glasses were extracted from Scott's built-in bar; a recent addition to the kitchen-diner, all dark wood and shiny chrome. Lee lined them up alongside the bottle of vodka.

"Not neat vodka!" Suzie said.

"Why not? The Russians do it!" laughed Lee.

Flic, without waiting for anybody else, or indeed for the game to start, poured a shot of vodka and downed it in one big gulp. The sharp drink burned the back of her throat, making her gasp and, appropriately considering her name, she flicked her head back, her long, dark hair falling softly around her shoulders. She looked seductively at Lee and held her glass out.

"Steady on!" Lee said, which was not a phrase he'd been heard to utter many times before. "Pace yourself. It's only half five, you want to be awake at midnight, don't you?"

He passed a glass to each of the others, pushing them so that they slid across the smooth, shiny table top.

"So, what's it to be? Truth or dare?"

"What are we? Twelve?" Mike asked.

"Yeah, I don't think so…" Suzie began.

"No, go on, let's do truth or dare!" Anna said.

Mike looked at her in surprise. "Really?"

"Why not? I'm feeling reckless. Anyway, we all know each other pretty well. Flic?"

"Why not? I just want to get drinking!"

"OK then," Lee said, "We'll call it Truth or Drink, though. Mike, you start. You need to choose somebody and ask them a question. They either answer truthfully or have a drink."

"Alright," Mike smiled, "I'll choose you, Lee. Did you really meet Kurt Cobain when Nirvana played the Victoria Rooms?"

Lee blushed. "Yeah, course I did."

"Lee!" Anna laughed, "This is meant to be *truth* or drink. I think you're going to have to drink!"

Lee looked annoyed for a moment but, accepting his game was up, he poured a large shot of vodka and necked it.

Mike laughed. "I knew it!"

"I didn't say I didn't meet him."

"OK, OK, whatever. Now your turn to ask someone a question."

Lee took his time, looking around the table, and ended up looking at Flic. "Have I got the biggest knob you've seen?"

"Lee!" Anna exclaimed again.

Flic just laughed, looking composed. "Erm, I think I'll drink."

Everybody else laughed then and Lee's face went redder.

"Well, it was a silly thing to ask, Lee," Suzie said.

Flic drank her vodka and licked the rim of the glass slowly, looking at Lee.

"Come on!" Mike said, impatiently, "There are three other people in this room, you know."

"OK," Flic said, looking at Mike, "You and Suzie have been together for two years. Why didn't you move in with her this year instead of going to Halls?"

"We all already know that," Anna said.

"Mike's got to answer," Flic insisted.

"No problem," said Mike. "We decided we were a bit young for moving in together, didn't we?" He looked at Suzie.

"Well, you did. And your mum." Suzie found the words escaping her mouth before she'd had a chance to think about what she was saying.

Mike looked annoyed. "No, we all did. I'm only eighteen, for God's sake. You've already had two years of freedom at university."

"OK," Suzie realised she should quickly diffuse this conversation. "You're right, that's it. Let's move on. Your turn again, Mike."

She hadn't meant to say that about his mum. And really, she was very happy living with Anna. Living with Mike would make things very different. And he was right, he was only eighteen. She was about to turn twenty-one.

"I don't know, I'm not sure this game's a good idea."

"Ask Anna a question!" Flic piped up, pouring herself

another glass of vodka.

"Don't you think you should wait for your next turn?" Mike asked.

"It's fine," Lee said, "It's new year. Let her enjoy herself."

"Glad you bought the pizzas," Suzie said quietly to Anna.

"OK," Mike said, "Anna... this one's for you. You've known me and Lee a long time. If we were in a sinking boat and you had a life raft but could only fit one of us in it, who would you choose?"

"That's a stupid question, Mike!" Suzie admonished. "Don't make Anna choose."

"It's fine," Anna laughed, "I think if it was a choice of one or the other of you, I'd have to let you both go. Anything else wouldn't be fair."

Everybody laughed at this.

"Fair play, Anna, fair play." Lee looked at her, "You'd choose me, though, wouldn't you, really?"

"I think I'll have a drink now," Anna laughed.

"Aha! So you would, you'd choose me!"

"Not necessarily, mate, you'd talk too much. I could sing songs and keep everybody's spirits up," said Mike. "It'd be me, wouldn't it, Anna?"

"Pass me the vodka!" Anna smiled. "Now, I've got a question for Suzie."

Anna managed to bring the tone of the game round to something more neutral, asking Suzie about her first kiss, and Suzie endeavoured to do the same. She asked Mike if he had fancied any teachers at school. He, in turn, asked Flic if she'd had a crush on any of her teachers.

"No!" she hiccuped, "but I did have a crush on a girl!"

"Really?" Lee's eyebrows raised. He filled her glass, "Tell me more!"

"I think we'll leave it there, shall we?" Anna said. "How about some music? And shouldn't we get going out soon?"

"Good idea," said Suzie, "You don't want to be stuck in with two couples when midnight strikes."

"Ooh, yeah, let's find Anna somebody for a midnight kiss!" Flic giggled.

"I think she's capable of doing that herself," Mike said.

"I don't think I want a horrible slobbery drunken snog anyway," Anna said, "but I would like to go out."

"OK," said Lee. "Good call, I'm just gonna get changed. Mike, put some more music on, will you?"

"I'll come with you," Flic said to Lee.

"Nah, don't worry, I'll only be a minute. You pour us a drink instead, eh?

Anna and Suzie looked at each other. Flic already seemed quite drunk. Her words were coming out slurred and she must have had a good five or six shots of vodka, on top of whatever she'd drunk at lunchtime and since.

"Have you got any snacks?" Suzie called after Lee.

"Yeah, loads, check in the cupboard next to the dishwasher. Help yourselves!"

"Here, Flic, what do you fancy?" Anna asked.

"Ooh, let's…" Flic let out a large burp, "actually, I don't feel great."

"OK, no problem, just sit down. Let me get you some water."

Anna could see Flic was looking pale. She sat her on the large black leather settee.

"Thank you, Anna," Flic said, sipping the water gingerly.

Mike sat down next to her, "Are you OK?"

"Yeah, I'm… Oh god…" Flic was sick over the settee, over Mike, and into her beautiful swinging hair.

Mike jumped up. "Urgh! I mean, are you OK? I mean, urgh!"

Anna rushed over. "Oh, Flic, bless you. Here. Let's get you up to Lee's room and out of these clothes. In fact, I think you're going to need a shower or a bath or something."

Anna ushered Flic out of the room while Mike and Suzie grabbed some cloths and a washing-up bowl full of hot, soapy water.

"You'd better go and borrow something from Lee," Suzie said, "You can't go out with sick all over you!"

"I will in a minute. Anyway, do you think we will be going out now? Flic can't, and Lee will have to stay with her. I suppose we could still go... with Anna..."

"No, no," Suzie said hurriedly, "You're right, maybe we are going to have to stay here instead."

"Silly cow, drinking so much!"

"Ah, don't, she's probably nervous. After all, we all know each other really well – especially you, Anna and Lee."

"I suppose," Mike conceded grudgingly. "OK, I'll go and see what I can borrow from Lee."

Upstairs, Mike could hear the shower going and Anna's gentle voice talking kindly to Flic, who seemed to be sobbing.

"Thank God for Anna, eh?" Mike said to Lee. "Got any jeans I can borrow? These are covered in puke. Though they're not nearly as bad as your settee."

Lee's face paled. "What? It's on the settee? Where else is it? Dad's goin' to kill me."

"It's OK, mate. Suzie's clearing it up. It's leather anyway so it should wipe clean, shouldn't it?"

"Shit, I don't know. Oh, fuckin' 'ell."

Anna came out of the steamed-up bathroom, with Flic wrapped in Lee's dressing gown, looking very sorry for herself.

"You've made a right mess downstairs," Lee said to her.

"Lee," Anna said warningly.

"I didn't mean to, I'm sorry," said Flic.

"Yeah, come on mate, we've all done it."

"Yeah, but Dad is going to KILL me."

"We'll sort it, I promise," said Mike.

"Yes, come on, Lee," said Anna, "It's not Flic's fault, we've all been drinking. We shouldn't have been playing that stupid game. Mike, how about you go back down and help clear the mess up? I'll stay up here and help Lee with Flic."

"OK," Mike said, "can I just get those jeans, mate?"

"Yep," Lee rummaged angrily in a chest of drawers, "there you go."

"Cheers. Look, I'll get the washing machine on, too. Anna, are Flic's clothes in the bathroom?"

"Yeah, thank you, Mike."

Mike smiled. You could always count on Anna. He didn't think he'd seen her really drunk. Well maybe once, back when they were about sixteen; he was pretty sure he'd held her hair for her while she'd been sick down the side of the Arnolfini, but ever since then she had always seemed so... in control.

"Some new year this is turning out to be," Lee muttered. "I'm going for a smoke."

***

"I don't know if we're going out or not," Mike said to Suzie as he walked into the kitchen. She was tipping the bucket of dirty water down the sink.

"How are things upstairs?" she asked.

"Wow, you've done a brilliant job," said Mike, admiring the clean, still-wet leather and floor. "Scott's not going to know anything went wrong. That's what Lee is most worried about, I think. Anyway, Anna's looking after Flic and Lee's gone for a smoke."

"Typical Anna," said Suzie.

"What do you mean? I can't tell if that's a compliment or not."

"It's got to be a compliment, hasn't it? Anna's perfect." Suzie sighed. "I don't mean it in any derogatory way to her. It's just... well she's got you and Lee wrapped around her little finger."

"No she hasn't!" Mike flashed back angrily, "She's not like that."

"No, she's not. I'm not doing very well here, am I? She's great. She's lovely. She's calm, kind, considerate. Beautiful." Mike said nothing so Suzie continued. "You've all known each other for years and I don't think anything could come between that. Not even me."

Mike put his arm around Suzie. "You don't have to come between us. You're... just you."

"Just me!" Suzie's laugh seemed muffled, half-hearted. "I think we need to have a chat, Mike."

***

Upstairs, Anna was stroking Flic's hair gently while Flic lay on her side in Lee's bed, groaning softly.

"Urgh, thanks for looking after me, Anna. God, I'm such an idiot. Lee's going to hate me."

"No he's not! It's not as if we haven't all done it, don't worry!"

"Yeah, but he was so angry about the mess downstairs. Kept saying his dad was going to kill him."

"Hmm."

"Do you know his dad, Anna?"

"Yep. Well, a bit."

"What's he like? Is he nasty?"

"He's... that's probably for Lee to say, to be honest."

"I feel awful."

"Look, why don't you get some sleep? It's only half nine, you might feel better in an hour or two, wake up and see the new year in with us."

Flic smiled gently, her eyes already closing. In the doorway, Lee was watching Anna. She looked up and saw him, mouthing 'shhhh'. He smiled and held up a bottle of champagne, beckoning her.

Anna smiled back, remembering she was meant to be being reckless. She had hoped to go out to celebrate new year, but really, what was the point? As she'd said, she didn't fancy a drunken, beer-fuelled snog with a stranger. Instead, she could spend the evening with her three best friends. She looked at Flic - who was snoring gently – and stood up slowly then crept over to Lee.

"Come on," he said, "let's have this in Dad's room, on his balcony."

"Are you sure?" Anna felt strange entering Scott's room. However, Lee was adamant.

He opened the door onto a vast space, carpeted in plush, soft grey, and housing the biggest bed Anna had ever seen – bigger than she could imagine was necessary for anybody. Even Scott, with his macho, man-size frame. Over the bed hung a large painting, surprisingly tasteful and low-key for Scott, Anna thought. She'd imagined him liking art – if he gave it more than a moment's thought – that was hectic, brash and loud. This was a soft oil painting of the back a woman, sitting on a bed, a thin sheet pulled around her, falling off her bare shoulders.

The other walls were as naked as those shoulders. No more artwork, no photos of Lee. In fact, Anna realised, there were no photos in any rooms of the house except for Lee's bedroom. Even Anna's parents had photos of themselves together and family pictures – posed and paid for in expensive studios of course, but they were there, they were present. Reminders that theirs was a family home, never mind the distance between the members of the family who lived there.

Scott's dark curtains were open, revealing floor-to-ceiling windows almost all the way along one wall, which opened up onto the balcony. Outside, the rough, bare trees were shaking in the wind, and between their branches Anna could just see the lights of the suspension bridge. She knew Scott had wanted to pull the trees down, open up his view across the Downs to the gorge, but they had been under a protection order. Not even persuasive, bullying Scott had been able to argue against it. He'd had to 'settle' for these occasional glimpses instead. She liked to think of him not getting his own way.

Lee sat on the edge of the bed, pulling two glasses from the inside pocket of his jacket. "Took these from downstairs. Mike and Suzie looked like they were having a bit of a chat so I thought we could have a drink up here."

"A chat? Are they OK?"

"They're fine, I'm sure. You know how serious they both are; they're probably talking politics or animal rights or something."

Anna sat down next to Lee and he pulled her back, tickling her so she giggled. They moved up the bed, leaning against the pillows. Scott's pillows, Anna couldn't help thinking, but she tried to put the thought from her mind. Otherwise she would never relax. Was he nasty? That's what Flic had asked. Yes. He was an awful man. Tall, well-built, good-looking and over-confident. Smooth-talking and a total bastard. She stopped herself from shuddering at the thought of his big, dark-haired head resting where she was leaning.

Lee popped the cork from the bottle and swooped his mouth down to catch the bubbles. Anna watched him. His blue eyes were framed by long lashes, just as they had been when he was four. It was strange sometimes, looking at Lee and Mike, at the men they were becoming and remembering the boys they had been. They still were boys, really, she thought, although she would never say that to them.

"What?" Lee noticed her looking and smiled.

"Oh, nothing," she said. "I was just thinking about primary school."

"A lot's changed since then."

"Yeah."

"It's weird, Anna, still weird not having Mum around."

"I can imagine," Anna said. "Has she been in touch again?"

"No. I don't know. Well, maybe. I don't know. Dad and Gran were talking at Christmas. He was pissed. I could hear him saying somethin' about some post or somethin'. Somethin' 'e'd chucked away. I just thought it might have been from Mum. I don't know, maybe it's just wishful thinking. Dad's such a bastard, though, he wouldn't tell me if it was." Lee took a huge gulp of champagne from the bottle before pouring them a glassful each. "Then again, she left me with 'im, so she's not much better, is she?"

"I don't know. I don't know, Lee. Your mum was... I'm sure still is... lovely. You said she was unhappy."

"Yeah, but she left me! I don't blame her for leavin' Dad but she could've taken me with 'er."

"I know. It doesn't seem right, does it? I know your mum loved you. I wish you could find her, ask her what happened."

"I... well I think I know, a little bit more than I did before. Dad got pissed on Christmas, started talking about her. Nearly crying, I thought. It was embarrassing. Gran made me leave the room, but I listened outside. That's when I 'eard 'im talkin' about that post."

"What else were they saying?"

"Said 'e'd never love anyone like Mum, said it was 'is fault she left. I think 'e told Gran that 'e 'it her. I think Gran already knew. I could 'ear 'er whisperin' to 'im. She was being nice to 'im! Why was she being nice to 'im? 'E's a cunt. 'E 'it my mum, and 'e 'its me. 'E's the reason Mum left me."

"She was being nice to him because, after everything, he is still her son and she loves him."

"Well, if that's what mums do, why did mine leave me?" Lee kicked the bed angrily.

"I don't know, I don't know." Anna put her hand on his arm. "I'm sorry, I really am."

"What are you sorry for? Not your fault."

"My dad's cheating on my mum," Anna said.

"What? How do you know?"

"I heard them arguing about it. On Boxing Day," she laughed. "Bloody Christmas! I heard Mum talking about his flat in London and some floozy he's got shacked up there. Such a stereotype."

"Will your mum kick 'im out?"

"No, she's on to a good thing. She can carry on doing what she's doing and just see him from time to time when he can be arsed to come back to Bristol."

"That's fucked up."

"Yep."

"So what will you do when you finish university?"

Anna took a gulp of the champagne, the cold bubbles nearly making her jump. "I... will go away. Anywhere. As far away as possible. Australia? Nursing's meant to be pretty good over there."

"You can't go, Anna, I need you."

"No, you..." Anna began to reply but then she saw the tears running down Lee's face.

***

Downstairs, Mike was arguing with Suzie, but not angrily. Indignantly, even pleadingly.

"It's not true, Suze. I do love Anna, yes, but not like that. She's like a... like a sister."

"You tell yourself that, Mike, but if... if it was you in the boat and you had to choose between saving me and her, you'd choose her. Every time."

"I wouldn't, I wouldn't," Mike insisted but he wondered if that was actually true.

"You would, Mike, and that's OK. You and I are... we're good together. We're friends. I think you're gorgeous."

"I think you're gorgeous, too..." Mike leaned forward to kiss Suzie.

153

"Stop!" she said. "Don't. I think this is it. Mike, I'll be twenty-one in less than a month."

"And I'll be nineteen in a few months," he said sulkily.

"It's not about age, really, though," she said. "It's about us. It's been great. I've loved being with you but life is about to change for me. I need to find a job, and I don't think I want to stay in Cardiff. You'll be there for two more years after me, you and Anna both will be."

"It doesn't matter, we can do the long-distance thing again, like before when you were in Cardiff and I was still here…"

"Do you really want to do that, Mike? I know you. You're reliable, you're kind, you're thoughtful. I love you, I do, but I don't think you love me. Not that way. Not like you love Anna."

"Fucking hell, Suzie, you're doing my head in."

"Sorry, I'm sorry, Mike. Look, I'm going to go. I'll head off down to the Vic Rooms and see who's about. My advice to you is to go upstairs and take Anna out. Leave Lee to look after Flic and take Anna for a meal somewhere. Tell her we've split up. See how she reacts."

"I can't believe this."

"Well, it's true. I've been thinking about it for weeks, ever since you both came to Cardiff. Look, I love Anna, too. I don't have any ill will towards her, or towards you. And I don't want to get to the point where I do. Go upstairs, leave Lee to his drunk girlfriend and see the new year in with Anna." Suzie kissed Mike on the cheek. "Please. Just do it."

Mike felt a tear run over the spot Suzie had kissed. "Suzie…"

"Don't, Mike." Tears glistened in her eyes. "This is right, believe me."

Mike watched her walk over the shining tiles, open the heavy oak door, and walk into the darkness. She closed the door gently and Mike stood shocked on the black-and-white tiles, the lights of the Christmas tree twinkling behind him.

He didn't know whether to laugh or cry. He felt like shouting, with frustration and confusion. What the fuck had just happened? He searched his pocket for his tobacco tin. All was quiet upstairs so he headed into the back garden for a smoke and to think about everything Suzie had just said.

Outside, the wind was getting up and it was hard to light his roll-up. The creaking of the branches swaying overhead seemed magnified in the dark. Mike stood by the house, and eventually had success. He walked over the damp grass, to the far end of the huge garden, where he could find some shelter under the trees. A light which had been on upstairs suddenly went off, taking from him any source of illumination. He waited a few moments for his eyes to get used to this new level of darkness.

He thought back over Suzie's words. Anna. Did he love Anna? Could that be true? Yes, he had no doubt that he loved her; as a sister, as a friend. But would he have chosen her over Suzie? Not to save her life – that was ridiculous – but who would he rather have in his life? He thought of the way Anna had made him feel earlier when she'd been sorting things out with Flic, and keeping Lee calm. The rush of warmth he'd felt for her, flooding through him. But what was that? Friendship, surely? He'd known her since she was four. The thought of a relationship with her – a romantic one – was... well, it was weird. But now Suzie had put that thought in his head and he couldn't seem to shake it out.

Maybe he would... yes, he would, he'd take Suzie's advice. There was no point him and Anna hanging around while Lee got drunk and Flic threw up some more. It seemed a bit mean to Lee but Flic was his girlfriend and he had to look after her.

Mike wondered which window the light had been coming from. It must have been Scott's, he thought – that was the only one with open curtains. Mike looked contemptuously towards Scott's bedroom. He hated Scott. He was a big, angry man, and selfish too. If proof was needed, all you had to do was look at the huge bedroom he had designed for himself in his state-of-the-art home, while his son's room was about a quarter of the size and tucked away in the darkest part of the house.

Mike saw movement on the balcony. One of the huge panes of glass had been slid open. He shouted up, "Hello? Lee?" and waved. However, the noise of the wind in the trees must have kept his voice from being heard. He waved his arms but realised that Lee wouldn't be able to see him, unless he noticed the glow of his cigarette. There was a corresponding glow coming from the window: Lee must be smoking.

Mike could just make out Lee's figure, and another, smaller one. That had to be Anna. "Hello up there!" Mike shouted and walked forward, out of the cover of the trees, but the wind must have been blowing away from the house, carrying his words towards the Gorge, to float forever unheard down the estuary.

He could make out the smell of weed, and he saw Anna take the spliff, put it to her mouth – and take a deep drag, judging by the amount of time he could see the red-hot glow. Mike stamped his cigarette out and moved to go back to the house. He'd go up and join them; he quite fancied a smoke, then he'd whisk Anna away, if she wasn't too stoned. She wasn't one for smoking, really, but maybe she'd succumb to the munchies. They could go and get a curry or something.

As he neared the back door, something made Mike look back towards the balcony. He stopped in his tracks. They couldn't be... but they were. Anna and Lee, his two best friends - one of whom he was seriously considering that he might be in love with - were kissing each other while the still-burning joint fell, forgotten, to the cold, damp ground below.

Christmas in Bristol

Anna was in two minds about the Christmas break. She'd certainly been working hard enough to warrant a rest, and a bit of time to collect her thoughts after the first term at university would be good, but the thought of returning to her parents' for weeks did not fill her with much enthusiasm.

With both of her brothers abroad, it would be just her, her mum and her dad. She knew her mum had booked leave from work that Christmas "to spend some time with you, darling," but it would be business as usual with her dad; literally, as far as Anna was aware. If previous years were anything to go by, he would have Christmas Day and Boxing Day off; he would drink and eat and give his wife an expensive diamond necklace, some earrings, or something else it was quite possible his secretary had picked out. He'd try to feign some enthusiasm for whatever gift Anna got him – often a book, although she didn't think she'd ever seen him actually read anything she'd given him, despite going to great lengths to choose something she thought he would enjoy. He'd sneak off to his study whenever he got the chance, calling absentmindedly down the stairs that he'd "just be a minute". Life was work for him, Anna knew that, and she was proud that he had a job he believed in. As a high-level barrister, he put everything into his cases and was a huge success, but he had little left for his family. Her mum, also a solicitor – they had met when she was an associate and he was a partner, married at the time to Steve's and Andy's mum - didn't seem to mind. She was also incredibly career-focused. How they had found time to have Anna, she had no idea. She had come to her own conclusion that she was a careless mistake.

Steve and Andy's mum, Alison, worked at an accountancy firm but from what Anna could tell, she had always put her job in second place to her family. Consequently, Anna's brothers had grown up within a warm, loving home, albeit fatherless and far smaller than the one Anna had grown up in. They would spend weekends and occasional other days at their dad's place and were free to come and go as they pleased, which they did, as well as many of their friends.

Anna's bus journeys to school and college would take her past the house on Gloucester Road where her brothers lived with their mum. On cold, dreary mornings, the windows looked aglow with a warm, welcoming light and sometimes Anna could see Alison at the kitchen table, reading her paper and eating breakfast, or sometimes chatting to one or other of her sons. Anna's stomach would rumble and, if she allowed herself to, she would feel a deep sense of longing, to be in that house... that home... where papers were piled on the table, and the paint on the windowsills was peeling, and the people who lived there would chat, laugh and eat together.

At least Mike, Lee and Suzie would also all be in Bristol for Christmas, she thought as she carefully folded some of her clothes into her bag. Already there was a plan in place for New Year's Eve; they would start at Lee's house then meet up with lots of their friends at College Green (where else?) and spend midnight outside the Victoria Rooms amongst the usual crowds who thronged there. Anna was looking forward to it but she wondered how it would be that year. Mike and Suzie would be together, Lee had invited Flic to Bristol for New Year's – although Anna couldn't imagine him having her to stay at his house, unless his dad was away - and she would... well, she could always just go back to her parents' house, she supposed. All said and done, it was just another night. She had bigger fish to fry.

Anna was absolutely determined that her nursing course, these three years at university, would be her chance to turn her life around. She would put her all into everything she did and, when she graduated, as much as she loved Bristol, she would find herself a job, and a place of her own, as far away as possible.

Lee couldn't wait for his friends to be back in Bristol. As much as he enjoyed his trips to Cardiff, if he was honest it was starting to grate on him that he had to make the trips over there so much. After all, he worked. He didn't just sit around attending a few lame lectures, drinking the rest of the time away.

He did his best to fight that attitude. He knew it was wrong; he could see how much Mike was into his course, and the girls were training to do one of the hardest jobs going, but nevertheless, it was how he felt.

What Lee was looking forward to most was things being how they had been before. He could stay over at Mike's, sit and chat to Emma, who he had also missed. Although Emma had told him to come round "any time", it just felt weird when Mike wasn't there. Like he was having an affair with his friend's mum.

Anna, back at her parents', would be just half an hour away, if that, and she'd have plenty of time for him. He knew Mike and Suzie would be spending time together but they were OK, Lee thought; more like friends than anything else, at least when other people were around.

What was troubling Lee was that he'd invited Flic to Bristol. What had he been thinking? Flic was hot, and a good laugh, but even so, it was New Year's Eve and he'd managed to effectively tie himself down for the night. In truth, Flic had really invited herself; his own fault, he supposed, for going on about his amazing house and what a great place Bristol was. Scott at least was going to be away over new year, otherwise it could never have happened. Ah well, Flic would just have to fit in. At least she knew Mike and the others already.

Christmas Day for Lee was going to be at his gran's house, as it had been every year since his mum had gone. That was something to look forward to. Despite his age, his job, and his car, his gran still treated him like a boy and, although he would never want anybody else to see it, he really quite liked it. As soon as he walked through her door, she'd be ushering him in, offering him a mince pie, a drink, giving him the remote control, along with an enormous, all-enveloping hug. Lee would hold his breath against the cloying smell of Lizzie's perfume but when he was at his gran's was when he felt most at ease, and most safe.

She was the one person whose opinion Scott seemed to value - almost to fear, it seemed to Lee - and he wouldn't dare put a step out of line while they were there. Sometimes Lee wished he could move in to Lizzie's, and be looked after. When he was there he felt an almost overwhelming sense of relief. It was a physical feeling, like a long, slow exhalation of breath.

Did Lizzie know what her son was capable of? Lee sometimes wondered, but surely she wouldn't allow him to continue living with his dad if she really did know? Her husband, Scott's dad, had died when Lee was a baby so Lee knew very little about him. Scott wouldn't talk about the man, and Lizzie didn't have much to say about him, either, only that he "worked hard" and "had a lot of problems". Did a bad temper run in the family? Lee hated to think of this as, if it did, it was clearly running straight through the male line and he was next on its list. His gran, though firm and no-nonsense, was not given to rage.

He pushed these thoughts to one side. He had a lot to look forward to.

***

Mike, Anna and Suzie all got the train back together at the end of term. They pooled their coins and bought some miniature bottles from the buffet car, drinking the spirits neat in the over-warm carriage, their faces flushing with the drink and the heat.

At Temple Meads they went their separate ways. Emma was waiting on the platform and she gave Mike an enormous hug before turning to greet the girls. "Suzie, you're looking as lovely as ever. And Anna, I've missed you! You can't be at university; it feels like only yesterday I was helping out with your first Christmas play."

After checking the girls had lifts home lined up, Emma took Mike's bag from him, despite his protestations, and they walked out into the darkening afternoon, their breath glistening in the cold air under the orange of the streetlights. They hurried into the car and Emma turned on the engine, along with the heaters.

"It's so good to have you back, Mikey!" she turned to him while they waited for the condensation on the windows to clear.

"Mike," he half-sternly reminded her.

"Yes, sorry, Mike. I don't know why that still slips out sometimes."

"It's good to be back, Mum."

"Is it? Really?" Emma looked pleased then her expression turned to one of concern. "You do like Cardiff, though? And your course?"

"Yes, of course I do! I love it, Mum, I really love it."

"Good, I can't imagine anything more perfect for you. But if you're ever unhappy…"

"Yes, Mum!" Mike smiled, "I will let you know! Of course I will! Now, how was Spain?"

"Oh, Spain, it was… I think I love it more each time I go

out there. It was still warm, there were even still oranges on the trees! At this time of year, can you imagine?"

"And how was Miguel?"

Emma actually blushed, Mike noticed, before responding, "Oh, fine. He said to say hello."

"I'm sure he did," Mike grinned and Emma gave him a playful push on the arm. "I'm really pleased you've met somebody you like, Mum."

"Oh, Mike, thank you for being a grown-up."

"Mum, you've been on your own long enough. I want you to be with somebody."

Neither mentioned the other reason that Mike was so relieved she had found somebody else – somebody nice – in fact, they had not mentioned the incident with Scott since the night it had happened.

Emma had wanted to, or meant to at least, but Mike had been so clearly set against it; he obviously wanted to forget the whole thing. Cowardly though she felt herself to be, she also wanted to pretend it had never happened so she accepted the situation and was just grateful that he had apparently not mentioned it to Lee.

She smiled, "Well I don't know if I can really be 'with' Miguel, what with him being in Spain, but I'll enjoy it while I can. Now, come on, let's get you home!"

1994

Friendship

On the last day of their first year at sixth form, Anna and Mike went to the pub with some of their fellow students but made their excuses and left early. They were meeting Suzie off the train from Cardiff then getting a cab up to Clifton to meet Lee. They'd made a plan, the four of them, to spend the evening living it up in the poshest part of Bristol. Fake IDs tucked safely in the pockets and wallets of the three younger ones, the city was theirs for the night.

Lee, who was taking a break from illegal substances on the advice of Anna, was having a drink or two at the Lamplighters with Scott and some of their workmates. He'd had his hair cut at the end of May, delighting Scott. Anna had been shocked when she'd seen him.

"Wow, Lee... what!" she'd exclaimed, having nearly walked past him on the street.

He'd laughed, "Like the new look, Anna?"

"I do, I really do," she'd realised she was telling the truth. Lee looked younger with his short hair; more clean-cut, and it suited him. He also looked healthier than he had in months - thanks, she thought, to cutting back on the drugs, and spending more time in the gym.

"Changed your mind about marrying me?" Lee had laughed again and she'd put her arm through his, feeling a lightness in her step. She hadn't known it had been missing until it returned, but Lee seemed like a fun person to be with again.

At the station, Anna had wanted to rush up and hug her friend, but she had to let Mike take precedence, with his status as boyfriend. She was relieved that the two of them greeted each other with a quick hug and a kiss on the lips – no lengthy snog. They never behaved like that around her, to be fair, and as they headed out of Temple Meads towards the queue of taxis, engines running and exhaust fumes puffing into the cold night air, Anna felt a thrill of excitement and comfort to be with two of the people she loved most in the world.

They clambered into the back seat of a black cab, Suzie sitting in the middle, holding one of Mike's hands and one of Anna's.

"Oh my God, it's so good to be back!" Suzie said.

"It's so good to have you back," Anna smiled and squeezed her friend's hand.

The taxi trundled through the heavy Friday night traffic, into town, along Colston Avenue and up Park Street. There was a light, cold rain in the air, which ran gently down the cab's windows. Late night shoppers and early night party-goers mixed on the streets, coat collars pulled up high and umbrellas held aloft. Despite the weather, the city seemed alive with people and high spirits.

On up into Clifton Village, stopping outside the Avon Gorge Hotel, where Lee was waiting for them.

"Suzie, you're back!" he smiled, stepping forward to kiss her on the cheek before greeting Anna and Mike.

"Wow, Lee, look at you! You look all grown-up!" Suzie exclaimed.

He smiled, and his cheek dimpled. Sometimes that dimple took Anna by surprise, and she thought it only appeared when the smile was genuine. It made her think of the younger version of him – before his mum left, when he seemed more at ease in himself and with life. Although it had been years now since Elaine had gone, Lee had never fully shaken off that sad air he had, and there was often a serious, troubled look on his face when he thought nobody was looking. He turned his smile to her, and offered his arm. "This way, m'lady."

They walked into the bar of the White Lion, Mike and Suzie right behind them. Their plan had been to sit on the terrace there but the weather had put paid to that. Instead, they pushed their way through the merry drinkers to a small amount of space near one of the windows. The lights of the Clifton Suspension Bridge shone proudly. Suzie looked at it and sighed.

"I love Bristol," she smiled, "and I love you lot. Come on, who wants a drink?"

"No, no, first round's on me," Lee had grinned, pushing off back through the crowd before anybody had a chance to disagree. He was gone for a while but when he came back he was brandishing a bottle of champagne while a barmaid followed with an ice bucket and glasses.

"Just here, love, thanks," Lee, slipped a five-pound note into her hand and winked.

"Lee, what… that must have cost loads!" said Suzie, wide-eyed.

"It's fine, Dad gave me a bonus today."

"Yeah, but you don't want to spend it all on us!"

"Why not? It's summer! Who better to spend a bit of dosh on than my best mates? I know life's hard for you poor students."

Suzie stared at him in wonder. She was nineteen, Lee just seventeen, but he'd acquired the air and confidence of somebody much older.

"Thank you, Lee," Anna had kissed him on the cheek, then Suzie kissed his other cheek.

"Er, yeah, thanks mate," Mike didn't seem quite as excited, but he accepted a glass of the champagne and they all clinked glasses.

"To friends!"

Suzie had kissed Mike then, just on the cheek as well, but

close to his ear. He'd felt the hairs on the back of his neck stand to attention.

When their champagne was drunk, they headed to the village and found a little Italian restaurant, where they were bustled along by a smiling waiter to a small, cosy table for four. After they had dried off, the four friends' cheeks were soon aglow, and all the moreso once they started on the wine. None of them were wine drinkers really, but they'd made up their minds to act like grown-ups for the night. They hadn't factored in that it would be very difficult to behave like grown-ups after a couple of starter drinks, a bottle of champagne, and two bottles of house red.

As they crunched breadsticks and tried to spike slippery olives on the end of cocktail sticks, they became very giggly, especially when Mike's olive refused to be contained and flew off the plate, hitting a nearby diner in the back. The white-haired, straight-backed lady appeared not to notice but it was hard to see how she could have failed to, with the amount of snorting and guffawing from the table behind her.

It felt good to be out, just the four of them. Mike found himself able to tease his friend in a way he'd not felt he could for some time.

"Any more saucy housewives then, mate? Opening the door and letting their dressing gown fall open?"

"'Appens every day, Mike, you'd better believe it."

"I do, just a shame it's wrinkly old women with saggy…"

"Mike!" Suzie cut in, feigning shock.

"Sorry, Suze," Mike grinned at Lee, who felt a warmth flood into him at a joke that felt like it was just his and Mike's.

"You didn't tell me about this, Lee," Anna said. "Has this been going on while you've been proposing to me?"

"Oh yeah?" Mike's attention was quickly taken. "Proposing?"

"I keep telling Anna she'll marry me one day, but she's

'avin' none of it. She'll soon change her tune, when the old man's retired and I'm runnin' the business. It'll be champagne every night then, love."

"OK, well give me a call when that's happening."

After dinner, Suzie wasn't feeling very well. "I did have a bit of this on the train," she said, extracting a bottle of vodka mixed with lime cordial from her bag.

"Bloody hell, Suze, that's not the grown-up way!" Mike laughed, taking it from her, having a swig, then passing it on to the others. Anna shook her head but Lee accepted it. "Better get you home," Mike continued. "Sorry, guys, but we'll see you again on Sunday, won't we?"

"Yeah, of course," Anna said. "Come on, Lee, you can walk me to my bus stop."

As Mike and Suzie headed one way, Mike gallantly shouldering Suzie's holdall, and Lee and Anna the other, Lee realised he was still holding Suze's bottle of vodka. "Ah well," he said, taking another slug of it.

Anna just smiled at him. "Don't overdo it, though, Lee."

"I won't," a slight crease crossed his brow momentarily but he soon smiled at her. "Listen, why don't you come back to mine? Just for an hour or two. Dad's out and it's only quarter to ten! I'll get you a taxi home. Got my bonus, 'aven't I?"

He pulled a thick wad of notes from his pocket and Anna's eyes widened. "Wow. That's some bonus!"

"Yep," Lee hiccupped, "Think Dad's trying to make up for being a prick."

Anna didn't respond to that, though she thought he was probably right. "Go on, then, let's go back to yours for a bit."

"Brilliant!"

They took a taxi back through Clifton Village, up past the zoo and over the Downs.

"Keep the change, mate," Lee slurred as he handed the

driver a twenty-pound note.

"Er, you sure… thanks," the driver quickly changed his mind about giving Lee the opportunity to change his.

The big house was dark as Lee and Anna went inside, their footsteps echoing on the polished tiles. The bright lights of the kitchen made them blink. Anna sat at the breakfast bar while Lee headed to the fridge and pulled out a bottle of beer.

"Drink?" he asked Anna but she knew she'd had enough.

"Got any Coke?" she asked.

"You know I'm not touching that stuff now," Lee laughed. "Wouldn't mind a bit, though."

"The drink, Lee, the drink," she smiled, wondering how she could persuade him to go for a soft drink, too. The warning signs were beginning to display themselves. He was on the tipping point.

They took their drinks up to his room, where he put The Wonder Stuff on loud then pulled a tin out of a drawer.

"Skin up?" he asked, throwing it to Anna.

"No thanks, Lee. I thought you were off this stuff?"

"Not smoking," he laughed. "Everything else, yes, but this is just to chill out."

He took the tin back and sat at his desk, scattering tobacco everywhere.

"Where's your dad?" she asked.

"Some new bird's," Lee said. "Been seein' 'er a few weeks. Don't think I'll see 'im till Monday."

"Does he know you smoke?"

"Fuck, no! Not draw. Caught me once, and… well, let's just say 'e wasn't 'appy."

Lee looked intently at his work, and Anna watched him, wondering why he was doing this when he was so scared of his dad. His stubborn streak, she supposed; plus, Scott was away – so it was disrespecting him behind his back, with no chance of being caught. Lee sat back, satisfied with his efforts, then went to the window to smoke. "Turn the lights off will you, Anna?"

She did so, and went to stand with him at the window. Outside, the rain had stopped but an unseasonal wind was building up, shaking the branches of the tall trees which shielded Lee's house from the rest of the world.

He put a friendly arm around her shoulder and she rested her head against him. She could hear his heart beating fast, and felt awash with affection for him. Here he was in this huge house. His mum had left him and his dad didn't seem to care, no matter how much money he dished out. It was a lonely life. At least her parents were around – just about, anyway.

Suddenly Lee stiffened. "Shit."

Anna heard the strong, crunching steps on the gravel and could make out a tall, dark shape heading up the drive.

"It's Dad," Lee was panicking suddenly, hastily trying to stub out the spliff.

The figure seemed to stop briefly, and look up.

Then the front door slammed.

"Lee, you little prick, are you smoking weed again?"

Lee put his light on, gestured to Anna to be quiet.

"No, Dad, I…"

"Don't you lie to me, I just saw you up there in the window. For fuck's sake, I can smell it."

"No, Dad, it was just a fag, I…" Lee had left his room and was walking across the landing.

Anna stayed still, feeling like she didn't even want to breathe.

"Don't you fucking lie to me, I can smell it. You little junky shit." Scott's feet were heavy on the stairs. Before Anna knew what she was doing, she was across the room and out of the door. Lee's white face had turned towards her. She saw terror written across it and the words were out of her mouth before she'd had time to think them through. "It was me, Mr

Lewis. It wasn't Lee. It's me smoking pot."

Scott stopped, unsteady on the stairs and clearly unsure of his next move.

"Anna..." Lee began.

"Don't worry, Lee, I can't let you get into trouble for something I've done. I'm really sorry, Mr Lewis, it's the last day of term, I'm a bit drunk. I shouldn't be smoking in your house."

"No, you shouldn't," Scott grunted then he turned and headed back down the stairs.

Anna walked to Lee, touched him on the shoulder, and led him back into his room. She could feel him shaking and, when the door was shut, he switched the lights back off. She put her arms around him and he collapsed into her, his shoulders heaving with huge, relieved sobs.

1993

Bristol, September 1993

University, college and work

A couple of weeks after Mike and Anna had started their A-Levels, it was time for Suzie to leave Bristol and head off to university.

"She's goin' to leave you, mate!" Lee had tried to wind Mike up when they were walking down Park Street to meet Suzie, Anna and a few of their other friends on College Green. Suzie had specifically requested that they meet there as so many of their good times had been there. It also removed the problem of her being legally able to drink while three of her best friends, including her boyfriend, could be chucked out of any pub they went to.

"Just get 'em a lemonade and some crisps," Josh, about to head off to Cambridge University to read English, had joked when they were talking about their send-off.

"I can't believe you're going to university to learn to read English, mate," Lee had come back quickly. "We all learned at primary school."

"Oh yeah, good one," Josh sneered, preening his long dreadlocks and wondering how he could convince his mum to let him keep them. She'd told him they were fine for his gap year but he'd have to get rid of them before he left for Cambridge.

Mike had grinned. Things had been cooler between him and Lee since the night Lee had hit him, but they'd gradually found themselves coming back together. Their bond was old,

173

and strong. Besides which, he knew Lee's dad was a bully and that his friend was having a hard time at home. It was hard to stay angry at Lee, and harder still when he took down pricks like Josh.

"She can if she wants," Mike had said in response to Lee's dig at him. "She's a free person."

"Oi, I was only jokin', mate. Anna says she's really into you, apparently has been for ages."

"Really?" Mike smiled. In honesty, he hadn't really thought of Suzie like that until they'd kissed that night up on the Downs. He certainly hadn't missed the fact that she was one of the most beautiful girls he'd ever met, but he liked to think he was above judging people solely on their looks. She was lovely, though. Caring, funny, clever, and into the same music and books as him. Emma liked her, too, although at his age, Mike knew that wasn't supposed to be a good thing. His mum wasn't like other mums, though.

Emma had also warned him that things might not last when Suzie went away, although in a more sympathetic manner than Lee had used. "Things can change fast when you leave home for the first time, Mike. I'm not saying they will, just that they can."

Both his mum and his friend were to be proved wrong, however. Suzie left for university, bundling into her dad's car with all her clothes, her stereo, extensive record collection, posters, and a box full of photographs from her life in Bristol. Mike had been there to wave her off and he'd seen her eyes fill with tears when she'd pulled away from their goodbye kiss.

"Hey, I'm going to come and see you next week!" he said, putting his hand on her cheek.

"I know, it's just... I think things are going to change. I'm scared," she had sniffled.

"You're going to have a great time! Cardiff's supposed to

be a brilliant night out, and think about all the bands you'll be able to see! You'll make loads of new friends... you'll forget all about us."

"I won't," Suzie said, "I really won't."

Just then there was a shout and Anna appeared, puffing up the hill. "Hang on, I wanted to give you something!"

She had in her hand a homemade book about Bristol – full of fliers from gigs they'd been to, maps of Bristol with their favourite haunts highlighted, carefully copied-out lyrics of songs: the Levellers' *Far From Home*, The Cure's *Close to Me* and *Friday I'm in Love*, which they always danced to. At the back was a photo of the four of them at that year's Ashton Court Festival – Lee and Mike on one side, with Anna and Suzie leaning into each other and grinning from ear to ear, the evening sun just setting over the top of the hill, its rays splaying out like shooting stars.

"Oh my God, Anna, I love it. Thank you so much!" Suzie's eyes filled again, and Anna hugged her friend close to her.

"I've been working on it all summer!" she smiled, happy to see her efforts appreciated.

"I love it, I'll look at it every day. I'm going to miss you so much. All of you," Suzie looked over her friend's shoulder. "Say bye to Lee for me, won't you?"

Lee was busy working with Scott, as he had been since the start of the month. He'd somehow managed to get his dad to agree to him having a summer to enjoy with his friends but at the start of the school year, when Mike and Anna had started college, Lee had begun work for his dad's business.

"We will," Mike said, "we'll all come over one weekend too, shall we?"

"Please, please do."

"And you'll be back in October for the week anyway!" Anna said cheerfully, though she too was feeling tearful, at the thought of her first really close female friend leaving. "Don't make too many new friends!"

"Especially not blokes!" said Mike.

"Only if you don't make any new female friends," Suzie said, half-jokingly.

"Don't worry, I'll keep an eye on him," said Anna, looking towards Suzie's dad, who was standing by the driver's door, waving his car keys. She missed the expression on Suzie's face change ever so slightly.

"Come on, Miss," said Suzie's dad, and ushered her into the car. Her mum was nowhere to be seen and Mike couldn't believe she wasn't there to see her only daughter safely away to university.

As the car pulled away, Mike and Anna stood at the end of the drive, waving Suzie off. Suzie looked back one last time to see her boyfriend put his arm around her best friend's shoulder as they turned together to walk away.

Good to his word, the following week Mike made the train journey over to Cardiff, leaving Bristol straight after college.

Suzie came to meet him off the train and threw her arms around him. He was surprised by how happy he was to see her, and just how relieved he felt that she seemed so glad to see him. Perhaps he'd been worrying more than he thought.

"How are you? How's uni? How was Freshers' Week?"

"It was great! Well, a bit mental, really. Lots of drinking, lots of throwing up, lots of snogging – not that I did either of those. I did drink, though."

"What are the people like that you're living with?"

"Oh, they're really nice. The girls on my floor are all lovely, and the blokes too, but they seem so young."

"As young as me?" Mike asked, as she led him towards the bus stop.

"Oh, you're much more grown-up than them. God, I always forget you're sixteen!"

Mike felt pleased. So his potential rivals were immature, something he knew Suzie hated. "Yeah, thanks," he said, "don't remind me!"

"It doesn't matter, Mike. It really doesn't. You're more grown up than bloody Ian, and he's twenty."

"Must be having a mum like mine," Mike said, as Suzie waved at the bus coming towards them.

"I think it is, I really do. Your mum is so cool," Suzie said. "Is she OK?"

"Yeah, she's off to Spain again in a couple of weeks. Seeing Miguel again."

"Is she? Do you mind?"

"What, having the house to myself? Not at all!"

"Is she going over a weekend?"

"Yeah, I think so. Why, what are you thinking?"

"Well, maybe I could have a sneaky trip back to Bristol, keep you company."

"That would be great. I think I'm meant to be doing something with Anna and Lee, as well."

"Of course. It'll be brilliant to see them, too. Nice if we get a bit of time together as well, though."

Mike smiled slowly. "Aren't we going to get that this weekend?"

"Yes, we are, but it's not quite the same. Halls are... well, you'll see."

And see he did. Mike found he felt very young amongst the eighteen- and nineteen-year-olds, although he did his best to stand tall and proud. He had no idea of the feelings of insecurity and homesickness that filled those small, pokey rooms at night time. To him, it looked like university life was just endless fun, from the moment of waking up (usually mid-morning, or so it seemed) to going to bed (usually early morning).

The boys, though, he noted with relief, did not seem nearly as grown-up as the girls. They were also very friendly towards him and made him feel really welcome, to the point that he was playing drinking games till the small hours with them, until Suzie gradually dragged him off to bed.

Through the wall, they could clearly hear the sound of her neighbour's music. "See what I mean?" she whispered. "Not much privacy."

"And not much space either," Mike smiled, nudging her further onto her narrower-than-a-normal-single bed.

She giggled, "We'll just have to cuddle up."

"I think I can cope with that."

Life soon settled into a kind of routine. Mike spent every second weekend with Suzie in Cardiff, unless she was coming back to Bristol for a visit. Anna would sometimes go over with him, for the day, and on the odd occasion, Lee would come too. He and Anna would stay long into the evening, catching the last train back to Bristol. On those nights it was almost possible to believe that nothing had changed between the four friends, but much had.

After their fight, although Lee's and Mike's friendship had quickly resumed, Mike found he sometimes felt wary of Lee and his increasingly unpredictable nature, exacerbated by an increasing intake of alcohol and experimentation with all sorts of substances. The College Green crowd were a mixed lot, in terms of background, ages, and mental health. There were the Joshes, who were having a great time playing at anarchists until the time came for them to move on to university, graduation, and high-paying jobs in the City. Then there were the college dropouts, who were more firmly committed to the alternative lifestyle and to trying to turn their dreams of making it in music, writing, art, etc. into reality. There were also the younger lot, such as Anna, Lee and Mike, who were really just starting out and finding their feet. And then there were the older, more hardened individuals, some of whom were homeless ('crusties', as they were unflatteringly called), and many of whom relied heavily on substance misuse and abuse.

They were people to be wary of, Mike thought, but Lee seemed to court them. He was in awe of their status in the group, and also their ability to supply him with whatever his drug of choice was. Once he'd handed over money for a bag of skunk and never seen the cash again, nor any drugs. Even Lee was not bolshy enough to tackle the scary, mohawk-sporting Rik about this, so the incident was never mentioned again. Another time, Lee bought some tabs of acid which turned out to be rice paper.

He never let it put him off, though. He was hungry for adventure, and, as Anna and Mike had agreed, determined to spend as much time off his head as possible. He was escaping reality and the misery of his home life, which his friends understood deep down, but were too young to know how to deal with.

Mike also worried that Lee resented him for going to college. Lee was working for Scott full-time, and seemed to be enjoying it. He certainly talked about it a lot.

"Got this fit bird we're doing some work for now. Fuck me, she's gorgeous. She's got to be twenty-five, got a rich 'usband 'oo works away. I'm pretty sure she fancies me."

"Oh yeah?" Mike had also found himself having to take quite a few pinches of salt when swallowing Lee's stories these days.

"Yeah, anyway Dad reckons she fancies 'im, but there's no way, 'e's an old git. We've got a bet goin', see who she gets off with."

"Right."

It was totally alien to Mike; although college had been a step on from school, and the teachers treated the students much more as adults, he was more than aware that they were still just teenagers. Not even anywhere near approaching twenty years old. He also found Lee's relationship with his dad strange. The way Lee seemed to hero-worship Scott, despite the fact he was bullied by him. Scott was a nasty bastard at times. Lee had told Mike so himself, when he was pissed. So why was he so keen to emulate him?

More than once, Mike had to intervene when Lee looked like he might get into a fight. Whether it was with one of the College Green lot, or a bloke in the chip shop, if Lee was in the mood then it was very hard to shake him out of it. The warning signs were becoming more apparent. First, he would get off his face. Then he would go through a period of melancholy, at which point Mike and Anna would try and convince him they should head off to Mike's house, or they would take Lee back to his own home. Sometimes Lee would be convinced, but other times he would become angry and defensive.

"I'm fine, fuck's sake, leave me alone," he would slur. "You two fuck off back 'ome to study or whatever, I'm lettin' my hair down, it's the weekend. That's what workers do."

The 'workers' thing was annoying, too. It definitely felt like Lee looked down on Anna and Mike for continuing their studies. As though earning a wage was the only important thing.

When he wasn't working or becoming inebriated, Lee worked out in a gym. Mike had been once or twice with him and was surprised to see how strong his friend had become. Lee, red-faced, would be lifting weights, grunting and determined. It was just another way of letting off steam, really, but it scared Mike. Together, the components of Lee's life did not seem to be pointing in a very positive direction.

Anna worried about Lee, too. She saw him more than Mike did. When Mike was in Cardiff, she would usually be with Lee. On these weekends, Lee seemed a bit calmer, although he would still drink too much.

"You're a good influence on me, Anna," he'd say, and his drinking would turn him more emotional. "I need a woman in my life."

"I'd say you've got plenty of women in your life," Anna

would smile. Lee had become a popular lad at College Green and frequently took advantage of the fact (however, he never did get off with the twenty-five-year-old client - though neither did Scott).

"They don't mean nothin' to me, I'm not interested."

"It didn't look like that last night when you were with Sophia."

"Ah, well, yeah, she's OK, bit of a slag though really, isn't she?"

"Lee! You can't say that! If anyone's a tart round here, it's you. You're with a different girl every week."

Only Anna could get away with talking to Lee like that. He smiled, put his arm round her. "Anna, we'll get married one day."

"Yeah, whatever you say, Lee." She smiled indulgently at her friend. He was much softer than most people knew. As he pulled away, however, his sleeve caught on her cuff and pulled back, revealing an arm criss-crossed with cuts and scratches.

"What's that, Lee?"

"What?" he asked, distracted, looking for his tobacco tin.

"On your arm. What are those marks?"

Lee stiffened. "Nothing. Just from work. That's what happens when you've got a physical job."

Anna didn't say anything else but she knew what she'd seen. Lee was self-harming, she was sure of it, but she knew better than to push it that night.

On the bus home, she desperately wanted to talk to Suzie. She missed her, and knew that Suzie would have an idea of what to do. But Mike was with her. They were probably out somewhere. Or in bed together. Anna tried not to think about it. She'd just have to wait till Sunday afternoon, when Mike would be on his way back to Bristol. She could phone the communal Halls of Residence phone and hope that someone would get Suzie for her, not just leave the phone hanging off the hook like they had done last time.

"I don't think you can do anything, Anna," Suzie said when she'd listened to her friend "Seriously, nothing more than you're doing now. Being there for him and giving him the chance to talk. If he's going to talk to anyone, it'll be you. Mike says they don't really talk much anymore."

It was hard for Anna to listen to Suzie talk about Mike, like she knew him better than she did. Which was possibly true – she knew a different side of Mike, at least. Anna pushed those feelings aside, though. This wasn't about her, it was about Lee.

"He gets so out of it, though, Suze, I'm worried about what he'll do. If he's hurting himself, if he gets really down, he might..."

"I know, I know what you're thinking. Shit. He wouldn't, though. Not Lee. He enjoys life too much. Some of it, anyway. Listen, Anna, now he knows you've seen those marks, maybe he will open up to you. Maybe he wanted you to see them?"

Suzie sometimes seemed so grown up.

"You're going to be a brilliant nurse, Suzie," Anna smiled down the phone line to her friend.

"I'm..? Oh thanks, Anna, I really hope so. You should think about it, you know. It's a great course. You'd be brilliant at it, too."

"I miss you, Suze."

"I miss you, too."

"Sure you don't just think I'm a stupid sixth-form kid?"

"Of course not!" Suzie laughed. "You're amazing. I love you. I just wish I saw you more. It's difficult, with Mike and..."

"I know," Anna cut her off quickly, "let's make sure we spend loads of time together when you're back at Christmas, eh?"

"Yes, definitely," said Suzie, "Listen, I'm going to have to go, there's about four other people waiting to use the phone. Sundays are a busy time."

"Of course. Write to me, then!"

"I will, tonight, I promise."

Something the girls had between them that was theirs and theirs alone was their writing habit. They wrote religiously to each other, at least once a week, and both kept hold of the other's letters. It was something special, Anna thought; no boys involved, just their friendship. Suzie drew stupid pictures in her letters; caricatures of people she'd met, while Anna wrote nonsense verse that she knew would make her friend laugh. She loved those mornings when an envelope would land on her doormat - covered in silly pictures and messages for the postman, so that it was sometimes near-impossible to read Anna's name and address - just as she was leaving the house. She'd read and re-read the letter on her bus journey to college but would tuck it out of sight before she met up with Mike. She didn't want him to see the letters, she wanted a part of Suzie just for herself.

End of the summer

Results days were approaching and a gathering had been planned for the day that the A-Level results were announced. These exams seemed far more important than GCSEs, somehow.

Suzie turned up at Anna's house that morning with red-rimmed eyes.

"Suzie, what's wrong?" Anna ushered her in.

"Ian's dumped me," Suzie sniffed, "Says there's no point us being together 'cos I'm going to uni."

"You're only going to Cardiff, for God's sake!" Anna tutted.

"Yeah, I think he was just saying that for the sake of having a reason. I think he's bored of me. He's always got loads of groupies hanging round him, especially that one I told you about, with the long red hair. She's older than him, got her own flat and everything."

"Then he doesn't deserve you, Suze. He doesn't." Anna found her own eyes had filled with tears. She pulled her friend tightly to her. "Come on, let's have some breakfast. You need to get your results today."

"I know, I don't really feel like I care anymore."

"Yes you do, you must. In fact, you should care more than ever. Don't let him get the better of you."

Anna didn't really know where these words of wisdom were coming from. She suspected she'd heard them on TV or read them somewhere, but they seemed to make sense and she said them with conviction.

"Thank you, Anna. Will you come with me to school?"

"Of course I will," Anna squeezed her friend's hand. "Now go and wash your face, you can borrow my make-up. Come out feeling great, like you deserve to."

By the end of breakfast, Anna had even managed to make Suzie laugh, although she felt like crying herself at the thought of her friend going away. However, as she had already pointed out, Suzie was only going to Cardiff. Just half an hour away by train. Even so, in comparison to the current five minutes' walk, it seemed much too far.

They walked together to the all girls' school that Suzie went to, where the hall was bustling and buzzing with girls hugging each other, crying, exclaiming and jumping up and down with excitement. Teachers were smiling and handing out cups of tea and coffee.

"Suzie!" squealed Fiona, a girl Anna recognised from a few nights out, "I'm in! I'm going to drama school!"

Very suitable, thought Anna.

"That's brilliant, Fi, will we see you tonight?"

"Yes, definitely, we're off to the Cadbury House first, want to come?"

Suzie turned to Anna, who shrugged.

"Sure, we'll see you there."

Suzie was shaking as they approached the table where she would pick up her results. Anna was right by her and could feel her friend's arm trembling. Would she feel like this next week when it was her GCSE results day? Somehow she couldn't imagine it. It felt like nothing particularly depended on her GCSEs, but she knew that Suzie's dream was to be a nurse, preferably working with children. These A-Level results were key to getting Suzie on the course. When she listened to Suzie talk about her hopes of being a nurse, Anna wished that she had such conviction about something. Suzie was adamant that Anna too should become a nurse, but Anna knew her parents would not approve. Not high-flying, nor well-paid, enough. Sometimes when Anna tried to look ahead into her future it seemed wide open, and somehow empty.

A teacher smiled widely as Suzie moved to the front of the queue and handed over the envelope, looking at her expectantly.

Suzie slowly opened it and pulled out the paper, which she looked at and promptly dropped, shaking and crying.

Anna picked it up while the teacher hugged Suzie.

"Well done, Suzie, you really deserve this. You've worked so hard."

Two As and a B! Anna grinned. Take that, Ian. Her friend had only needed three Bs to get her place. Suzie was thanking her teacher, wiping her tears away.

"You're going to have to do your make-up again, you know," Anna smiled. Suzie hugged her.

Anna tagged along for a while as Suzie spoke to teachers and friends, then she made her excuses and left. Phil, the boy she had been seeing for a few months, was getting back from France that morning with his family and she wanted to phone to let him know about the party that night.

"Oh, hi Anna," Phil's mum sounded a bit distant, Anna thought. "No, he's not here at the moment."

"Oh, OK, did you have a good holiday?"

"It was lovely, thank you, smashing."

"That's great. Would you mind asking Phil to phone me when he gets back, please? A few of us are going out tonight and I wondered if he wanted to come."

"Yes, yes, I'll do that. Bye, Anna."

"Bye," Anna said lamely to the sound of the other phone already being put down.

She sat in the lounge, feeling the sun burning down on her through the window and watching the delicate specks of dust twirl in the shaft of light.

Suzie was leaving. And next week Anna would find out her exam results and whether she was going to sixth form. Really, she knew she would be. She had worked fairly hard, and had found the exams OK. She and Mike were hoping to go to the same college and had one subject, Sociology, in common, but after that he was doing arts subjects whereas she was planning on studying sciences.

The clock ticked away and Anna wondered why Phil hadn't phoned back. Her instinct was to phone again, in case his mum hadn't passed on the message, but she fought it. She had no desire to appear desperate. Instead she picked up the phone and rang Mike.

"Hi Emma," she said when Mike's mum answered.

"Oh hi, Anna! How are you? Any news on Suzie's A-Levels?"

How was it that Mike's mum was always so interested not only in her son but in his friends? It felt to Anna like her parents were barely aware of their own daughter's existence at times.

"I went with her, she did brilliantly! Two As and a B."

"That's amazing! Tell her well done from me. Now, if you're looking for Mike, I'm afraid he's over at the third musketeer's!"

"Ah, OK, I'll phone there, then."

"OK, have a great time tonight."

"Thanks, Emma, see you soon."

Instead of phoning Lee, Anna decided to have a bath. That way she could keep away from the phone and hopefully Phil would ring and have to face the answerphone. Then *he* could wonder where *she* was.

She started the taps going, watching the steam rise and

pouring a good glug of her mum's bath oils into the water. The oils formed a thick slick on top of the water and Anna stripped her clothes off, slipping in through the steam as the taps continued to run. She let out a long, involuntary sigh as the hot waters momentarily closed over her body, at once shocking and soothing her. She closed her eyes and thought of the night ahead.

As midday passed, the sun seemed to burn increasingly intently. Anna's hair had already dried in the stifling heat by the time she'd passed St Bonaventure's church. She'd decided to walk to Lee's, but was regretting her decision not to wear any sun cream as it felt like her shoulders were burning already.

Lee answered the door wearing shorts and no top. He had a baseball cap on backwards and was carrying a can of Strongbow. "Come in, Miss Harper," he bowed lavishly and Anna laughed, walking into the cool hallway where the heat seemed to vanish instantly.

She took off her sandals, the cold of the tiles a relief for her tired, hot feet.

When she'd got out of the bath and wrapped herself in a towel, the first thing she'd done was check the phone in her parents' bedroom, treading wet footprints across their dark wooden floorboards. To her surprise – she hadn't heard the phone go - there was a message. Her heart had leapt at the sound of Phil's voice. "Hi, er, Anna, sorry I missed you before. Give us a call back, yeah?"

It was hardly a romantic overture, but it was exciting to hear him nevertheless. Only when she'd called him back, according to his mum he was out again.

"Oh, OK," Anna tried to disguise her deep disappointment, "I'll see him later, probably."

"OK." The woman could hardly have sounded less enthusiastic if she'd tried.

So – Lee and Mike it was.

Up in Lee's room, Mike was lounging on the small settee, guitar – as ever – in hand. He looked up and smiled at Anna as she walked in, then continued playing. It was something that sounded familiar to her. Anna took a seat on a beanbag and watched Mike. Every now and then he'd look up at her, and she couldn't work out if he was staring into her eyes or concentrating so hard on his music that he was looking right past her. It made her feel weird. She smiled at him and, after an instant, he smiled back, but he missed a beat.

"Ah, fuck it," he said, laying the instrument carefully down. "It's too hot!" He walked to the beanbag and flopped down next to Anna. "You OK?"

"Yeah, just – hot. Tired."

"Here, have one of these," he passed her a Strongbow.

"Thanks," she held the chilled can in her hands, enjoying the feel of it against her skin, then clicked it open and took a glug. Cider was OK when it was properly cold like this. Warm cider, however, was quite a different matter.

"You two coming for a smoke?" Lee asked.

Mike looked at Anna and she shook her head.

"Suit yourselves," he stuck the joint behind his ear and walked out of the room, whistling. Scott would put up with, if not actively encourage, his son drinking, and smoking fags, but anything illegal was strictly out of bounds. Funny what ethics people set for themselves, Anna thought.

Mike was humming to himself. She looked at him and could see a smile playing around the corners of his mouth.

"You're in a good mood!" Anna said.

"Yeah, must be because you're here," he smiled at her.

"I thought so. You coming to the Cadbury later? I said I'd meet Suzie there."

"What, you've walked all the way up here only to turn round and pretty much walk home again?"

"Yeah. Must be because you're here."

What was going on? Were they... flirting? Anna felt herself flushing at the thought.

"Thought so," he nudged her. They leaned against each other, listening to The Cure playing quietly on Lee's hi-fi, occasionally catching the soft scent of their friend's joint as he smoked below his window.

In the late afternoon, Mike cooked pasta for the three of them in Scott's kitchen. "Got to line our stomachs before tonight. It might be a bit late for you, though, Lee!"

"Fuck off!" Lee said amiably – at least Anna hoped it was amiably. He was far more drunk than she had seen him for some time. It set off a series of warning bells but she would do what she always did – be there for him. And at least Mike would be, too.

"This is lush," she said, hungrily pushing forkfuls of pasta into her mouth.

"For a small girl, you've got a massive appetite!" Lee laughed. "Where does it all go?"

"She burns it off, don't you, Anna?" Mike smiled at her.

"She burns it off, don't you, Anna?" Lee mimicked and Mike looked annoyed.

Anna looked from one to the other. "Idiots!" she said and laughed, diffusing the tension which seemed to have popped up from nowhere. "I'll be a total lardarse by the time I'm thirty, anyway."

"I don't think so," said Lee.

"Yep, can't see that, somehow. Anyway, Mum said Suzie got the grades she needs for her course?" Mike asked.

"Yeah, she's done really well. Here, let's have a toast to her." Anna lifted her Coke can, clacking it against Mike's Strongbow and Lee's Newcastle Brown. Anna had made a mental note that Lee was mixing his drinks. "We'd better get going soon, I said I'd meet her at six."

"I don't know if I can be arsed to go to the Cadbury," said

Lee, "why don't we just go over the Downs, wait for Suze there? Unless you can't wait that long to see her, Mike?"

"What? Don't be a dick. I can wait. But Anna, you want us to come with you, don't you?"

Anna's ears had pricked up at Lee's words. Was Mike interested in Suzie, then? That was news to her. She realised she hadn't mentioned that Ian had dumped their friend and for some reason she couldn't fully understand, Anna decided she still wouldn't. "No, it's fine, I'll get the bus down there, and see you lot up at the Downs."

"We'd better get moving," Lee said, "Dad'll be back soon." He quickly whipped away their empty plates while Mike busied himself gathering up the empty bottles and cans, putting them all in a bin bag.

"I'm going to get going, if you don't mind," said Anna.

"Sure," Mike looked up and smiled, pushing some hair away from his eyes. "Have fun."

"You too."

The Cadbury House was a hive of sixth-former activity and chatter. Anna walked right into the middle of it all, seeing faces she vaguely recognised but not stopping until she saw Suzie, who was standing by the door to the beer garden. She looked slightly on edge.

"Hello, old bird!" Anna said, swooping in and kissing Suzie on the cheek. "Had a good day?"

"Hi Anna!" Suzie seemed falsely cheerful. "Oh yeah, not bad, thanks. Had enough of this place now, though, shall we head off to the Downs?"

"I've only just got here!" Anna laughed. "And I've pretty much come from the Downs, I've been up at Lee's. Can't we stay for a quick drink here? I kind of just fancy a lemonade, I'm thirsty more than anything."

"Oh, er, OK... I guess..." Suzie didn't look too enamoured with the idea.

"Could you get it for me? I'll give you the money. I know it's only lemonade but even so, I probably shouldn't really be here. I feel very… sixteen, somehow."

"Half the people in here shouldn't be!" Suzie snorted. "Course I will, though. Come on."

"Do you mind if I wait out in the beer garden? It's boiling in here and I've just run from the bus to get here." Anna pressed a pound coin into her friend's hand then wafted her loose, thin cotton top about below her red face, to prove her point.

"No, don't do that…"

It was too late. Anna was already on her way through the door to the beer garden and it didn't take long to see why Suzie had been so keen to move on. Straight ahead, sitting on one of the beer garden tables, was Fiona – the girl she'd seen earlier at Suzie's school, legs around Phil, who was too busy nuzzling Fiona's neck to notice his girlfriend.

Fiona noticed, however, and her eyes locked on to Anna's, accompanying a smug, triumphant smile.

"Ah," Suzie arrived just behind Anna, practically bumping into her. "You've seen, then?"

"Yes," said Anna angrily. "I've seen."

At the sound of her voice, Phil turned round, open-mouthed. Anna considered throwing her lemonade over him but she was thirsty. Instead, she stood there, taking in the sight of Phil with Fiona. Saying absolutely nothing. She raised the glass to her lips and downed her lemonade then turned to Suzie. "Come on, let's go. We've got better things to do." She stifled a burp which was bursting out of her, walked out on to Richmond Road and promptly burst into tears.

"Both of us dumped within twenty-four hours," Suzie sighed. "Amazing."

She rubbed Anna's back as they tramped across the grass of the Downs – sparse and dry from the summer heat, exposing patches of cracked earth beneath the girls' sandals.

"Shit!" said Anna.

"Yep."

They could hear the fire crackling almost before they caught the first whiff of it on the slight breeze. From a small copse a steady, wispy stream of smoke was rising, and the girls slipped between the trees to see a small group of their friends gathered around. Mike sat with Tash and Vicky, while Lee was busy prodding the fire, laughing with Matt. It seemed that most of them gathered there were Anna's age; Suzie's lot, now old enough to drink in real pubs, considered this kind of gathering beneath them – until they ran out of money, at least.

Mike looked up and smiled while Lee jumped to his feet, ran over, and hugged them both. "Group hug!" he laughed, breathing alcohol fumes into their faces.

"Stop slobbering on me," laughed Suzie, "and stay away from the fire, your breath'll catch alight!"

"I'm just glad you're talking to me," Lee said, putting his arm around Suzie's shoulder. "Miss Brainbox. You're going to make me a lovely wife one day."

"Dream on, mate!"

Anna walked over to Mike and sat down. The ground was hard so she took the jumper she'd tied around her waist and folded it up into a cushion, adjusting it until she felt more comfy. "How's he been?" she asked quietly, looking at Lee.

Mike followed her gaze. "Oh, he's OK, I guess. Started on the spirits now, though."

"Shit. That's not good."

"No."

"Has he said anything about his dad to you?"

"No. Why?"

"I don't know. Just a feeling. He hasn't mentioned him to me for ages, the only time I've heard him say his name was when he said we'd better get out of there earlier. I worry that the less he says, the worse it is at home."

"Well he's never really told me anything, you know that. You're the one he speaks to."

"Shh," said Anna, seeing Lee coming their way.

"What you two whisperin' about?"

"Nothing!" Anna said ever-so-slightly too brightly. Lee looked from her to Mike.

"Suze just told me about Phil," he said. "And Ian. What a pair of pricks."

"What's this?" asked Mike.

Anna, who had just been thinking how nice it was to be amongst friends, and far away from Phil and Fiona, was jolted back into reality.

"Ian broke up with Suze last night," she said, twisting a piece of grass around her finger.

"And Phil?"

"Cheating on me."

"No!"

"Yep. Just saw him at the Cadbury, with one of the girls from Suzie's school."

"I'm sorry." Mike put his arm around Anna's shoulder. "Bloke's an idiot."

"I knew you never liked him."

"No, it's not that," Mike laughed. "Well, maybe."

"Or maybe he was jealous," Lee put in. "Wants you for himself, Anna."

"Don't be stupid, Lee," Mike looked annoyed.

"Yeah, don't be daft, Lee. You know you and Mike are like my brothers."

"Exactly."

The conversation was halted at this opportune moment by the arrival of three teenage boys who Mike didn't recognise. They looked slightly older than the group already around the fire and, judging by their rapidly-chewing jaws and wide eyes, were under the influence of something a little stronger than alcohol.

"Told you it was a party," one of them said. He had a neat ginger ponytail and matching beard and was wearing baggy linen trousers and a Mudhoney t-shirt.

"They're just kids," his mate – also sporting a ponytail, but paired with a hooded top and baggy jeans – laughed.

"Fuck that," said Lee, and stood up. "Alright, gents?"

"Gents! I like it," the ginger one scoffed, and his friends laughed.

"Some fit birds 'ere, though," the tallest of the three spoke up, looking at Suzie. "Alright, darlin'?"

"Yep," Suzie looked him in the eye, holding his gaze and not smiling. She did not suffer fools gladly, thought Anna, wishing fervently that she could be as strong as her friend.

"Mind if we sit down?" the guy in the hoodie asked, and promptly did so without waiting for an answer. He reached into the pouch of his jumper and fished out a tin. Taking out papers, tobacco, and a bag of skunk, he began to construct a huge joint. "Enough for everyone, yeah?" he grinned. "Just to be friendly."

"Fuck me, that's a massive spliff!" Lee, always too easily impressed by people like these, seemed to have a change of heart. He moved to crouch next to the fire, closer to the drugs.

"Move along, mate," the ginger one said, pushing Lee with his foot so that he almost toppled over.

Anna felt Mike straighten up beside her. Lee looked annoyed but didn't say anything. The two other newcomers sat down, either side of their mate, and Lee moved back to Anna and Mike. Anna put her hand on his arm, and gave it a squeeze.

The atmosphere had changed rapidly; nobody seemed at ease to chat now that these three interlopers had arrived. Who were they, and what did they want? More importantly, were they going to go again soon?

"Come and sit down, darlin'," the tall one called to Suzie.

"No, you're alright."

"Stuck-up cow," he muttered.

"What was that, mate?" Lee was back on his feet.

"Nothing."

"Better fuckin' not be."

"Alright, chill, mate," said the guy who was skinning up. "And keep your mouth shut, Dan. There's no need for that." He carried on licking and rolling, until he'd produced a fat, cone-shaped joint. "There. Let's all have a bit of this. Then we'll move on, leave you good people alone. I'm Meader, by the way, on account of the fact I'm from Southmead, that's Dan, and this-" he gestured to his ginger-haired friend, who was chewing his gum rapidly and grinning widely, "is Baker."

He put the spliff in his mouth and lit it up, shielding the flame of his lighter with his hand. "Aaahhhhh," he grinned, exhaling a great cloud of smoke which enveloped his face. He then reached past his friend and handed the joint to Lee who, pacified slightly by the gesture of friendship, smiled and took a great big drag then passed the joint on. It went twice round the whole group and by the end of it, peace seemed to have been restored. Until Suzie, who had mellowed a little and moved to sit down near the fire, let out an exclamation. Dan was leaning over, saying something to her.

"I said no!" she said, and suddenly both Lee and Mike were on their feet.

"What's up, Suzie?"

"Nothing I can't handle."

"That's right, boys. She's a big girl," Dan said, looking at her lasciviously.

"Don't talk to her like that," said Mike.

"Or what, mate?"

"Just... just don't."

"I'm meant to listen to a little geek like you?"

"Come on, Dan," Baker said, "don't get like this."

Mike felt his friend tense beside him and before he was able to stop him, Lee was lunging for Dan, his eyes intensely dark and his hands grabbing for his neck.

"Fucking hell," Dan was on his feet, and quickly secured Lee in a headlock. "What do you think you're playing at, you little shit?" Lee's face was red with fury but he couldn't free himself, no matter how hard he pushed. He kicked Dan on the shin. "Ow! You little fucker! I should get you for that, but I don't beat up kids."

"Come on, Dan," it was Meader this time. "Let him go."

"Yeah, let him go," Mike said. "You lot must have somewhere better to be. And Lee didn't mean any harm, did you?"

Lee glared at Mike.

"Oh, fuck it," said Dan. He rubbed Lee's head, hard, and let him go then slapped his cheeks and Anna winced. "Don't try anything like that again. Come on, boys, let's go."

All was quiet around the fire as the three disappeared, Meader casting an apologetic look back over his shoulder. "Enjoy the rest of the night."

"Are you OK, Lee?" Anna asked but Lee didn't answer, he was too busy lunging for Mike.

Thwack. A hard right hook struck Mike's left cheek, stunning him for a moment.

"Oi!"

"Lee didn't mean any harm."

"Come on, mate, I was just trying to get him to leave you alone. He was massive. He could have really done some damage." Mike was rubbing his cheek.

"I don't need your 'elp. And I could've 'ad 'im."

"Oh yeah!" Mike laughed and Lee's face grew darker.

"Just watch it, Mike."

"Oh shut up, Lee."

Anna stood between her two friends. She looked at Mike, then turned to Lee. "Lee, let's go for a walk, OK? Have a chat? You don't want to do this."

Lee's blue eyes were glassy, not focusing on Anna, but

then they connected with hers and it was like he'd returned to himself. "OK," he muttered, like a small boy. He let her take his arm and he followed her, trying not to stumble.

"Are you OK, Suzie?" Mike asked.

"I'm fine," she said. "Sorry, I feel like that was my fault."

"It wasn't." Mike sat down next to her and put his hand against his sore face.

"Are you OK?" she asked him, and moved closer so she could squeeze his arm. He just nodded. He looked sad, Suzie thought, and leaned against him. It had been an eventful day.

Matt, who had disappeared after Lee and Anna, emerged from the trees and threw some more dry sticks onto the fire. They watched the flames consume the wood, tossing handfuls of sparks into the air.

As dusk set hard, Lee and Anna walked across the flat expanse of grass towards the dark, gaping mouth of the Avon Gorge. When they reached the wire fence, they could see the bridge all lit up, bulbs strung along its support ropes like giant fairy lights.

Behind them, to their right, somewhere beyond those dark trees, was Lee's home with Scott. In the other direction were their friends, gathered around the fire. Enjoying themselves again, no doubt, now those other blokes had gone. And now that Lee was out of the way, Anna thought.

"What's going on, Lee?" She was annoyed at her friend, for hitting Mike, and for putting her in this position once more, of his carer. She would do anything for him, and Mike, but this was getting annoying. He couldn't handle his drink, and he couldn't take responsibility for himself. She wanted to be back by the fire, celebrating Suzie's amazing results with her. Messing about with all their friends, making the most of the end of the summer. In just a few weeks, Suzie would be gone, off to study in Cardiff. Leaving her behind.

"Huh?"

"You just punched Mike!" Anna wished she'd said something to Mike. She wondered what he thought about her going off with Lee when he had just punched him. She hoped it didn't look like she was taking sides.

"He deserved it."

"No, he didn't."

Lee said nothing.

"That other bloke deserved it. He was the one you should have hit – if you had to hit anyone," she hastily added. "Mike was just trying to stick up for you."

"Oh, Mike's so fucking perfect, isn't he?"

"No. Nobody's perfect."

"Yeah, but he's cool, isn't he? Mike. With his guitar, and his writing. Next week you'll be celebrating, you two. Nine GCSEs each and on your way to college."

"Don't!" Anna snapped. "Don't turn this into something it isn't. That bloke just then – Dan – he made you feel like shit. Not Mike. Lee. Lee..."

"But Lee didn't answer. He was leaning against the wall, being sick, the lights of the bridge and the city shining brightly behind him.

By the time Lee had finished being sick, and sobered up a bit, he was full of remorse.

"Oh God, I'm such a loser," he said, and again Anna felt a stab of annoyance. Why did he have to feel so sorry for himself? But she knew he had a lot to put up with, living with Scott.

They all had problems, though; she'd seen her boyfriend kissing somebody else.

Suzie had been dumped, and Anna should be commiserating with her as well as celebrating those wonderful results.

Mike had been punched. By his best mate. Anna had watched his expression change from one of shock to anger, which had then quickly reduced to a look of sadness. Confusion, even. He'd looked at his friend in disbelief, although really, thought Anna, nothing should surprise them when it came to Lee. She should be with Mike now. She realised that she wanted that more than anything.

Yet here she was, dealing with Lee's problems. Again.

"Right, this is what we're going to do. We're going back over there to our friends. You are going to apologise to Mike. I am going to celebrate with Suzie, and I'm going to have a drink. You, however, are not going to have a drink. Maybe a can of Coke. You can't carry on like this, Lee. It's not fair."

She took him by the hand. He looked so forlorn, and part of her wanted to just take him over to his house, get him cleaned up, tucked into bed. But that wasn't her job. And tonight, she deserved to be cheered up, too. She was determined to pull the day around before it was over, to head home on a happy note.

As they neared the copse, the light from the fire could be seen through the branches. There was music again, and laughter. Anna felt an involuntary sigh of relief escape her. Nearly there. She squeezed Lee's hand and smiled at him. As she pulled him through the trees, he knocked against a couple who were kissing against a tree.

"Sorry, mate," said Lee, and the pair pulled apart. "Fuck me!" he laughed and Anna turned around. Her breath escaped her more quickly this time. It was Suzie and Mike.

Study leave

Months of freedom stretched ahead of them. School had broken up for the fifth-years in good time for study leave to begin and the newfound independence was a joy. Although Anna had surprised herself by shedding a silent tear during her last ever Maths lesson, she was really overwhelmed with relief that she was going to move on, to college, where she felt she might have a chance to be herself.

Secondary school had been OK, she thought, but she'd always felt the need to keep her head down. It meant not answering questions that she knew the answer to, not taking part in any extra-curricular activities, and generally keeping a low profile. To do otherwise was an invitation to be given a hard time, by many of the boys in their year and often some of the girls too.

She was neither a swot nor a rebel but since she'd begun to dress differently out of school – tasselled skirts, black DMs or Ruccanor baseball boots, stripy tights, music t-shirts – this change had begun to come across in school too, in subtle but noticeable ways. She wore DM shoes, not being allowed to wear boots to school, and her bag – which she'd bought with her birthday money at Catse in St Nick's Market - bore an embroidered elephant complete with sequins and intricate embroidery. It didn't take long for these things to be noticed and Anna to be singled out. 'Gypsy!', 'Jitter!', 'Hippy!' Accompanied by much laughter and self-satisfaction.

It wasn't that Anna particularly minded. Those that made the most noise were not people she wanted to be friends with anyway, but it wasn't a very nice way to be treated and made coming to school even more of a drag. She had outgrown school, and she knew it.

Still, when it came to the thought that it was the last of her school days, and she was soon to move on into the unknown, she couldn't help but feel a little bit sad.

Mike and Lee, meanwhile, were just delighted to be getting out of there.

For Lee, knowing that it was the end of his studying years was a huge relief. He'd never really taken to any of the subjects at school, though he had a good mind for Maths, if only he applied himself properly – according to his Maths teacher, Mrs Sterling, at least. None of that mattered now, though. His dad was taking him on as an apprentice and Lee knew that his status as boss's son put him in a privileged position. He just had to get through his exams, and that would be it.

Lee had experienced a growth spurt during this last year at school and was now getting close to Mike's height. He was also becoming stocky, like his dad, but did very little to maintain this physique, other than biking around town, and that was just for ease of transport rather than exercise. He kept his hair chin-length, Kurt Cobain-style, usually tied back. Scott regularly derided him for this but Lee was determined that on this front at least, he would be his own man. He didn't want to be a townie like his dad.

Mike, like Anna, had found himself increasingly frustrated with school life. He worked hard, and enjoyed much of the work, but he had developed a deep resentment of having to wear a uniform. He also struggled with getting out of bed on time to get to his lessons, although Emma never allowed this to become a problem.

So, exams aside, when May came round and study leave began, it was with an overwhelming feeling of excitement and relief that the three friends found themselves finally free. Beside the small matter of exams, of course.

Despite the need to 'knuckle down' (in the words of Head of Year, Mrs Greene) and do their best in their exams, there was suddenly a lot of time to play with. This might mean hanging out at Mike's house, or up in the open, unblemished sunshine of the Downs, school books cast aside in favour of musical instruments or, if they were feeling energetic, frisbee or football.

Often they would meet up with other friends from school or some of their new friends from College Green. Suzie was a regular in the evenings but during the day she really was knuckling down. She was approaching her A-Level exams, which seemed a lot more vital than GCSEs, as she was hoping to get on a nursing course at Cardiff university.

Since their first meeting just months earlier, Anna had quickly formed a very close friendship with Suzie, who treated her as though the two-year age gap didn't matter in the slightest. The girls had similar natures, and not dissimilar family backgrounds in some ways. Whereas Anna's family were well-off, however, Suzie's were somewhere at the other end of the financial spectrum. Her dad worked, and her mum drank, and together they had as little time for her as Anna's parents had for their daughter. From the first time Anna and Suzie had shared a smoke on College Green, a bond had been formed. The friendship had grown strong very quickly.

Lee, meanwhile, had a huge crush on Suzie. It was obvious to everyone, including Suzie, but she tended to go for older 'men'. That summer she was seeing twenty-year-old Ian, a member of one of the local bands, Storm Trooper Heroes. Sometimes Suzie's life made Anna feel she was still a little girl.

Lee, who was popular with girls his own age, liked to flaunt his success in front of Suzie, trying to make her jealous, but it had no effect. Nevertheless, he flirted outrageously with her, making Mike almost wince at times.

"So, Suzie, when you goin' to leave that loser for me, then?" Lee would say.

Suzie would just laugh. "When you've got your own car."

"Won't be long now, Dad's goin' to get me one for my seventeenth. So is that a promise, then?"

"I'll be long gone by then, love!"

"You'll be back."

During the long, early summer evenings, when the daylight stretched far into the night, and the setting summer sun cast long shadows across the Downs, large groups of teenagers would gather on the grassy expanse, laughing, shouting, drinking, playing music, singing and dancing. Some would sneak off in pairs into the small copses, their exit usually accompanied by wolf-whistles.

Lee would sometimes take a girl away into the trees. He was not too bothered which; he fancied most of them.

Anna, Mike and Suzie would generally remain with the main group. Sometimes Ian and his friends would be there too and Anna would find herself tongue-tied, unable to think of anything she could say that would be interesting. She would chat quietly to Mike instead. Although she never asked him, she sometimes wondered why he never took a girl off the way Lee did; in fact, why he never really showed interest in any girls. He had become quite intense about his music, and loved to jam with some of the others. *Been Caught Stealing* by Jane's Addiction, *Far from Home* by the Levellers, and sometimes songs that they'd written themselves. Mike loved to write the lyrics more than anything and Anna loved to hear them. They said a lot more about Mike than he said about himself.

Anna's own love life had taken off since their group of friends had expanded. She had been going out with Phil, a boy from Bristol Grammar, for about three months. He was in the lower sixth there and he too was mad about music, though he couldn't play anything, or sing that well. He loved going to gigs, though, and Anna had started going with him. They had tickets lined up for Mega City Four at the Bierkeller, and plans to go to Ashton Court Festival together. Tall, with dyed black hair and a long black trench coat – even in the summer – over his tight black jeans, Phil was highly sought-after by many girls so Anna had been extremely flattered when he'd singled her out one night and sidled up to her. They'd got talking, sitting in the dancing light from the bonfire somebody had started (although fires weren't strictly allowed on the Downs) and by the end of the night they'd been kissing, Phil's hand snaking under her top and stroking the smooth skin of her stomach.

Although Anna had kissed boys before, this seemed different. Phil had stubble, for one thing. She found the feel of it enticing, although the next day her face felt sore. Used. She found herself touching the pinkish skin, conjuring up memories of the night before.

The one thing she wasn't too happy about was that Mike didn't seem to like Phil. He never said so as such, but she could tell. He didn't engage with Phil, if the three of them happened to all be together. Anna also noticed that Mike would smoke more, or drink more, or sometimes just go home early, if Phil was around and there weren't many other people to dilute the atmosphere.

Sometimes it crossed Anna's mind that Mike might be jealous, but she quickly admonished herself. That couldn't be it. He was like a brother to her, as was Lee. No, it was maybe just that Phil was more of a superficial muso, not as deeply besotted by music as Mike was. Mike was incredibly earnest about it all, to the point of music snobbery, which in turns amused and irritated Anna.

1992

Emma and Scott

Emma was surprised to see Scott at the Labour Party campaign meeting. She had decided that this was the year she would get involved. With Mike soon to turn fifteen and becoming more independent with every passing day, she felt she could commit to campaigning without feeling like she was neglecting him.

More often than not, Mike would come home, do his homework after school, have an early tea, then head off on his bike to meet up with Lee and Anna, and any of the other kids who they were keen on at any given time.

It had been a long time since she had seen Scott, or even given him much thought. She saw Lee at least a couple of times a week, of course, and she tried to fill the gap that his mother had left in his life as subtly and tactfully as she could: a warm, home-cooked meal; a few well-aimed questions about his school work or how his day had been. She knew, however, that whatever she could offer would have little effect. Her heart broke when she looked at Mike's friend, and she couldn't help but still see that small four-year-old, skinny little legs sticking out from knee-length grey shorts. Now she had seen him change from a boy who already looked under pressure - the bags under his eyes suggesting sleepless nights and worry - to somebody quite different. He had grown loud, almost brash, at times, but Emma could see past all that. When Mike left the room, when Lee didn't know she was looking at him, he would seem to sink into himself. His eyes would turn down, and it was then that she saw the little boy inside the increasingly strapping fifteen-year-old he had become.

How his mum could have left him, Emma had no idea. Her one-time partner, Mike's dad, had not stayed around long enough to even see his son. He'd missed the chance to hold that tiny bundle of warmth, and Emma was sure that if he had stayed that long, there was no way he could have left. It had been difficult, bringing up Mike alone, but despite the at times achingly hard work, she had never once wished for it to be different. She couldn't bear the thought of not having him in her life. He was what kept her in Bristol; he was settled, he had friends, and she already felt like she had let him down by not keeping his dad around for him. She knew sensibly that it wasn't a failure on her part. She knew exactly what she would tell somebody else in her situation – "It isn't your fault, he's behaved like a wanker!" – but when it came to applying her own advice to herself, she struggled.

She had not really had a relationship since then. There had been the odd flirtation with men she had worked with, a close-call with a married man, but she'd come to her senses before becoming embroiled in that. Now Mike was older, Emma felt that she might be in a better position to think about herself. For the time being, however, she was just enjoying her newfound freedom, feeling able to leave Mike alone at home, knowing he was safe and could look after himself – for a few hours, at least. She would never leave him for too long. The thought of abandoning her son, or of something happening to her – an accident, an illness - and Mike being left alone, made her stomach lurch.

Now here was Scott, one of the last people she had expected to see. He stood out immediately, being a good head taller than most of the other people there. And, though she hadn't seen him for years, Emma immediately recognised that dark, close-cropped head, even from behind. She didn't expect him to recognise her, though.

"Emma! Mike's mum, isn't it?" Scott smiled widely, stopping her in her tracks as she made her way to the coffee machine. He kissed her on the cheek. "It's great to see you again."

Emma had forgotten how tall he was. She felt dwarfed by his size, her face on a level with his toned biceps. She'd forgotten how good looking he was, too. She could see the ease with which he turned on his charms, no doubt instrumental in helping him develop his business. It was a good job she wasn't easily swayed by such superficialities.

"Hi, Scott, how are you?" His hand took hers and she was surprised at its warmth. There were tiny black hairs along the back of it, which half-tickled, half-prickled her own hand. She had to fight the urge not to jump.

"I didn't know you were a Leftie," she decided to make light of the situation. She really had assumed that he was Tory through and through. Self-made man and all that. A fine example of the Conservatives' social mobility, if ever there was one.

"Too bloody right. Can't 'ave these sods in a moment longer. I know I've done alright for meself but I 'aven't forgotten the working man. Still am a working man." He smiled disarmingly.

"Well, that's... brilliant. Have you done this before, then?"

"No, to my shame I 'aven't. Now that Elaine's... gone... and Lee's getting older, I seem to 'ave a bit more time on my 'ands, know what I mean?"

Emma looked at him, surprised at the mention of his wife. And yes, she knew exactly what he meant. It was lovely having some freedom again but she realised that the stage of her life when Mike needed her – *really* needed her - was coming to a close. Did Scott really feel like that, though? Both she and her son had suspicions about Scott's behaviour towards Elaine, Mike convinced that it was Scott who had driven Lee's mum away. Mike said Scott was a bully and Emma knew that when she had seen Lee's parents together, years ago - at primary school plays and functions - Elaine had always been very quiet, while Scott had been confident; gregarious; smooth-talking parents and teachers alike.

Elaine was a thin, beautiful woman, but Emma, despite the many times she had tried to spark up conversation, had found her hard work. At first she had thought her snobbish, then adjusted this opinion to just shy. They had to talk, of course, to arrange times for their sons to play together, but Elaine had always been happy for Lee to come to Emma's unaccompanied, and rarely invited Mike back when the boys were little. On the very rare occasion that Emma had come with Mike to Lee's house (there was no way she was going to leave him unaccompanied when he was so small), Elaine had been... nice. Welcoming, but making very little in the way of conversation. Emma would find herself talking quickly, filling in the gaps with nonsense, she thought, just trying to avoid the awkward silences. Trying to put Elaine at ease. It had been important to her to be friends with Mike's friends' parents but eventually she had accepted it just wasn't going to happen and, to be honest, the amount of work she was having to put in, she was finding it exhausting.

She looked at Scott, unsure that she wanted to be standing with him, given her suspicions. However, the campaign co-ordinator rescued her, switching on his microphone and calling for quiet, and they were off. He did an excellent job of rallying the troops and ensuring that nobody in the room could be in any doubt that this time the Labour Party was going to be successful.

The room was full of an exuberant energy and Emma felt an excitement pick her up and whoosh her along. Life had been steady and sturdy since she'd had Mike. There was work, there was Mike, there were her parents, and there was the very occasional night out with friends. She'd settled into it. She was… content. But it was a long time since she had been really excited about anything. Despite her misgivings, she looked up at Scott and smiled.

Throughout the following weeks, Emma became involved in leaflet-dropping, in manning Labour party stalls in Broadmead and attending hustings. As the election date drew nearer she agreed to try some doorstep campaigning. She had found her confidence grow as she realised that she could talk to people. They could see that she knew what mattered to them, that's what she thought made all the difference. She was not a rich, successful business person, or privileged product of the public school system.

Even when people were staunch Tories, they were usually polite to her. Only very occasionally would she get any form of abuse from householders. It just so happened that on one of these occasions - the worst - Scott was on the other side of the road, talking to a nice old lady who had voted Labour all her life.

Emma had walked into a neat front garden, slightly nervously eyeing the 'Beware of the Dog' sign on the gate. As she rang the doorbell, she heard a lot of barking, and shouting, inside – "Shut up! Fuckin' dogs."

The man who opened the door was wearing a neatly ironed shirt and had a closely-shaven head. He was half bent over, holding the collar of some kind of terrier. Was it a pitbull? Emma wasn't sure, she didn't know that much about dogs, but she did know she didn't want the man to let go of this growling beast.

"Good afternoon, sir," she began, "my name's Emma Sawyer and I'm representing the Labour Party in this area…"

"I can see that," the man sneered at her rosette, "well you're not gettin' my vote."

"I'm sorry to hear that," Emma said as politely as possible, hearing her voice become posher and inwardly kicking herself. She had a feeling that sounding more middle class wasn't going to endear her to this man. "May I ask why not?"

"You lot'd let in all the darkies, place is already over-run by 'em. Pakis in the corner shop. Fuckin' rastas smokin' weed on the streets. You're s'posed to be representin' the British working male…"

"Well, that's not quite true, sir…"

"Labour, in't it? LABOUR. Representin' the working class."

"Well, yes, to some extent that's true, but…"

"Look, love, I don't want some bird comin' round tellin' me what I should be votin' for. I know me own mind, I can see what's 'appened to this city over the last twenty years, somebody needs to sort it out. I don't reckon you lot's up to it, do you?"

"I'd appreciate it if you didn't call me a 'bird'," Emma said, feeling her hackles rising, just as the dog's were settling. It sat down and looked interestedly at this woman who was apparently stupid enough to be challenging its owner.

"My house, my rules, I'll call you a bird if you like. I didn't ask you to knock on me door, did I? I'll call you a fuckin' stupid bitch if I like."

"I'd watch your mouth if I were you, mate!" The voice came from over Emma's shoulder.

"Oh yeah? And 'oo the fuck are you?"

Scott walked up, stood next to Emma. The dog was back on its feet, muscly shoulders pushing forward. The shaven-headed man assumed a similarly aggressive stance. "'Oo the fuck are you?" he asked again.

"I'm a white working class man, that's who, but one who knows how to talk to a lady."

Emma flushed, hating herself for not standing up to this idiot, and kicking herself for feeling flattered by Scott calling her a lady. What had happened to her strong, feminist principles? Pathetic. They had clearly shrivelled up and wriggled off to hide in a corner.

"Go fuck yourself," the man pulled his dog back and Emma and Scott found the shiny red door shut in their faces.

"At least he painted his door the right colour," Emma tried to smile.

"Didn't want it painted black, did 'e, though? Racist prick. Are you alright?"

"Oh yeah, I'm fine," Emma realised she was actually shaking.

"No, you're not, come on. There's always going to be people like 'im." Scott's voice was throaty with anger. This was not what Emma expected from a man who bullied, possibly beat up, his wife. "Let's go and get a drink, shall we? We can come back and carry on where we left off in 'alf an hour."

Emma found Scott's strong arm around her shoulder, persuading her away to the dark, cosy confines of a smoky bar, conveniently tucked around the corner of the street where they'd been canvassing.

"Two large single malts please, mate," Scott called to the barman, at the same time pulling a chair out for Emma at a table by the window. She didn't think it would be polite to tell him she didn't like whisky.

In the end, Emma found herself quite enjoying the drink. The burning liquid calmed her nerves as she traced its progress down her throat, spreading warmth through her chest.

"Don't let 'im get to you, will you?"

"I won't, I promise. I think I was as scared of his dog as I was of him. Maybe more than."

"I don't blame you," Scott chuckled. "Scary-looking bastard."

"I don't think it liked you much."

"No!" he laughed again and Emma noticed those straight teeth once more. "Thought you were an animal lover, though?

Bit of a 'ippy, the boy reckons."

"Oh does he, now?" Emma couldn't help but smile to think of Lee telling his dad this about her.

"Yeah," Scott quickly replied, "'e don't mean it as an insult, though, I think he wishes I was more like you. I've told 'im if he turns veggie I'll kick 'im out!"

"You wouldn't."

"No, I wouldn't. Shouldn't make jokes like that, really, with Elaine…"

"You didn't mean it, I know." Emma thought she could detect a sadness in Scott's eyes and wondered if she and Mike really had misjudged him. "Do you miss her?"

"Elaine? Yeah, I reckon I do. We were only a bit over twenty when we got together. She's been around a long time. I coulda been a better 'usband to 'er."

"Well…" Emma found she didn't really know what to say.

"Listen. Let's not get into all that," Scott said. "We'll drink up and get back to it."

"Sure." Actually, Emma would have liked to have stayed for another drink. Talked some more. Adult male company was a novelty for her; especially good looking company. She shook her head. What was she thinking? Maybe it was time she took her mum's advice and started dating. For now, though, she had a job to do.

Emma found herself waking on election day morning with butterflies in her stomach. She had invested a huge amount in this election – emotions and time. This was the first time she had really felt involved in politics and she was excited to think that she had played a part in what she was sure was going to be a much-needed change in government for the country.

"There's no way those Tory bastards are getting' in for a fourth term," Scott had said in his gruff voice when they'd been arranging what to do on election day. She sincerely hoped not.

When Mike left for school, she went to cast her vote, then stood with Nigel, another local campaigner, outside the polling station. It was a surprisingly warm, dry day for early April. Emma hoped it signified brighter days to come.

Nigel was a very affable and seasoned campaigner, who engaged voters going in and out of the centre, chatting with them and passing the time of day. Emma soon picked up a few tips from him and was smiling and greeting voters, asking who they would be voting for. Could it possibly make a difference at this stage? She wasn't sure, really, but she was a part of this. It was vitally important to her that everything she did that day was about the election.

There was a widely-held belief that Doug Naysmith was going to do it, knock Michael Stern off the perch he had occupied since 1983. Nobody Emma knew was really happy with their government. Even those friends and neighbours of hers who had voted them in previously were getting fed up. Her plan was to stay at the polling station until mid-afternoon, go home and eat, and then it would be off to the pub with a few of the others before heading to the campaign headquarters, to see the results come in. The Bristol votes weren't likely to be announced until 3am so it was going to be a long night. Emma had wanted her mum to come and sit in with Mike but he'd insisted he'd be OK.

"I might go up to Lee's, anyway, his dad'll be out with you lot, won't he?"

"I guess so. OK, that's a good idea," Emma kissed Mike. "Just think, next time you'll be voting, too."

"Yeah, can't wait to put the Tories back in." Mike grinned and Emma gave him a cuff round the ear.

Emma bought half a cider at the bar and walked over to where Scott was sitting with some of the others. He pulled a chair over from another table for her. Emma found she was shaking slightly, with nerves, adrenaline, excitement.

"You OK?" he smiled.

"Yeah, great, just can't wait to see Doug get in!"

"Me neither, reckon this could be it, eh? And all thanks to us!" Scott grinned and raised his glass to hers.

"Cheers," Emma said, then made a point of clinking her glass against everyone else's at the table. She didn't want Scott thinking he was special.

Throughout the night, Emma and Scott remained sitting next to each other and at some point she found his hand on her knee. Her halves had turned into pints and she was more drunk than she had been in years. Possibly since before she'd had Mike. Still, it was a special night.

When last orders were called, the raucous group got up, gathering coats and bags, scraping back chairs and chanting Doug Naysmith's name, to a few cheers from some of the other drinkers. Outside, they agreed to get taxis and meet up once more to see the results come in.

"We'll stop at mine to get a few bottles," Scott offered, taking possession of Emma with an arm around her shoulder. She let him. It felt good.

Back at Scott's, he opened the door as quietly as he could, bearing in mind the eight pints he'd consumed that evening.

"Shhh," he said, "case the boys are asleep."

Emma took off her shoes, fearing that they might make too much noise on the shining black-and-white tiles. She stood upright and suddenly Scott was lifting her off her feet, kissing her. It happened so fast her breath was whipped from her and before she knew it, she was being carried upstairs into Scott's huge bedroom.

There was no time to think, and besides, this was a day for celebration, enjoyment. A momentous day, when things were going to change. She let Scott slip her jacket off her as he continued to kiss her – her mouth, her neck, her shoulders, as he pushed back her loose-necked top. Soon, she was pulling at his clothes to even things up. Then they were together on his bed, and that was that.

Scott nibbled her neck, "That was fuckin' brilliant."

"Er, yeah," Emma was still trying to catch her breath. It had been brilliant, but unexpected, unplanned. Probably stupid. No doubt.

"Better get those bottles, though, go and celebrate Doug's victory with him." Scott pulled her to him, "Not that I wouldn't rather stay 'ere with you."

Emma smiled. "No, that's fine. The others'll be wondering where we are. And I really want to see this, anyway."

"Great." Scott began pulling on his clothes while Emma picked up hers, which had been scattered around the room.

As she was still wriggling into her top, Scott opened his bedroom door. "I'll go and dig out some booze... oh, alright mate?"

Emma stopped sharply and looked up. There was Mike in his t-shirt and boxers, coming out of the bathroom. He looked straight at her and she felt all the blood rush to her face.

Scott looked from one to the other. "Shit."

When Emma had tried to talk to Mike, while Scott made himself scarce downstairs, he'd just answered, "It's fine," his voice flat and unconvincing. "Shouldn't you be out finding out who's won the election, though?"

"Yeah, but Mike, you're more important. I didn't mean you to see that... No, I don't mean that, not like that. I mean, I didn't even mean that to happen, it just..."

"I said it's fine."

"I – oh, shit. I'm drunk."

"Yes, I gathered that."

Emma felt like the teenager all of a sudden. Mike the disapproving parent. Then she thought of something else. "Is Lee still awake?"

"No, Mum," Mike sounded annoyed, "and I won't say anything, if that's what you're worried about. You and Scott can have the pleasure of telling him you're going out with each other."

"We're not..." They weren't and they wouldn't be, she was sure of that. But how bad was it to be caught having casual sex by your fourteen-year-old son, especially when that sex was with his best friend's dad? Worse still, a dad they suspected of having driven his wife away with bullying and possibly even violence. She had to keep calm, at least give the impression she knew what she was doing. "Listen, I'll talk to you tomorrow properly, OK? I do need to go now."

"Sure." He let her kiss him and stalked off back to Lee's room.

In the taxi, Scott tried to talk her through it, but she felt awful. Suddenly her head was throbbing and she was starting to feel sick.

"Guess that's it for us, then," Scott said cheerfully. "You were fuckin' brilliant, though."

Emma smiled thinly.

The candidates were lined up on stage to hear their fates read out. Exit polls had been hard to read, the Conservatives seeming to have garnered more support than expected, but Emma was sure. It was going to be a Labour win.

"Doug Naysmith, Labour Party, 25,309."

"Yes!" Emma smiled at her friends but realised they were not returning her smiles. They looked nervous.

"John D. Taylor, Liberal Democrats, 8,498."

"Michael Stern, Conservative Party, 25,354."

All around Emma were gasps and cries of disappointment while just beyond were cheers and jeers.

The candidates shook hands with each other and the terrible ending to Emma's day was complete. Suddenly her world felt very small. She sat on a chair at the edge of the room, watching the new day unfold before her and the new world she had hoped for fade away. She closed her eyes and a vision of bright, sunny Spain came unbidden to her.

Growing up, going out

The drinking had begun in earnest early on in their fifth year of secondary school, when attention should have been on GCSEs but of course, being fifteen years old, much of it was elsewhere. Girls, or boys (depending on preference), drinking, music, going out. Starting to stretch those wings of independence, which had been just nubs since they were ten or eleven, fighting hard against parental efforts to clip them.

Lee, Anna and Mike would meet regularly, either in St Andrew's Park or up at the Downs on a Friday night, clubbing together to buy a bottle of cider, maybe a packet of cigarettes. At first they would stick together, just the three of them, huddling in the cold of autumn, then winter, in the shade of the trees. Sometimes Mike would bring his guitar and they'd mess about with lyrics and tunes, but only Mike was really serious about music. They all loved to listen to it but Lee, despite owning a Fender Precision Bass, had never really progressed in terms of skill. It wasn't that he couldn't do it, more that he couldn't be arsed. It required effort, learning to play, and Lee was finding that he wasn't too bothered about putting much effort into, well, anything really, except perhaps for girls and football.

It was usually Mike who had to procure the drink and cigarettes, being a full head taller than Lee, and even more over Anna, whose slight frame and fresh face made her look very much her age – even when she tried to create an older effect with thick black eye-liner and mascara. She just looked endearing to most adults, which was not at all the kind of impression she was hoping to make.

Occasionally, a friend or two from school would join forces with them and there would be two or three bottles of drink going round. Sometimes just cider, but other times there would be neat vodka or martini added to the mix, with disastrous consequences. Amongst their group, which, extended, also included David Manworth, Matt Evanton and twins Louisa and Sarah Smith, there was not one of them who had not had cause to lean on their friends and allow them to hold their hair from their faces – all the boys had long hair by now - or rub their backs, while they were being sick.

For Anna, once had been enough. Emma had given her a lift back home and helped her up the steps to her house where she was met with an "Oh Anna," from her mum, who stood under the stained glass of their doorway, over-sized glass of red wine in hand.

The following day had been awful; Anna hadn't been able to leave her bed and had never experienced a headache like it. She vowed never to mix her drinks again and limited herself to a can of cider, maybe one cigarette, knowing that it would still be enough to make her feel giddy and that she would be able to enjoy the rest of the weekend.

The boys were not so sensible. Mike, who had a very strong constitution, had only had cause to be sick once as well, but in contrast to Anna, Emma had picked him up, taken him home, and given him a bit of a talking to before he'd gone to bed. He'd woken the next day with a slight headache and a huge appetite. Downstairs, Emma made him a fried breakfast – eggs, veggie sausages, toast, beans, mushrooms, and he was soon right as rain, and happy to carry on experimenting with drinking whenever the occasion arose. He paid lip service to his mum's admonishments to 'be sensible' and 'keep a strong head on your shoulders'. She also warned him, embarrassingly, about doing the right thing by girls. He didn't want to end up a dad at sixteen, she said, and she didn't think many of the girls – or their families – would appreciate a baby at this stage of life, either.

Lee was a very different matter. It was as if the phrase 'drinking to excess' had been invented for him. He always had money to spend on drink and cigarettes, and this he gladly did. "Go on, Mike, go and get us a bottle of Thunderbird, I'll go twos with you."

Mike didn't mind doing this for his friend, but what he was starting to mind was the number of times that Lee was getting properly drunk, to the point of being sick or, worse, getting aggressive. Rarely with Mike, unless he was being defensive when Mike was trying to calm him down, but often with some of their other friends or even passers-by. It was embarrassing and it was worrying. And often it ended in tears - usually Lee's.

As Lee's house was only just at the edge of the Downs, it was easy enough to get him home and often the place was empty so it was a case of getting him out of his vomit-stained clothes, into his joggers and a hoodie, and putting him into bed. Sometimes Mike would phone Emma and tell her he was staying at his friend's. He'd heard tales of people choking on their sick during their sleep, and he couldn't get the thought of Jimi Hendrix doing just that out of his head. Lee was annoying when he was drunk but he was still his friend and he needed looking after.

On these occasions, Anna would get a lift home with the twins' parents, and Mike would give her a hug before she left. She'd kiss him on the cheek then go to Lee and do the same to him.

"I love you, Anna," Lee had murmured on more than one occasion.

She'd look up at Mike and smile. "Love you too, Lee. You too, Mike."

Mike would wait to make sure the girls had been safely collected – usually having left Lee slumped against a tree or the water tower, before picking his friend up and supporting him across the darkness of the Downs. The pair would stumble together, Lee talking gibberish (or so it seemed to Mike) until they got to the house. Mike would have to pat Lee down till he found the key, then let them both in. Despite the size of the house and its being full to the brim of expensive home comforts, it somehow never felt like a home to Mike. Whatever the season, it felt cold, and the slightest sound seemed to echo around the spacious hallway. Mike always wished he was going back to his own house, waking up in his small bedroom, the walls of which were now covered in posters pulled out from the NME. Mega City Four, Ned's Atomic Dustbin, Mudhoney. Anna's big brothers had more than proved their worth in introducing their little sister and her friends to band after band; dispensing knowledge which Mike, Anna and Lee all eagerly pounced upon.

In Lee's room there were proper posters, bought from Rival Records, of bands like The Cure, tastefully framed as per his dad's wishes. Scott would not tolerate anything being stuck to the wall with blu-tak. Any photos in the house were few and far between, whereas at Mike's place they were spilling off shelves, stuck to noticeboards, the fridge, the backs of doors. People, places, pets. It would be Scott's worst nightmare. Lee cringed at the thought of Scott and Emma meeting. They'd hate each other, for sure.

At the end of March, when the clocks changed and the longer nights of spring and summer were seductively close; GCSEs less seductively so, Lee suggested that they venture further afield.

"Matt Evanton's started hanging out at College Green," he said, "Reckons it's great. People playing music, drinking, smoking, fit girls…" he looked at Anna and laughed.

"Probably blokes, too. What do you reckon?"

Mike, who was lolling against a tree, smoking a roll-up and trying to squeeze into the last bit of sunshine that was falling their way before it disappeared for the day, looked interested. "Yeah, Matt mentioned that to me, too. It can't hurt to give it a go. What do you think, Anna?"

"Erm, OK. I think my brothers used to go there, too. If it's really dodgy can we just go back to this, though? I like it up here."

Mike smiled, "Course we can. If it's shit, we're out of there. OK, Lee?"

"Sure," Lee was standing up, jiggling his keys in his pocket. "What are we waiting for?"

"What... go now?" asked Anna.

"Why not? We can get a bus down and get another back here if your mum's coming to collect, Mike."

The three of them raced each other across the grass to the top of Blackboy Hill where, as luck would have it, a number 1 bus was just drawing up at a stop. They piled on, Lee paying for all their fares. Mike had the cider bottle hidden inside his coat, and he walked confidently to the back of the bus with Anna close behind.

The three sat, chatting nervously as the bus travelled down the hill, past the BBC building and the Victoria Rooms, on past Habitat and then down Park Street with its trendy shops and nice-looking restaurants. Lee pressed the bell and the bus stopped almost directly opposite College Green.

It was already nearly dark as they shuffled off the bus and looked across the street. They could hear laughter from the archway near the building, and the sound of an acoustic guitar being played. Suddenly they were unsure of themselves.

"What do we do? Just walk over there?"

"Well, I guess so."

"Can you see Matt anywhere?"

"I can't see anyone, it's dark."

"Maybe we should just go back," Anna suggested nervously.

"No, come on," said Lee, pulling her arm and pressing the button on the pedestrian crossing. "We're here now. Let's just go over there."

Mike felt suddenly very young but he wanted to look after Anna. "Look, let's just go and sit on one of the benches for a bit and have a drink. We'll see what's going on and keep an eye out for Matt."

"OK," Anna didn't sound convinced.

"The bus stops are right there, at the side of the green," he reassured her. "We can just get straight back up to the Downs if we need to."

They walked across the road and Mike noticed Lee had adopted the strut that he seemed to have been cultivating of late. What was more, instead of going to one of the benches, he walked straight in underneath the archway. Mike and Anna stopped some way behind him.

"Alright?" they heard him say.

Nobody answered for a minute then there was an 'Alright' in return.

"Mind if we hang with you lot?" Lee gestured to Mike and Anna in the dusk and they moved forwards.

"Whatever."

"Great. Want a smoke?" Lee offered his nearly full packet of twenty B&H round. It disappeared into the darkness and came back empty. Lee laughed, screwed the packet up and tossed it on the floor. "Give us a rollie, Mike."

Mike fished his tobacco tin out of his pocket. "Here you go." He spotted some space on a stone ledge that wrapped around the bottom of one of the pillars. "Come on, Anna, let's sit down." He made space for her and handed her the cider bottle, whispering, "We'll just stay for a bit."

The two of them sat close together and tried to hold a

normal conversation, trying to bluff over the fact of their self-consciousness. Meanwhile, Lee had taken it upon himself to start talking music with a couple of long-haired blokes in combats and German army parkas, who looked a bit older, maybe seventeen or eighteen. It was hard to tell whether they were taking the piss out of Lee or genuinely engaging in conversation with him.

Mike was wondering how he was going to get Lee away when a voice came from next to him. "Hi, haven't seen you here before."

He looked up to see a tall, pretty girl with a ring through her nose and long, curly hair. She was wearing a black leather jacket and had a bag slung over her shoulder.

"No, we, erm, haven't been here before," he said. "I'm Mike, this is Anna."

"Hi," the girl smiled widely at them both. She took a packet of Marlboro from her pocket. "I'm Suzie. Do you want one of these?"

She offered them to Mike, who took one, and Anna, who didn't.

"Don't smoke?" Suzie asked.

"Not really, not much, I mean, every now and then."

"What about weed?"

"W- no, not really. Well, no, never, not yet anyway," Anna admitted.

Suzie laughed. "Do you want to try some?"

"Erm," Anna gulped. She knew she did want to give it a go sometime, but here seemed a strange place. And she didn't know Suzie. Or anybody else, other than Mike and Lee. It was dark and she could hear Lee's voice from somewhere in the arches, still talking music. Maybe he'd actually hit it off with those two guys.

"That would be brilliant," Mike said before Anna had a chance to answer.

"No problem," Suzie squeezed in next to them and took a

large tin from her bag. She opened it up and set up a large cigarette paper on the rim of the tin. Mike and Anna watched closely as she ripped off a small piece of cardboard and rolled it into a little funnel, placing it carefully at one end of the paper, into which she sprinkled tobacco from a cigarette. Then she got a little brown lump from the tin and proceeded to hold it above the flame of her lighter and crumble some of it onto the tobacco. Within moments, she'd rolled the whole lot up and twisted the other end, tapping it against the tin lid.

"Want to spark up?" she asked Mike.

"Erm, I don't... no, you do it, I've never had any before, either."

"Really? No worries." Suzie lit the twisted paper and it glowed brightly in the dark, a plume of white smoke twirling upwards from it.

She took a deep drag as the red glow reached the tobacco, then she inhaled deeply. Mike looked across at Anna, who smiled and shrugged.

Suzie took another deep drag then passed it to Mike.

"Watch out for blim burns."

"Blim..?"

"Hot rocks. They fall from the spliff. They can burn you, or your clothes - just tiny holes, mind, you're not about to catch on fire." Suzie laughed, exhaling the last of the smoke.

Mike put the joint to his lips and took a drag. He could taste something different to tobacco but could he feel anything different? He tried again.

"Do it more deeply," Suzie said. "Hold it in."

He did, and suddenly he felt light-headed. He passed the joint to Anna, who tentatively put it to her lips.

Sucking deeply, Anna saw the end of the joint glow a strong red. She let the smoke go right to the back of her throat and somehow resisted the urge to cough. She held it, exhaled slowly.

Suzie smiled at her, "It suits you."

Anna felt warm, and fuzzy, she wasn't sure whether it was the smoke or Suzie's words. She went to pass the joint back to its owner.

"No, have another go, there's plenty to go round."

As Anna was taking another deep pull on the joint, Lee appeared.

"What's going on?" he asked, his eyes alighting on the spliff.

"This is Suzie," Mike said, "and this… is a spliff…"

Suddenly he was laughing and Suzie and Anna were joining in. Lee was trying to smile but had the feeling he was missing something.

"Want some, mate?" Suzie asked and his eyes lit up.

"Please," he inhaled deeply, feeling the smoke fill his mouth and his lungs. "God, that's good."

Mike wondered if Lee really did feel something straightaway; he was sure he hadn't. However, he was feeling a bit lightheaded, in a nice way, so perhaps it was taking effect.

"Nice to meet you, Suzie," he said, "and thanks for that, do you want any money for it?"

"No, don't be daft, it's just a spliff. Share and share alike. What's your mate's name, by the way?"

"I'm Lee," Lee held out his hand and she shook it. "I was just talking to Boz and Si over there."

"Ah yeah, they're nice guys. Obsessed by music. So, are you two together?" Suzie turned back to Mike and Anna.

"No," both Mike and Lee seemed to rush to answer, possibly for different reasons.

"OK!" Suzie laughed. "Just good friends?"

"Something like that," Mike said.

"Methinks he doth protest too much," Suzie laughed again.

"No, it's true," Anna said, "we've all been friends since we were four years old."

"Really? That's really cool," said Suzie. "I don't think I've known any of my mates anywhere near that long. We only moved to Bristol a few years back."

I'll be your friend, Anna's internal voice was shouting. She was aware that would not be cool, however. Instead, she smiled and said, "We've all grown up here. It's a brilliant city. So much going on. Loads of gigs..." Anna realised she was babbling. What was it about this girl that made her want to make her stay? "It's a brilliant city," she repeated slightly redundantly.

"I'm getting to like it," Suzie smiled widely at Anna then her eyes turned to Mike.

1990

Lee's loneliness begins

One day, not long after Lee's thirteenth birthday, he came into school looking pale and withdrawn. Mike greeted him but received little more than a weak smile in return.

"Do you know what's wrong with Lee?" he whispered to Anna during English, keeping half an eye on Miss Tomlinson, who had surely borrowed her super-sensitive hearing from the animal kingdom.

"I haven't seen him today," Anna whispered back, "did he say anything about his parents?"

"His parents? No." Mike was puzzled. What did she know about Lee's parents that he didn't? And how? He supposed it was something that had happened while he was in Spain. He sighed and returned to his exercise book.

Anna looked worried.

At breaktime, Anna said she'd catch up with Mike in a couple of minutes then she sped off. He went to their usual hangout, a doorway next to the science block, but there was no sign of Lee. Mike sat on the cold step and bit into his apple. He looked over to the tennis courts where a game of football was in full swing, but Lee was not there either.

A group of girls were positioned between Mike and the school sports hall, chatting and giggling. When they moved off, he saw his two friends huddled together, looking deep in conversation, over by the entrance. What was going on?

Lee looked over, saw Mike looking, and said something to Anna. She put her hand on his arm and they walked over.

"Alright?" Mike said, unsure of himself suddenly.

"We're fine, aren't we, Lee?" Anna asked, falsely bright.

"OK. Well, I was just about to go and play a game of footie. You two don't mind, do you?" Mike framed the question as though it was him leaving them but he felt confused and hurt. He didn't know how to act around them so the best thing seemed to be to just go. He was welcomed onto the tennis court/football pitch, and was soon stuck into the game, but every now and then he'd risk a quick glance at his friends, only to see them deep in conversation once more.

At lunch that day, Mike decided he'd leave them to it again. He wasn't sure if he was being grown up, respecting their need for space, or very childish and churlish, feeling left out. Maybe it was a bit of both. As they did every day, the three of them queued together in the noisy, hot dinner hall, with their trays – idling alongside the serving counter and trying to decide between chips and sausages, chips and pizza (that was the only choice for Mike, being vegetarian) or chips and some kind of dubious-looking gammon. All three dishes were accompanied by squashy-looking peas and mushy carrots. Bypassing the interestingly-coloured trifle, they all took apples for dessert and then moved along, paying the cheery cashier and taking their seats together at one of the long formica-covered tables.

Mike reached for the water jug and poured a glass for each of them, playing for time. There was something going on, but who knew quite what? Well, Lee and Anna, clearly, but Mike had no idea. He looked at both of them as he slid their glasses across the shiny surface. "Cheers, mate," said Lee glumly, while Anna smiled brightly and falsely. Mike had had enough.

What was that weird expression his Grandma used? The elephant in the room – that was it. What the hell did that mean? Mike ate quickly and made his excuses, standing to take his tray over to the clearing station and heading out of the stifling atmosphere into the chilly but bright Bristol day, heading straight for the school field where a very muddy game of football was taking place.

There was no sign of Lee and Anna all that lunchtime, and in French class, Mike found himself withdrawn. He didn't want to be, but somewhere inside he realised he was feeling really hurt. He wasn't even really sure why. However, he could barely talk to Anna.

"What's wrong?" she whispered.

"Nothing," he answered unconvincingly. He spent afternoon break in the school library and then left the Maths classroom in a rush at the end of the day, barely saying goodbye to Anna.

Of the three of them, Mike was the only one who could walk to and from school so he hurried back home, to find Emma on her afternoon off.

"What's up, petal?" she asked him.

"Nothing," he stormed, "And don't call me petal."

Emma knew better than to push it so she let him go off to his room. Mike put on a Rolling Stones album he'd borrowed from her and lay on his bed, not quite understanding just why he felt so upset.

He didn't hear the doorbell go, or Anna's light footsteps on the stairs. When she knocked, he thought it must be Emma.

"What?"

"It's me. Anna. I just wanted to check you're OK."

"Is Lee with you?"

"No, his gran picked him up tonight."

"Oh, right." That in itself seemed a bit strange. Lee's gran ran a shop over in Easton, so the only time Lee usually saw her was on a Sunday.

Mike turned his music down and Anna came softly into the room.

"Is Lee OK?" he finally asked.

"Not really," Anna answered quietly. "His mum's left."

"She's what?"

"She left, last night, without him."

"Oh my god. Poor Lee. Poor Lee's dad."

"Hmm," Anna laughed in a way that seemed to Mike very grown up. He found himself looking at her and seeing her differently. How did she suddenly seem so much more adult than him?

"What?"

"I don't think you should be feeling sorry for him, that's all."

"Well, why not? What's going on?" Mike felt embarrassed that his eyes were starting to prick with tears. This was not good.

"Mike, oh Mike, don't be upset. I've felt really bad not telling you..."

"I'm not crying," Mike huffed, wiping his eyes hastily, "and not telling me what?"

"Well, it's only because it's not my secret to tell. And it's not that Lee didn't want to tell you," Anna quickly added. "But he says his dad's been hitting his mum."

"What?" Mike couldn't believe his ears. Scott was certainly a 'man's man' – Mike always felt slightly intimidated and wimpy in his presence – however, a man beating his wife was another matter entirely.

"I know."

Both of them fell silent, thinking of Lee.

***

At that moment, Lee was heading down the Portway in the front of his gran's car.

She looked pale, and he could tell she was trying hard to be cheerful for his benefit.

"Don't, Gran, OK? You don't have to. Mum's left but it's not your fault."

"Oh Lee, it's not that. I don't think it's my fault. But it certainly isn't your fault, OK?"

"But…"

"What, love?"

"But she left… she left without saying bye." Lee was engulfed by tears and his gran drove until she could find somewhere she could stop. She pulled the car over, her own sight blurred by tears, and pulled her grandson to her while he sobbed.

Lee thought of the Friday before, the shouting had been worse than ever. Lee had actually been in his room, working hard at his Geography homework. He'd promised his mum that he'd try harder this year, and he was trying. He wanted to get back in the same class as Anna and Mike, anyway. Sometimes it felt as though they were drifting – more like speeding - away from him, with their clever brains and high exam scores.

So there he'd been, reading about Aust Cliff, his mum downstairs cleaning up after tea. His dad, as usual, had not made it back for dinner and his mum had saved a plate for him. Elaine had seemed distracted, and had snapped at Lee a couple of times over his slouching at the dinner table. She wasn't usually the type to snap. Then, which Lee couldn't believe, when she'd been tidying away their plates, she'd just tipped his dad's dinner away. The whole lot. Chicken, potatoes, carrots, peas, gravy. All went sliding into the gaping mouth of the bin.

"What are you doing, Mum?" Lee had gasped, knowing his dad's reaction wouldn't be good.

"Well, I'm fed up of this, Lee. How many times have we eaten together as a family – ever?"

Lee thought. It was usually just his mum and him, but that was OK. He loved his dad, sometimes. His dad could be a brilliant laugh and full of fun, but if he was in a bad mood he was very hard to be around. Lee found himself watching his every word, and his mum was even worse. She seemed to shrink into herself when Scott was in the room.

"Not many," he admitted.

"Well, do you know what, Lee? It's not just you who's going to change this year. You're working so hard, and I'm really proud of you. And I'm going to change, too." She poured herself a glass of wine. Lee watched as the ruby-red liquid glugged into the glass.

"No more," she'd said, "no more." She was looking intently at her glass. She seemed to be talking to herself.

Lee had felt swamped by fear. He knew things weren't right with his parents. He knew it was his dad in the wrong, if he looked into his heart of hearts, but he still believed they loved each other. His dad just worked too hard and maybe drank too much.

"Mum," he'd watched her gulp back her wine.

"Lee, I love you so much. You can't imagine how much. Hopefully you'll know one day, if you have your own kids. I can't let you live like this anymore, and I can't live like this anymore, either."

"Mum," he began again.

"Look," she'd spoken over him, "just you get up to your room, get on with your homework, and I promise you when you come down later on, things are going to be different."

"But..."

"Just go! Listen, that's his car."

Lee had cast a worried glance at his mother but done as he'd been told. His stomach felt like it was folding in on itself.

All was quiet as Lee got out his Geography exercise book, covered in old wallpaper to protect it. All the class did this, so there was a pretty, sometimes gaudy, array of workbooks on display across the classroom, or piled on the teacher's desk when there was homework to be handed in.

The front door slammed.

No more sound.

Lee began reading the notes they'd made that day. Miss Jeffries, his teacher, had mentioned something about a field trip to the Severn Estuary but he'd forgotten about it, what with his mum's strange mood.

An angry voice. His dad's. Lee put on his headphones, put a Guns'n'Roses tape – *G'n'R Lies* – into his tape player. Turned it up loud so that the speakers in his headphones crackled.

There was shouting, he could just make it out. Not just his dad this time – extremely unusually, his mum too. What had got into her? Whatever it was, maybe, just maybe, this was going to be the night that turned it around. Maybe her standing up for herself would show his dad he needed to change.

Lee continued trying to read the notes, to ignore the shouting from downstairs, and singing the lyrics of *Patience*. At one point there was a huge bang. Broken glass. He'd heard that before. Then... was that the front door slamming? His dad back off to the Lamplighters, no doubt. Lee decided to give his mum a few minutes then maybe he'd go down and check on her. Then again... something inside him told him to wait.

When he had eventually gone downstairs, it was into a house of darkness.

"Mum? Dad?" Nothing.

He switched on the lights in the hallway. His mum's car keys were there, hanging on their usual hook. His dad's were nowhere to be seen. Lee went from room to room, starting in the kitchen where he'd last seen his mum, switching on the lights so that the outside seemed darker than black. Neither of his parents were anywhere to be seen.

Lee had thought about phoning Anna, maybe Mike, but what would he say? He couldn't put his finger on it but he felt very, very bad somewhere deep inside.

He got a packet of Monster Munch and a can of Coke and

took them up to his room. On his way past his parents' bedroom, he heard his mum sobbing. He felt panicked. Should he knock? No, he had taken the coward's way, as he now thought of it. He'd ignored his mum's sadness, gone back to his bedroom. Putting his headphones back on, he played tape after tape, until at some point he must have fallen asleep.

On Saturday morning, Scott had driven him to Lizzie's shop in Easton. "Be a good lad, for your gran," he said gruffly, pushing a couple of five-pound notes into Lee's hand. "I'll pick you up tomorrow night."

"What about Mum?"

Scott paused. "Or your mum."

***

Anna put her hand in Mike's. It had been a long time since she'd done that and somewhere deep in the recesses of Mike's mind, a memory offered itself – a small, pudgy four-year-old hand being thrust into his own. Anna in a grey pinafore, her hair in cute little bunches, smiling shyly at him. They'd been friends forever. As a rush of warmth and affection flooded him, Mike realised that she wasn't betraying him, deliberately pushing him out. She wouldn't. She was just trying to do the right thing by Lee, when he needed her.

"Poor Lee," he said.

"Yes," she sighed.

"Should I phone him, do you think?"

"He won't be in, he's staying at his gran's tonight."

"I feel awful. I feel like I should do something."

"You can't. I can't, either."

"But he talked to you about it. Why didn't he talk to me?"

"He will, I think it was just because he told me about his mum and dad in the summer, so I already knew they weren't getting on."

"Imagine your mum leaving you." As Mike said it, he

238

thought about the fact that his dad had left him. Before he'd even met him. But it had never bothered Mike, it had always just been him and Emma. He didn't miss his dad because he didn't know him. Besides which, of Lee's two parents, it would surely be better if it had been Scott who had left. Lee's mum was quiet, but she was nice. She was kind and she loved Lee. Mike sometimes felt like Lee was trying to prove something to his dad. It felt uncomfortable when his dad was around.

"I'm not sure I'd notice," Anna laughed, then quickly apologised. "That's not true, or fair, sorry. I shouldn't make jokes like that when Lee's mum really has left. It's just, well... you know what my mum's like. I wish she was more like yours."

As if on cue, Emma called up the stairs, "Want to stay for tea, Anna? Then I can give you a lift home."

"Yes please, Emma," Mike's friends had always called his mum by her first name, never Mrs - or Miss - Sawyer. "If you're sure that's OK."

"That's no bother, as long as you don't mind being veggie for a night!"

Anna never did. In fact she had made up her mind to tell her parents she was going to be vegetarian full-time. She just hadn't got round to it yet, and they had so few meals together that she wasn't sure they'd even notice.

"Mum," Mike began at the dinner table and Anna gave him a look. She knew what he was going to say, it seemed. Mike continued undeterred. "Lee's mum's left."

Emma's fork stopped halfway to her mouth. "Oh my god. That's awful."

Nobody spoke so Emma, realising she couldn't expect two twelve-year-olds to fill in the gaps unprompted, asked, "When?"

"Last night," said Anna.

"Do you know where she's gone?"

"No, and I don't think Lee does."

"Oh my god," Emma said again. "Poor Lee. How was he today?"

"Awful," Anna said, "he hadn't slept and he looked ill."

"I'm not surprised, the poor boy. Mike, you need to invite him round at the weekend. Get him to ask his dad if it's OK."

"OK," Mike said, trying to read his mum's face. She looked sad, but not shocked. He wondered if it was because she was used to people leaving. Not for the first time, he wondered if she was lonely and if she wanted a boyfriend, or wished his dad would come back.

"Poor boy," she said again.

The three of them sat quietly then Anna politely asked Emma about her day and the conversation took a different turn, from Emma's work, to school, to what films were on at the cinema that weekend, but Lee never strayed far from any of their thoughts.

The three of them walked out to the car after tea, and sat in it for a few minutes, exhaling visible breath into the cold air while the heaters got going and the windscreen cleared.

The lights were on at Anna's house when they got back. "That's something, at least," Mike heard his mum mutter but Anna, in the back, appeared to hear nothing. Mike got out and pulled his seat forward so that Anna could clamber onto the pavement.

"See you tomorrow," he said.

"Yeah, see you, Mike," she smiled and laid her hand briefly on his arm. He watched her walk up the steps, fish her key out of her school bag, and let herself in, then he got back into the car. All the way home, he could still feel where Anna's hand had touched him and he wished she were still with him, slipping that very same hand into his.

Bristol, February 1990

Lee left alone

Lee trudged home from the bus stop, feeling the weight of four more days at school until the weekend. It was early February, the weather was dismal, and there was nothing left to look forward to. His birthday had been good – but that seemed like weeks ago, although in truth it was just ten days. So much since then had happened, and the weekend had been the worst. Not that he minded spending time in the shop with his gran. He liked it, and being taken back to her warm, cosy home, where she plied him with pizza and cans of pop from her shop. But something was wrong with his mum, and he had no idea what he could do about it. He hadn't seen her since before the argument she'd had with his dad on Friday night. Lizzie had dropped him off at school that morning and he'd found it very difficult to concentrate all day.

His dad hit his mum. Lee had to acknowledge it, although he hated to. What he really wanted to know was whether or not it was normal. It was wrong – undoubtedly – but then so was shouting at each other and he knew just from TV that people argued all the time. It didn't mean they didn't love each other. Boys at school sometimes fought but by the afternoon could be like best mates again. Still, Lee knew deep down that his dad hitting his mum wasn't quite the same thing as that.

He put his key in the door, feeling his stomach knot tightly inside him. A familiar feeling.

"Alright, mate?"

His dad was home – very unusual for this time of day.

"Hi Dad," he said tentatively.

"Good day?"

"It was OK."

"Monday's a shit day, eh?" Scott laughed and ruffled Lee's hair. "Tell you what, how d'you fancy coming down the Lighters with me and the lads?"

"Really?" Lee's head shot up and he looked at his dad's face. Was he winding him up?

"Yeah, why not? You're a teenager now, aren't you? My old man gave me my first pint at twelve."

"Your first pint? Grandad did that?"

"Yeah, guess he wasn't a total bastard! Mind you, I think he gave me a belting later that night. Still, that's not gonna happen to you," Scott said quickly, looking slightly anxiously at his son. "And I ain't saying you're gettin' your first pint, right? Maybe a 'alf a cider, 'ow's that sound?"

"What about..."

"Your mum? Don't worry about her. Let's go, eh?"

"Can I change out of my uniform?"

"Go on, then. Be quick. I'll wait here for you."

Lee flew up the stairs to his room. His dad had never taken him to the pub before. He felt nervous about hanging out with Scott and his workmates. They were always friendly to him if they ever came to the house, but they were big, loud men and Lee felt very much his age when he saw them. He chose his clothes carefully but quickly – new jeans, and the Guns'n'Roses t-shirt Mike and Anna had bought him for his birthday. A quick ruffle of his hair so that his schoolday parting vanished, and he was ready.

Scott was standing at the bottom of the stairs, jangling his keys. "Come on, then!"

The pub was smoky, but there were only a few drinkers in at that time of day.

"Get us a pint, will you, Joy?" Scott called to the barmaid. "And, er, 'alf an apple juice for the boy."

Joy winked. "This Lee, then? I 'aven't seen you since you were a babe in arms, love."

Lee felt his face flushing.

"That was a long time ago, though," Joy carried on kindly, "I can see you're all grown up. Here's your apple juice."

Lee looked at his glass. It looked a bit like apple juice, but darker, and it had a far stronger smell.

"Happy birthday, son," Scott was already halfway through his first pint.

Lee took a sip. The drink was sort of sweet, and it did taste of apples, but of something else too. His first half of cider.

"Cheers, Dad!" he grinned up at Scott, who clinked his glass against his son's and winked at him.

"Cheers."

The pub quickly filled up over the next hour or so, and Lee found himself at a table with Scott and six or seven of his mates. The cider had gone to Lee's head so he didn't feel quite as shy as he might have but still he found it difficult to make conversation, preferring instead to listen in. The only thing was, the men kept interrupting their stories to apologise to him for swearing. Like he hadn't heard it all before.

"So she opens the door in 'er dressing gown, with 'er tits – sorry, Lee – pretty much 'angin' out, and bends down to get the milk. 'Shall I come back later, love?' I asked 'er, but she just dragged me in through to the kitchen." This was Fred, one of the guys that sometimes worked for Scott.

"Fuckin' 'ell – sorry, son – what did you do?"

"Well, I didn't quite know where to put meself but the phone rang, and it were 'er 'usband - on the road – and it put a dampener on the 'ole thing. Felt a bit wrong, to be honest."

"Wrong?" Scott scoffed. "You must be gettin' soft in your old age."

"Less of the old, you cheeky sod!"

"I wouldn't touch 'er with a barge pole, mate, she's been round 'alf o' Shire, an' 'ave you seen her 'usband? Bloody 'uge bloke. He'd beat the shit out o' you."

"Well she seems to 'ave got away with it so far."

"Best steer clear, believe me."

Lee quietly went off to the toilet; the conversation, the smoky atmosphere and the cider had all gone to his head. He stood for a moment in the relative peace of the gents, resting his head against the cool tiles of the wall. He tried not to think when the last time they had been cleaned might have been. He was loving this night. He felt like one of the lads – well, nearly. Would his dad let him stay out late? On a Monday night? His stomach rumbled and he thought of the homework that lay waiting for him in his school bag at home. He'd get in some shit if that wasn't done for the next day. Still, he'd have to take it.

"... I'd fuckin' kill 'im," Lee could hear Scott saying as he walked back to the table. "I'd be sneaky about it, though, so nobody'd know it was me that done it. Fuck up his boiler or oven or somethin'... fill 'is 'ouse with gas, make it look like a leak."

The men all laughed then Fred, spotting Lee, nudged Scott.

"It's alright, lads," Scott said, "I was just saying what I'd do to any bloke that tried it on with yer mum."

Lee's face flushed. Scott laughed. "Ah, it's OK, mate, don't be embarrassed. Not goin' to 'appen."

Bill smiled at Lee. "Just a stupid conversation."

"Yeah, we was just talkin' about that woman from earlier. Not right 'avin' it off with someone else's missus."

Lee smiled weakly. Suddenly he felt really hungry, and uncomfortable. This place, this pub, wasn't yet for him. These blokes were too old for him. The nagging feeling about the English homework grew more severe and he just wanted to get home. To his mum.

After another hour, Scott noticed Lee yawning. "Come on, son, best get 'ome, eh?"

"Thanks, Dad," Lee smiled. He had a headache and he just wanted to go to sleep. He'd have to get up early and do his homework.

He walked to the car with Scott. How many pints had his dad drunk? He shouldn't really be driving, Lee knew that, but he didn't dare say anything.

"You know I love you, boy, don't you?" Scott said when they were in their seats.

Lee looked up. This was really not normal. "Um, yeah."

"Good, 'cos it's gonna be just you and me from now on, son."

What?

Lee felt like his heart had stopped. "Wh- what do you mean?"

"Yer mum's left. She's gone."

"Gone where?" Lee tried to make sense of things quickly in his cloudy mind.

"Gone, not coming back. She's left me. And you. And good riddance too, the bi..." Scott seemed to realise he had said enough.

"Is this a joke?"

"No it's not a fuckin' joke!" Scott slammed his fist on the steering wheel and Lee jumped. He couldn't help wondering how his dad could go from the jovial, jokey bloke in the pub to this so suddenly.

But his mum couldn't have left. She wouldn't have. Not without him. This had to be some nasty joke of Scott's.

Lee said nothing and looked down at his lap, willing his dad to get driving, get him home. Thankfully, Scott did just that and the two of them sat in silence all the way back. Once they were in the house, Lee deliberately tried to keep calm. He didn't want his dad to see his panic, his weakness. But there were no lights on. And his mum's car was not in the drive.

Had it been there earlier? He couldn't remember. He wanted to rush from room to room, sure that she must be there somewhere, but he knew somehow that his dad was telling the truth.

"Up to bed, now, right?" Scott sounded tired himself and Lee followed him mutely, up the stairs. As Scott wandered down the hallway and fell onto his bed, where he was soon snoring, Lee found himself suddenly wide awake, with no chance of sleep. His mum had gone. She hadn't even said bye.

In the morning, somehow, Lee got up and ready for school, even though he was sure he hadn't slept all night. He sat in the kitchen, trying to force down some Sugar Puffs but they felt dry, like they were filling his mouth, stopping him breathing. He couldn't stop thinking that his mum should be there. He felt shrivelled and shocked.

He put his bowl in the sink and went upstairs, where he put on his uniform. He wanted to fall on his bed, to sob, and call for his mummy, like when he was little. But he was twelve years old now. He hadn't called his mum 'Mummy' since he was about five. Some instinct kicked in that he couldn't let Scott see his weakness. If she had really left him alone with his dad – the thought made him feel physically sick - then he would just have to get on. He would have to toughen up.

He walked down the stairs, got some change from the jar in the hallway for his bus fare and lunch, and walked, on autopilot, to his bus stop. All the way to school, all he could think of was telling Anna.

1988

Starting secondary school

Life at their new school was a shock to the system for the three friends. There were timetables to get to grips with, and seemingly endless corridors which were vast and confusing to unaccustomed young eyes.

The dynamics of the friendship were to change for the first time when school began. Mike and Anna, if not effortlessly brainy, were both intelligent and hard-working, and although the school claimed not to stream students in the first year there, it soon became evident that there was some kind of differentiation at work. Mike and Anna were placed in the same class for all their subjects while Lee was put with an entirely different set of students, none of whom would have been termed brainy or particularly studious.

The forms were organised differently, however, and Lee and Mike ended up together, with Anna on her own. She didn't seem to mind too much, although evidently she was very quiet in her formroom. So much so that Mike and Lee had to put an end to some of the boys from her form calling her names - behind her back, in true cowardly fashion. Also behind her back, her two gallant friends threatened to kick the boys' heads in, which seemed to put an end to the problem.

In class, Mike noticed Anna was quieter than she had been at their old school. He knew she knew the answers but she never put her hand up to volunteer them. He found that annoying, though he didn't really know why.

So now Lee was cast out from the threesome most of the time, although they would normally get back together to eat lunch and hang around in the playground, unless Mike or Lee were tempted off into a game of football. They rarely both played at the same time, as that would have meant leaving Anna alone.

Whether or not Anna needed such protection was another matter. She had made friends with a few of the girls in her form, and of course there were some of their classmates from their primary school who she already knew, but somehow there existed an unwritten, unspoken, rule that at least one of the boys would be with her at all possible times.

One day during November of that first term, Mike was off ill with tonsillitis and Lee, who had been playing football, was keeping an eye out for Anna. She'd gone to the library after they'd eaten but said she'd come and find him once she'd exchanged her books.

As she rounded the corner towards the playing field, Lee noticed two boys from the year above them following her. His hackles immediately rose; there was something about the way they were laughing together that suggested bad news. However, he knew how proud Anna was so he kept his calm, watched from a distance.

One of them called to her but Lee couldn't hear what was said; however, even from a distance, it was obvious that her face was flushing. Lee moved closer.

"Shouldn't you be in primary school?" the boy's mate was now calling. "You got no tits. Don't know what you've got a bra for."

Anna steadfastly ignored them, keeping her head down and walking more quickly. Lee walked towards her and she almost stumbled into him. When she realised it was him, her face was a mixture of embarrassment, annoyance, and relief.

"You OK, Anna?" Lee asked her, his hands on her arms.

She nodded. He looked up at the two boys who had been harassing her, now innocently walking away. Something in him snapped. "Stay here," he said.

Before he knew it, Lee was running after them and had launched himself, feet first, at the back of the knees of one of them.

"Argh! What the fuck?"

The boy landed on the floor and his friend turned round to find the first-year's face right up against his own.

"Who the fuck do you think you are, talkin' to 'er like that?"

Anna had never seen Lee like this before. She watched him, aghast. Wanting the world to swallow her up. Worried for Lee; she didn't want him getting hurt, but also slightly in awe that he was going up against two second-years just for her.

"We weren't doin' nothin', mate." The boy shoved Lee while his mate sat on the ground, rubbing his legs.

"Liar. I 'eard what you were sayin'." Lee, though shorter than his aggressor by a couple of inches, pushed back.

"What's it to you? She your girlfriend? You some kind of paedo or somethin'?"

Lee laughed. Then he headbutted the boy, straight on the nose. Lee rubbed his own head, his vision blurry for a moment. As it cleared, he was gratified to see that both boys were now on the ground, the one he'd just nutted had blood streaming from his nose.

A crowd had gathered and the teachers on lunch duty were running across the grey playground.

Mr McDonagh took hold of Lee's arm and marched him straight into school without giving him a chance to explain. "You'll get your chance in the Head's office."

Miss West took a look at the other two, knowing them to be trouble-makers, and unsympathetically ordered them up on their feet. "To the first aid room for now, boys, then it's off to the Head for you. She'll be very interested to hear what's been going on."

Unnoticed by either teacher, or by the crowd of kids which was dispersing as quickly as it had gathered, Anna stood shakily with her back against the wall. Everything had happened so fast, it was going to take her a while to process it all. She felt shocked by the boys' meanness, and embarrassed about what they'd been saying. Without thinking about it, she'd worn a blue cropped-top bra that day and it could clearly be seen through her white school shirt. Those two second-year boys, who had been in the library as well, had been sniggering about it. They'd followed her out into the playground and she'd had no idea what to say to them.

She hated violence of any sort and she knew she should be disgusted by Lee's behaviour but when she thought of what he'd done for her, she felt nothing but gratitude.

By the time Mike returned to school, Lee was still undergoing his week of detentions.

"What's going on?" Mike had asked Anna and she told him, missing out the part about her bra and the insults regarding her flat chest. Lee had never mentioned the boys' words to her and when she'd thanked him for helping her, he'd shrugged it off. "They're just dicks, Anna, and you're my mate. You'd do the same for me. Well, maybe not exactly the same." He'd grinned.

Mike wished that he'd been there to help out too, but he knew he wouldn't have done what Lee had. He knew he didn't have it in him, and he felt ashamed of that.

Nevertheless, despite the new challenges they all had to deal with, the three of them kept their friendship steady, strong and firm. On Wednesdays, Anna would go to Mike's house after school, and they would do their homework together before Emma got home from work. This would be followed by tea and then Emma would drop Anna back at her house, at just about the time Anna's mum would be arriving home, complete with trouser suit, high heels, and a briefcase full of work to keep her busy that evening.

Weekends would be spent with the three of them perusing the record shops on Park Street, looking at posters, learning the names of bands whose music they couldn't afford to buy, dreaming of the day that they could.

They would drink glass bottles of lemonade as they sat on the cold concrete of the harbourside, dangling their legs over the water, watching boats and people pass them by. Anna would gaze at the deep, dark water, and scare herself with thoughts of falling in – fighting what seemed almost an urge to jump. The thought at once thrilled and terrified her. Who knew what lurked in those murky depths?

If they could afford the bus back home, it was a rare occasion. Usually they would have to walk up Park Street, then Whiteladies Road, where they would stop at the charity office where Emma worked. They could sit in the foyer and then Emma would either drive them back to their own homes or they could all pile back to Mike's for tea and a video before Emma would drop Lee and Anna back home.

Emma seemed to do a lot of picking up and dropping off.

Secondary school was a big change in their lives but they had managed to make that transition together. It was a huge relief to Mike, and Anna, who had both been worried that things would change. Lee, however, had never even considered that possibility. They were friends for life, and that was that.

A summer apart

The summer before they started secondary school, Mikey had gone away to Spain with Emma for three weeks, staying with friends she had made during her days teaching English as a foreign language. He had returned with a golden tan, a new language, and having dropped the 'y' in favour of being Mike. A new name for a new school.

Anna and Lee, meanwhile, had spent the majority of their spare time together. They were too young for their parents to be worrying about their relationship – if their parents had been the type to worry about such a thing. Anna's mum may have done, if she hadn't been so tied up with her work, while Lee's mum was just happy he had such a nice friend and wasn't missing Mike(y) too much. Scott of course swung between thinking it was great his son had a girlfriend and worrying that he might turn out to be a bit of a puff. Anna's dad, away in London for much of the working week, barely noticed his daughter from one day to the next.

So it was that Lee and Anna had shared a happy, carefree summer (carefree save for the odd niggle about what life at secondary school was going to be like).

They had explored Bristol on their bikes, spending long, lazy days circling the Downs and pooling their pocket money for ice creams, or else popping into Lee's house to top up on snacks. They had spent a day at Bristol Zoo, paid for by Lee's parents, and had even managed to get across the Suspension

Bridge for part of Ashton Court Festival without their parents knowing (that was something they would have been concerned about). Now *that* was a revelation. Loud, live music. Plastic pint pots of cider. Families picnicking happily. Hippies by the campervan-load. All sorts of interesting and unusual smells, even the odd naked person. Lee and Anna wandered around, wide-eyed. At one point, when a man with a long, wispy beard and paintings on his bare chest came dancing up to them, Lee took hold of Anna's hand. They stayed that way for the rest of the day, until they crossed the Suspension Bridge and returned to the relative normality of Clifton Village. The crossing had seemed symbolic, almost magical, like they were returning from Narnia or some other magical land – one to which they weren't entirely sure they wanted to return.

In the week following the festival, a couple of days before Mike was due to get back from Spain, Lee phoned Anna. It was late afternoon and she had the house to herself; her mum wasn't due back till six at the earliest, and her stepbrothers were out at band practice.

"Can I come over?" Lee asked. He sounded a bit sad, Anna thought.

"Yes, of course," she said, "can you get a lift?"

"No, Mum's... in bed. I'll bike over."

"Oh, OK, I'll see you in a bit."

Anna put the phone down and picked up her book. She was reading *Are You There, God? It's Me, Margaret* for about the fifth time. It was an interesting read, one her mum had bought for her; Anna supposed it was in lieu of having to tell her too much about periods and 'becoming a woman' herself, but she didn't mind - she thought a book was probably the preferable option.

It was the friendships in the book that intrigued Anna as much as anything. Margaret had Gretchen, and Nancy – close female friends who she could talk to about anything. They all seemed so eager to start their periods, too! Anna thought she was in no hurry. However, she did wonder about those kinds of friendships. She got on with the girls at school, but it had always been her, Mike and Lee, ever since they were four years old. She couldn't imagine talking to them about puberty! Anna tried to imagine their faces if she told them she'd started her period. Which she hadn't – and judging by her childlike body still wouldn't for some time.

About half an hour later, a red-faced, slightly out-of-breath Lee appeared at the window. He knocked and grinned.

"Hi," Anna said, opening the front door and letting him past. She picked up a postcard from the doormat. "A card from Mikey! Did you get one?"

"Yeah, yesterday. Sounds like he's having a good time."

Anna read the card as she walked to the kitchen, where Lee was already helping himself to a drink.

"Want a Soda Stream?" she asked.

"Yeah! Brilliant."

"Mike says he's been snorkelling, and learning to speak Spanish."

"Yeah, I know. Says he's got some new records, too. Feels like he's been gone for months."

"He's back next week, we should do something good before we go back to school. Bike to Pill, take a picnic, maybe. What flavour do you want?"

"Cream Soda. Got any biscuits?"

Anna threw him a small packet of shortbread. "Mum brought these back from a meeting, want them?"

"OK."

The Soda Stream buzzed and bubbled and Anna poured two drinks into tall, dark green glasses. "Shall we go in the garden?"

"OK."

They sat on the swinging seat together, Lee talking about

Mike being in Spain and what music he might be listening to.

"Steve and Andy are at band practice at the moment. They reckon they're like U2!" Anna laughed.

"They are pretty good, though," Lee was quite in awe of Anna's older brothers. "Think they'd let us come to one of their gigs?"

"In a pub? I don't reckon, we'll have to wait till they're at the Colston Hall." Anna laughed again.

Lee leaned his head onto the back of the seat, watching the slow progress of a large, delicate cloud drifting overhead. A familiar *whoooosh!* took his and Anna's attention and they turned to see a hot air balloon high above, flames bursting in its heart as the pilot pushed it on.

"Fiesta next week," said Lee, "We should definitely go to that."

"With Mike," Anna added.

"Yeah, with Mike," he agreed.

"So why's your mum in bed?" Anna asked, as they watched the balloon float higher, above the streets, out of view. "She ill?"

Lee sighed.

Anna looked at him. "Is she? Ill?"

"No. Not really."

Anna remained quiet.

"She's... her and Dad keep arguing."

"Oh."

"I don't know. They've always argued, always. Do yours?"

"Do they argue?" Anna thought hard. Her mum and dad were really only ever together at weekends. Then they would stay in bed late, rise to collect the morning paper and sit reading that while they drank coffee and ate croissants and olive bread from Joe's Bakery. "I don't think they do, not really. They snap at each other quite a lot. They're not often in the same place, really. Do yours argue a lot? Bad, I mean?"

"Yeah," Lee sighed. Pretty bad."

"Is that why your mum's in bed? 'Cause she's upset?"

"She won't let me in to see her. I think they had a really bad one last night. I was in the den, watching *The Lost Boys*. Have you seen it? It's brilliant. Anyway, I heard him yelling. Really, really yelling. Then he threw something. I heard the smash. I opened the door but I didn't know what to do. Mum was crying."

"God." No, her mum and dad certainly didn't argue like that.

"Anna," Lee sniffed, "I think Dad hit Mum."

"Hit her?" Anna's eyes sprung open wide. "No, that wouldn't... he wouldn't... Did you see him?"

"No, I was in the doorway of the den. I shut the door again straightaway. I should have gone, should have gone to help Mum."

Lee's eyes filled with tears, which spilled onto his cheeks. Anna didn't know what to do. She put her arm around her friend's shoulders and let him cry.

"You don't know that he hit her, then, if you didn't see?"

"No, I heard it. He did hit her. I know he did."

Anna had heard of husbands beating their wives before – she'd seen things on TV – but she had never really thought it happened, not in real life, to people she knew.

"What had your mum done?" she asked. "Why was he so angry?"

"Mum hadn't done anything," Lee was angry all of a sudden, "she never does. Dad goes to work, she stays in. Dad goes to the pub, she stays in."

"So why was he..?"

"I don't know. I don't know."

"Shhh," Anna said, and squeezed him.

The two friends sat close and quiet as the swinging seat gently rocked in the heat of the afternoon.

When Mike returned, he was so excited to see his friends. He wanted to know everything they'd been doing – although he found he actually didn't really want to know, either. As they filled him in on their adventures, he started to feel a bit left out. He was particularly disappointed to have missed the festival, which Anna and Lee had managed to build up into some kind of spectacular event, without having planned to do so. The two who had remained in Bristol had also developed some new in-jokes during Mike's absence and they didn't seem particularly interested to hear about his time in Spain. He had enjoyed it immensely, but on his return he started to resent the fact that he'd been dragged away and missed all the fun.

However, they still had some time to go until the start of the new term and the beginning of the next stage in their 'school career', as their primary head, Mr McDonald, had insisted on calling it.

First off was the balloon fiesta. The friends set off on their bikes mid-morning, meeting at the Downs so they could cycle over the Suspension Bridge. Emma had sent a picnic big enough for the three of them in Mike's rucksack. She'd offered them a lift as she'd be going up there herself but they'd declined the offer; this would be their big day out.

Anna had realised Mike was feeling a bit put out that he'd missed the festival and she wanted to make sure they all did something special together. She had managed to get some money from her mum, to spend on hot dogs and drinks, while Lee's mum had also given him some cash.

Elaine had come out of her bedroom by the time Lee had returned home that day when he'd visited Anna, and was sitting in the kitchen in her dressing gown, looking pale and washed-out. Lee couldn't see any bruises, despite looking closely when she wasn't looking at him.

He didn't ask her about it, and although he listened behind lots of closed doors, he never heard his mum or his dad mention it to each other, either. Perhaps he had been mistaken?

The day of the balloon fiesta, between the three of them, they had twenty-three pounds, a box of sandwiches, a whole multipack of Walker's crisps, three apples, a big bottle of water, and three Curly Wurlies. Again, Mike felt slightly like an outsider when he realised the others had cash. There was no way his mum could spare that kind of money, but then his mum had made a picnic and nobody else's had. He knew Emma did everything she could. He didn't have a dad. They didn't have much money. That was life.

At the meeting point by the water tower, the air was already stifling hot. Not quite as hot as Spain, Mike thought, but he didn't mention it to his friends in case they thought he was showing off.

They split the picnic items between their three bags, to ease the load on Mike's sweating back, and pedalled off towards Clifton. It cost two pence each to cross the Suspension Bridge by bike. The bridge moved slightly with the weight of the traffic moving across it, and Anna felt her stomach turn slightly but she just tilted her face upwards, towards the sun, and tried to ignore it. Far below them, the muddy Avon twinkled, regardless of its thick brown consistency, and above them mere breaths of clouds skittered past. It was a perfect day for balloons.

At Ashton Court, they wheeled their bikes into the woods, chaining them together, before walking up the steep slopes to the crest of the hill. Here was where the festival stages had been just weeks before but now there were balloon crews, setting up ready for the big day. Vans were strewn around the grass as the teams unloaded baskets and huge swathes of material. Lee, Mike and Anna sat down a little way away, opening the bottle of water and eating their Curly Wurlies.

"I'd love to go in one of them," Mike said.

Just then, the first of the balloons – the Hoffmeister Bear – came to life. As it inflated and rose up, it pulled its basket –

crew already inside – vertical. A local TV crew rushed towards the basket, interviewing the pilot, who shouted his answers down to them while the balloon rose – tethered – a little way into the sky.

Already, crowds were gathering and the food vans were opening for business. Soon there were twenty or thirty balloons fully inflated, including a dinosaur, a National Express coach and a British Gas flame. Lee ran off to get a programme of events, and came back with three bags of candy floss as well.

The fluffy spun-sugar was soon gone, dissolving on their tongues in a deliciously sweet way. They moved on to the picnic, devouring that almost as quickly, then the three ran off to play in the woods for a while. They had not yet become too cool for hide-and-seek, and the game provided lots of giggles as they found the most stupid places to hide. Lee won when, clearly visibly to the others, he stood in the middle of the path, holding a twig in front of him.

It was hot in the afternoon sun and the shelter of the trees provided some welcome relief.

Later in the afternoon, Anna bought chips for them all and they settled down to watch the mass balloon launch. It was an incredible sight as the balloons all lifted off the solid ground, rising surprisingly quickly into the bright sky, where they cleared the Avon Gorge and headed off across Bristol; over the city streets and suburbs, where children ran into gardens and up roads, waving and shouting, and dogs barked redundantly.

A tired but happy trio of friends retrieved their bikes and cycled back across the bridge, past Clifton Village and back to the water tower. There was just enough cash left for an ice cream each before they went their separate ways home.

Bristol, February 1988

Turning eleven

Lee was the first of the three of them to turn eleven. As luck would have it, his birthday was in the February half-term, and he had asked Anna and Mikey to come bowling, then to McDonald's for tea. He was extra excited because this year it would be his dad taking them out.

He loved his mum, but he sometimes felt embarrassed by her. She wasn't like Mikey's mum ("Call me Emma"), who was young – well youngish, younger than his own mum anyway – and liked cool music, and even wore quite cool clothes. His own mum was so quiet, too. When he had tea round at Mikey's, the small kitchen was noisy and full of chatter and laughter. If Anna was there as well, or one of Emma's friends, even moreso. Lee knew his mum didn't really have any friends; nobody who came round to see her, anyway. She was always fine with him having friends round and she was a really good cook but having tea there, in the spotless kitchen of the huge new house they'd had built for them, was somehow stifling and awkward. Mikey and Anna were always polite but the fun seemed to get sucked out of them as soon as they entered the room.

He felt bad thinking like that, and he'd never say those things to anyone. His mum was the one he could rely on. Even at this young age, he knew that. He also knew somewhere very deep down that she wasn't happy but he couldn't really admit that to himself, never mind anybody else.

His dad was out most nights, down the pub after work. Even though they'd moved up to near the Downs, Lee's dad still drank in the Lamplighters down at Sea Mills, where he'd grown up and where Lee had been born. Despite drinking pints of cider, he still drove home. Something else Lee didn't want to think too much about.

It was exciting to think that his tall, cool dad was taking him and his mates out, though. They'd be able to ride in the work van. Sometimes Lee was allowed to go in the back, when it was empty, which was brilliant. He'd ask if all three of them could do it on the way back home. The plan was that they'd have their day out, his dad would drop Anna back at hers, then Mikey would come back for a sleepover. Lee had already chosen two videos from the Blockbusters in Westbury-on-Trym – *Ferris Bueller's Day Off* and *National Lampoon's Vacation*. He'd seen them both before, more than once, as had Mike, but they liked to watch them again and again, repeating the lines to each other. They'd roll around laughing, at each other as much as the film. Lee's dad hadn't seen the films yet and had promised he'd come and watch them as well. He was going to love them.

"You ready then, boy?" Scott's voice boomed up the stairs.

"Coming, Dad!" Lee was still getting used to the size of the new house. It was really cool, though. Huge stairs down into the hallway, a games room, and an enormous garden. His own room was way bigger than the box room he'd had at Sea Mills. He had a full-sized double bed, his own TV, and he was hoping he might get a Sega Mega Drive for Christmas, if his dad could get hold of one somehow (and he almost certainly could).

"Have a nice time, Lee," his mum came out of the kitchen and kissed him.

She looked sad again, he thought, but he pushed the thought away and pulled on his coat. "Bye, Mum."

At the bowling alley, Scott teamed up with Anna and the pair of them beat Lee and Mikey hands-down. Scott had never been one for letting his son win anything ("He needs to win it himself or it don't mean nothin'.").

He whipped Anna into the air and twirled her round. "Come on girls," he turned to Lee and Mikey, "let's get those gay shoes off you and get to McDonald's."

Lee looked at Mikey, who was just grinning. He'd always been laidback, it was very hard to offend him, and so Lee relaxed. His dad was just treating them like he treated his own mates. Lee couldn't wait for the day he could go down the Lamplighters with him and buy him a pint.

They traipsed over to the desk to the very pretty girl who was in charge of the shoes. While Lee and his friends sat down to sort themselves out, Scott stayed chatting to the girl and Lee looked up to see him handing his business card to her.

"What was that, Dad?" Lee asked, suddenly at Scott's elbow.

"Oh, nothing, son. Lyndsay here just needs a plumber, so I said I was the man for the job." He winked at Lyndsay, who giggled. Lee smiled. His dad was funny, everyone liked him.

Nearly everyone.

At McDonald's, Scott let them choose two burgers each, although Anna and Mike only wanted a Filet-o-Fish. Mike didn't eat meat, and usually not fish either but his mum said that he could have it occasionally, to make life easier at birthday parties and friend's houses. Scott himself ate two Big Macs, barely chewing them, it seemed to Lee, and washed them down with a big glug of cola. Lee had thought to do the same but a quarter of the way through his second burger, he couldn't eat another bite. No problem, Scott devoured the rest of that, too.

"How does it feel to be eleven, son?" Scott asked.

"Good," Lee grinned.

"Secondary school next, eh? I can't believe it. Look at all you lot." Sometimes Scott had these softer moments. "I remember your first Christmas play. Do you – Anna, you was Mary and Mikey your bloke, Joseph. Knew they wouldn't make you Joseph, son. Too much of a puff!" Scott laughed loudly and Lee looked at his friends. Perhaps he'd misread Scott's mood.

Mikey spoke up for his friend, "Lee was the Angel Gabriel the year after."

"Gay-briel's about right!" Scott snorted then, seeing Lee's face, "Oh don't be like that, son, I'm only 'avin' a laugh. We all know 'e's not a gaylord, don't we?"

Anna had gone very quiet. Even Mikey was struggling to keep a cheerful look on his face.

"I don't know, you lot've got no sense of humour," Scott sighed and crumpled his paper cup in his fist. "Come on, then, let's get Anna 'ome then I'll drop you boys off."

"Aren't you staying in tonight, Dad? We've got Ferris Bueller and National Lampoons to watch!"

"Ah, no son, don't worry, I'll watch 'em some other time. You've got Mikey round tonight 'aven't you? Maybe your mum'll watch 'em with you," he snorted derisively.

Lee was quiet all the way back. He sat on the seat in the front with his dad while Anna and Mikey were in the back of the van, trying to maintain balance as they took corners and roundabouts, watching a spare spanner and a balled-up dusty sheet sliding about.

"Is Lee alright, do you think?" Anna asked quietly.

"I think so," Mikey whispered back.

"His dad's…"

"Alright back there?" Scott shouted.

"Yes thanks, Mr Lewis."

At Anna's house, both she and Mikey jumped out of the back.

"Can you just wait a minute, please? I need to get Lee's present." Anna ran up the steps to her tall townhouse. Her parents were out as usual. Tucked just inside the doorway, there it was, the Woolworths bag. Her dad hadn't forgotten to get it, then. She trotted neatly back down the steps and up to the van.

"Here you go, Lee. Happy birthday, I hope you like it." Lee took the bag. "Sorry it isn't wrapped," she added.

Lee peered inside the bag and his face lit up. "The Housemartins! Thanks Anna, that must have cost you loads."

"I've been saving up, don't worry, you can do me a tape of it!"

"Me too," Mike was looking enviously at the LP Lee held in his hands.

"Course I will. Both of you. Thanks, Anna!"

Lee's face was broken by a huge grin, and his sombre mood was broken too. Anna waved them off, delighted to have been able to make Lee smile, then she walked up the stairs to her empty home.

Scott dropped the boys off without bothering to come in. "See you later, boys!"

Lee and Mikey said hello to Elaine and went straight up to Lee's room, where they listened to the new album back-to-back twice. Then down to the games room, where they played table tennis and eventually settled down to watch the videos, eating pizza and crisps. They brought their sleeping bags down and made beds for themselves on the beanbags and cushions from the settee. Eventually, they fell asleep.

Much, much later, in the deep dark of the night, Mikey woke and at first was struck by the sound of silence. At his house, the M5 could be heard not that far away, it created a comforting background hum. Lee's new house was on its own, its huge garden and trees separating it from its neighbours.

Had the quiet actually woken him up?

Then he heard it. Somewhere in a seemingly remote corner of the house, Lee's dad was shouting. He must have come home drunk. Was he on the phone to one of the men who worked for him? There was a slam of a door, or something, then quiet. Mike's over-tired mind began to drift off back to sleep but somewhere, in his dreams or in the real world, he thought he could hear someone crying.

1981

Bristol, December 1981

The beginning

The warm, cosy classroom was verging on stuffiness. Underneath the glow of the bright striplights was a hive of activity as the children struggled into their costumes, largely assisted by their teacher, Mrs Donovan, and a handful of mums.

The large safety-glass windows were steamed up but Emma could see that it was already dark outside. Having just rushed to the school from the bus stop at the end of the road, she knew it was also bitingly cold out there; a stark contrast. She could feel her cheeks burning red. It had been a stretch getting from work to the school on time: cutting off her boss perhaps slightly rudely, she had grabbed her coat and was still struggling into it as she'd run for the number 40. That too had been unnaturally warm; a breeding ground for germs, her mum would say. It didn't bother Emma, although she had astutely taken a seat a few rows away from the beige-coated man who'd been coughing and spluttering into his handkerchief.

From the bus stop she'd run again, getting to the school just as the end-of-day bell went.

She had promised Mikey she'd be there to help him get ready, and there was no way she was going to let him down.

The comfortably large, middle-aged secretary, Mrs Brown, had smiled at her as she'd panted her way in. "Come to help out, Mrs... *Miss*... Sawyer?"

The Miss thing. A lot of people did it. Emma was well aware that there weren't that many other single mums around at the school Mikey went to. It wasn't that Mrs Brown was trying to make a point but somehow Emma felt it just the same.

"Yes," she opted for a smile, feeling her heart rate slowly begin to relax.

"The others are in the staffroom at the moment. Please go on through, have a cup of tea. Mrs Donovan will come and get you in a minute or two. The children are very excited!"

"I can imagine," Emma smiled again and wandered towards the sound of female laughter coming from the room that was normally the staff's sanctuary.

Mike had not been particularly bothered about the play at first.

"Joseph?" Emma had asked, "You're going to be Joseph?"

"Yeah," he shrugged, looking curiously at his mum's apparent excitement.

"But that's brilliant! You know who Joseph was?"

"Erm..."

"Jesus's daddy!"

Even as she'd said it, Emma realised that it would mean very little to her son. She was not a church-goer and consequently neither was Mikey. In fact, until he'd started school she very much doubted that he would have heard Jesus's name, perhaps apart from as an expletive.

"Who's Mary?" she asked.

"Mary?"

"Yes, Mary. Joseph's wife."

"Dunno."

Emma just hugged him to her. It had been hard seeing him go off to school, so small; too small, it seemed to her, but despite her concerns he had settled in remarkably well. Parents' evening, which Emma had felt herself too young to be attending as a parent, had been a joy, and she'd had to keep herself from crying when Mrs Donovan told her that Mikey was progressing well and was very popular with his classmates.

"He could just do with a little bit more confidence at times," the teacher had added, and at that Emma had given a large sniff.

"Oh, but that's not a bad thing," Mrs Donovan had laid a kindly hand on Emma's. "I always think it's better for confidence to develop naturally, instead of coming as part and parcel of a child. As this year goes on, he'll come out of himself more and more. You wait and see."

Emma could have kissed her. When she got home, she kissed her mum – who had been looking after Mikey - instead.

"Mikey's doing really well!" she practically sang.

"Well, of course he is!" her mum smiled.

"Without a dad."

"Because he's got you," Sandra hugged her daughter. "Because he's got you. You're doing really well, too."

"Oh, Mum…"

"Well you are, and you need to hear it. Every day, if possible."

Emma crept up to Mikey's room where he was sound asleep, his little mouth puckered open, his round cheeks rosy and apple-like. She kissed his smooth, warm face and went back downstairs where Sandra was taking her tea from the oven.

Emma had no idea how she would keep the tears from falling during the play but right now she had a job to do. There were twenty-nine children with costumes ranging from shepherds to donkeys and just half an hour to get them all wriggled in to the right clothes, make sure they'd all had a wee, and calm them down ready to perform their first school play.

She had been allocated six children. Mikey, his friends

Anna and Lee, and the Three Kings, who were a comedic assortment of sizes, from the very tall Simon - who had turned five on the first day of the school year - to the almost minuscule Oscar, who would not be five until the next summer. Despite the difference in age and size, these two were already firmly best friends.

Lee seemed to be Mikey's closest friend, Emma thought, although she could see he also had an attachment to Anna – but then, so did Lee. Those two were as different as could be, she thought – Lee chatty and cheeky while Anna was quite solemn, although she could really beam sometimes and when she did it was as though somebody had turned the sun on. Emma had only gathered this from a couple of children's parties she'd been to. She would always stay with Mikey, even though he seemed happy to go off and play – but four seemed awfully young to her to be dropped off and left. However, that was exactly what Anna's parents seemed to do. Anna had two older stepbrothers and Emma suspected she was treated in a more mature fashion than her years demanded. Lee's mum – Elaine, she thought it was - would usually stay at the parties too, but she kept herself to herself, despite Emma's occasional attempts to draw her out a little. It wasn't that she was unfriendly but she seemed withdrawn, which made Emma wonder where Lee's outgoing demeanour came from.

She hoped she would meet Anna's parents that evening after the play, as she wanted to invite Anna round for tea sometime; Lee too, though possibly not on the same night. She wasn't ready for three children at the same time, not just yet.

"Are you excited?" she asked her charges, pouring them all a drink of orange squash from the tin jug Mrs Donovan had passed to her.

"Yes, yes, yes!" shouted Oscar who, despite his height, was also something of an extrovert. Mrs Donovan looked round and smiled at Emma.

"Do you think you should save your voice for the play?"

Emma asked, ruffling Oscar's hair.

"Are your parents coming, Anna?" she turned to the little girl who, it had transpired, was playing Mary to Mikey's Joseph.

"Yes, I think so," Anna answered shyly.

"I think you're going to make a lovely Mary," Emma said, "in fact I think that you're all going to be brilliant."

"Mikey's Mum..." James, the middle king, pulled at her sleeve.

"Yes, James?"

"I need a wee."

Unfortunately, James's warning came a bit too late and from beneath his kingly robes, a little puddle appeared. Suddenly it was action stations and Emma found herself at Lost Property, trying to get alternative pants and trousers for the little boy. The best she could come up with that looked about the right size were a pair of pink pants decorated with a picture of a little girl chasing a butterfly, and some P.E. shorts. They would have to do. She dashed back to the classroom and smiled at the sight of Mikey holding hands with Anna, already queuing up ready to go backstage. She got James into the clean clothes, ignoring his protests of them being girl's pants, and – given the nod by Mrs Donovan – headed off to the school hall.

Emma slipped in quietly through the doors at the back just as Mr McDonald, the headmaster, was addressing the waiting parents.

"Thank you for coming to this very special performance. I know as a parent myself that of all the events at school you come to over the years, this is the one you'll never forget. And the children have all worked very hard learning their lines and the songs but that doesn't mean they won't forget them when they're faced with being on stage! Just be patient, bear with them, whether they get through their lines or they fall asleep! Now, please, sit back, relax, and enjoy your children's first-ever Christmas play!"

Emma slid into a seat in the back row, smiling at the couple next to her. Anna's parents! Great. She determined to speak to them afterwards. She looked further along to where Lee's mum was sitting, at the end of the row. And could that be Lee's dad standing next to her? He was tall and good looking. His eyes flicked over to her and she quickly looked away. The room went quiet and the children filed onto the stage, lining up to sing the opening song. There was Mikey, next to Anna, and on the other side of Anna was little Lee, looking the epitome of an angel. The opening bars of *Little Donkey* began and before she knew it, but as she'd fully expected, Emma's eyes had filled with tears.

She looked along the row of children and back to Mikey and his two new friends. Anna was looking down, singing into her chest. Lee and Mikey looked straight out, however, into the audience, as Emma knew they'd been primed to by Mrs Donovan.

Emma admonished herself for her tears but she couldn't help it. She wiped her eyes and clapped along with the rest of the audience as the song drew to a close and the children took up their positions. They had already taken their first big step into the world away from home. They were so small, so innocent. It was hard to believe they could ever be anything else.

2003

Bristol, July 2003

The end

Suzie heard the blast as she leaned over Barney, changing his nappy before she laid him down in his cot, praying that tonight he would go to sleep without a fuss. Maybe even give Suzie and Jacob a few hours' uninterrupted sleep.

The *boom* echoed around the Cumberland Basin, loud enough to make Suzie look up sharply. Thankfully it didn't seem to have made any difference to Barney who was otherwise occupied, trying to grab his own feet.

By contrast, the *click* as Lee reached the bottom of the stairs, wallet in hand, had been barely perceptible, followed as it was by the huge explosion. Marking the end of a life which, like so many others, had started with such promise.

Did he have time to realise what had happened, as the dial on the timer Mike had set prior to his departure – meant only to switch the light on and off, giving the impression that somebody was home - turned slowly around and inevitably reached its destination?

The tiny spark was mighty enough to ignite the flood of gas from the oven and bang went Emma's house.

So ended the turmoil of Lee's life. His mixed-up conscience; his anger, his rage; his sadness. All gone in a flash.

The future

Anna and Mike had taken their time driving up to Emma's place. They'd had a lot to talk about, and Anna found a huge relief in not having to constantly worry that somebody might hear her. Bristol was a big city, but not big enough, as she'd discovered the time that Lee's mate had reported her behaviour on her hen do. The recent weeks of subterfuge had been a stressful time for her.

"I know he's been a bastard."

"More than a bastard," Mike grunted. Inwardly he was confused; he knew Lee had been a total bastard to Anna, but he couldn't quite let go of the feeling he'd had last night when he'd been out with his old friend. It seemed it was very difficult to accept such a long-standing friendship was over.

"Yes," Anna tried not to feel defensive towards Lee but despite everything that had happened, and against all her better judgement, she still felt a degree of sympathy for him. Or sadness. Maybe just sadness, she thought, at what had happened to the boy she had grown up with. "He'll be getting home about now. I can't imagine what he'll do. I hope he doesn't hurt himself."

"I don't know how you can still care about him, after what he's done to you. Don't look at me like that," Mike could see the irritation on Anna's face. "Please don't think I don't care about him. I do, of course I do. He's Lee. I'd give anything to go back a few years and – well, I don't know, exactly. But find a way, somehow, to make things turn out differently."

"There's no going back now, though," said Anna, opening her window and taking in the depth of the Spanish heat, which had hit her as she'd stepped out of the plane and walked onto the runway in the midday sunshine. It had been hot in Bristol but this was something else.

"Let's just hope he sorts himself out."

Emma was waiting nervously at her house. She'd sorted out Mike's flat, packed up his clothes, his books, his computer, as he'd asked, and piled them into the spare room instead.

She'd stocked the little kitchen in the flat with basics, and filled a wooden bowl with huge, juicy oranges and lemons. Next to Anna's bed was a small wooden table with a jam jar bursting with tiny blue-and-yellow flowers.

They should be here by now, she thought to herself, and then she heard the engine. Unmistakeable amidst the quiet of the evening, the only other sounds the cicadas chirruping and crickets burring.

She clenched her hands into fists and then stretched her fingers, taking a deep breath. A new beginning. She had fought against every instinct inside herself which hoped this would be a fresh start for Mike as well as Anna. When she had tentatively voiced this tiny hope to Miguel, he had vehemently told her to forget it. "This is not the time, Emma. This is not the way you should be thinking. The girl needs to recover, not have a new relationship."

Emma knew he was right. She thought of Lee, too; of the lad she had known, and she hoped that he could make this right for himself. But he had hurt Mike, and he had hurt Anna, in different ways. Emma had found her protective, angry maternal instinct flashing with spite. She tried to tone it down and remember what he too had been through. An image of Scott popped into her mind and she flushed at the memory.

Now that Anna was out of harm's way, Emma hoped she

could find a more peaceable level of feeling towards Lee.

For now, though, there was going to be a lot of mending to do.

The car appeared at the end of the winding drive, a cloud of dust in its wake. As it pulled slowly up to the house, Emma stayed in the doorway for a moment, where she knew the shadows would obscure her presence. She just wanted to watch the two of them together, just for a moment.

Mike opened his door and jumped out of the car, stretching his arms behind him. Emma felt a burst of love inside her. He walked round to where Anna was opening her door, a near-silhouette against the setting sun. Mike pulled the door back and said something which Emma couldn't catch. Anna laughed and got out, taking in her surroundings.

Time to make her presence known, Emma thought, feeling like a voyeur.

"Hello!" she said, stepping out from the doorway and sweeping Mike and then Anna in turn into all-enveloping hugs. "Welcome home."

If you have enjoyed this book, we would be very grateful if you would take the time to review it on the Amazon website. A positive review is invaluable and will be greatly appreciated by the author.

Please also visit the Heddon Publishing website to find out about our other titles: www.heddonpublishing.com

Heddon Publishing was established in 2012 and is a publishing house with a difference. We work with independent authors to get their work out into the real world, by-passing the traditional slog through 'slush piles'. Please contact us by email in the first instance to find out more: enquiries@heddonpublishing.com

Like us on Facebook and receive all our news at: www.facebook.com/heddonpublishing

Join our mailing list by emailing: mailinglist@heddonpublishing.com

Follow us on Twitter: @PublishHeddon

Writing the Town Read by **Katharine E. Smith**
ISBN: 978-0-9932101-2-9

On July 7th 2005, terrorists attack the city's transport network, striking Underground trains and a bus during the morning rush hour. In Cornwall, journalist Jamie Calder loses contact with her boyfriend Dave, in London that day for business.

The initial impact is followed by a slow but sure falling apart of the life Jamie believed was settled and secure. She finds she has to face a betrayal by her best friend, and the prospect of losing her job.

Writing the Town Read is full of intrigue, angst, excitement and humour. The evocative descriptions and convincing narrative voice instantly draw readers into Jamie's life as they experience her disappointments, emotions and triumphs alongside her.

Looking Past by **Katharine E. Smith**
ISBN: 978-0-9932101-3-6

Sarah Marchley is eleven years old when her mother dies. Completely unprepared and suffering an acute sense of loss, she and her father continue quietly, trying to live by the well-intentioned advice of friends, hoping that time really is a great healer and that they will, eventually, move on.

Life changes very little until Sarah leaves for university and begins her first serious relationship. Along with her new boyfriend comes his mother, the indomitable Hazel Poole. Despite some misgivings, Sarah finds herself drawn into the matriarchal Poole family and discovers that gaining a mother figure in her life brings mixed blessings.

Looking Past is a tale of family, friendship, love, life and death – not necessarily in that order.

Lightning Source UK Ltd.
Milton Keynes UK
UKHW020535241118
332859UK00001B/6/P

9 780993 487040